HELEN S. WRIGHT

A MATTER OF OATHS

POPULAR LIBRARY

An Imprint of Warner Books, Inc.

A Warner Communications Company

AN IRREGULAR PULSE
OUT OF PLACE
ON THE EDGE OF THE WEB
CAUGHT HIS ATTENTION.
IT WAS GROWING STRONGER...

(Immediate. Disengage.) He broke into Churi's practice with the order.

(Acknowledged. Disengaging.) The youngster in the web replied promptly. Rafe sensed him begin to obey, then halt abruptly.

The intrusive ghost was still getting stronger, interfering with the signal circuits, threatening to cut them off from each other. He had to get the youngster out now.

Rafe triggered the override, using it to forcibly eject the youngster from the web. For an instant, it worked, then dropped them both back into the ghost-ridden web. He swung uncontrollably between the unstable web and the horrible awareness of sharing a body with Churi, not sure which of their bodies he felt struggling for breath.

Close to panic, Rafe fought desperately to isolate himself—from Churi, from the web, from the insane combination they had become...

A MATTER OF OATHS

From introductory material for new members of the Guild of Webbers:

The web is based on a simple concept: a direct link between mind and machine. The systems of a ship become an extension of the webber's body. But this simplicity is deceptive, and will vanish the first time you enter the shub. Breathing a liquid does not come naturally, and is only the first step...

When you have mastered survival in the shub, you will be ready to take the next step. Through sockets at your neck and wrists, your nervous system will be linked to the ship, and to the other men and women who share the web with you. Through the sockets at your wrists, you will communicate with your web-mates. Through the socket at your neck, you will help to control and monitor the ship. It will take several months to learn this use of your nervous system, and several years before you can claim to have mastered the techniques...

Having a web is a privilege and a responsibility. You must never forget that your web-mates' lives depend on your self-control. Leave all other concerns behind you when you step into the shub. Forget your body. Focus only on control of the web...

THE OATHS BETWEEN THE GUILD OF WEBBERS, ITS MEMBERS, AND THE EMPERORS JULUR AND AYVAR

The Member's Oath to the Guild

I solemnly dedicate myself to the Guild of Webbers. On my honour, on my life, and on any lives I have to come, by all that is sacred to me, I swear:

That my loyalty is to the Guild before all others, and then to those to whom the Guild owes loyalty.

That my obedience is to the law of the Guild before all other laws, and then to the laws to which the Guild gives obedience.

That I will serve the Guild to the best of my ability, and in every way that I am able to serve.

That I will cherish each member of the Guild, respecting their beliefs and taking responsibility for their well-being.

That I will keep this oath so long as I shall live.

The Guild's Oath to the Emperors

We solemnly dedicate ourselves to the worlds that bore us and to the people of those worlds. On our honour, on our lives, and on any lives we have to come, by all that is sacred to us, we swear:

That our loyalty is to our people before all others, and then to the Emperors who govern our people.

That our obedience is to the law of the Guild before all other laws, and then to the just laws to which our people give obedience.

That we will serve our people to the best of our ability, in every way that we are able to serve, respecting their beliefs and taking responsibility for their well-being.

That we will cherish each member of the Guild, respecting their beliefs and taking responsibility for their well-being.

That we will keep this oath so long as one of us lives.

The Emperors' Oaths to the Guild

I, the Emperor Julur, solemnly dedicate myself to the worlds of the Old Empire and to the people of those worlds. On my honour and on my immortality, I swear:

That my loyalty will be to my people before all others.

That my laws will be just.

That I will serve my people to the best of my ability, in every way that I am able to serve, respecting their beliefs and taking responsibility for their well-being, and causing no harm to any unless for the protection of the Old Empire.

That I will cherish the Guild of Webbers, and each member of the Guild, respecting their beliefs and taking responsibility for their well-being, causing harm to no member of the Guild unless for the protection of the Twin Empires.

That I will keep this oath forever, or forfeit the loyalty of the Guild of Webbers.

I, the Emperor Ayvar, solemnly dedicate myself to the worlds of the New Empire and to the people of those worlds. On my honour and on my immortality, I swear:

That my loyalty will be to my people before all others.

That my laws will be just.

That I will serve my people to the best of my ability, in every way that I am able to serve, respecting their beliefs and taking responsibility for their well-being, and causing no harm to any unless for the protection of the New Empire.

That I will cherish the Guild of Webbers, and each member of the Guild, respecting their beliefs and taking responsibility for their well-being, causing harm to no member of the Guild unless for the protection of the Twin Empires.

That I will keep this oath forever, or forfeit the loyalty of the Guild of Webbers.

SHIP IDENTIFICATION:

OE-S32176040-8 *Bhattya*	Patrolship class 89/F
COMMISSIONED	240/5003, Keruil Zone
ASSIGNED	089/5043, Achil Zone (refitting)

SPECIFICATION:

WEB	Standard 20 + 4
DRIVE	Samansa
	(High Performance Option)
ARMAMENT	Class 2 weaponry;
	Class 2 shielding

CREW:	6 senior; 30 junior; 2 apprentices

COMMANDER	OE-P3987-49596 Rallya
CAPTAIN	OE-P2143-95277 Vidar
WEBMASTER	OE-P5971-17529 Joshim

FIRST OFFICER	Vacancy
SECOND OFFICER	OE-P7921-58712 Jualla
THIRD OFFICER	OE-P6417-75249 Lilimya

JUNIORS	. . .
	(No vacancies)

APPRENTICES	. . .
	(No vacancies)

"Now, there's pretty," Rallya said appreciatively, seeing the young webber who had paused just inside the entrance to the Guildhall rec-room. He must be recently arrived in the zone; otherwise she would have noticed him before, with his distinctive curly hair, contrasting shades of grey and brown, and that short, svelte figure.

"He is, isn't he," Vidar agreed, turning to look. "Young for you though, Rallya," he added, grinning at her with the immunity of ten years of close friendship.

"Looking isn't touching," Rallya defended herself. She leaned back, tipping her seat onto two legs, to get a better view. The stranger was looking around as if a familiar face would be welcome but unexpected. He noticed her continued scrutiny and nodded a courtesy to her rank, the cocky little scut, before moving out of sight behind a group of juniors.

"Anybody else notice his insignia?" Joshim asked.

Rallya nodded. The stranger wore them on his upper left arm, the only distinguishing marks on his plain grey tunic. He had a Second's badge and two Oath markers but no ship's patch: a shipless Second who had crossed the Disputed Zone once.

"Looks young for a Second," Vidar commented. "Probably just made it before he came across and that wasn't so long ago."

Joshim shook his head. "That second Oath marker isn't new, nor is the Second's badge," he pointed out. "It might be worth talking to him."

Rallya looked at him in tolerant amusement. "We need a

qualified First, remember? Not a pretty Second to feast our eyes on.''

''We've eliminated all the available Firsts and most of the unavailable ones.'' Joshim argued. ''Unless we want to sit in dock for the foreseeable future, we'll have to find a Second ready to be bumped up.''

''We haven't talked to *Chennya*'s First yet,'' Rallya objected.

''Now who's looking for pretty?'' Vidar teased. ''Anyway, she'll be on patrol for another six days.''

''And *Vasir*'s Three are courting her,'' Joshim added. ''Their First accepted the Captain's berth on *Hashil*.''

Rallya frowned. She wanted Lina, *Chennya*'s First, a skillful webber with the reputation for being a steady influence in the web-room, and with the potential for command rank in a few years' time. However, if she was being courted openly, etiquette prevented *Bhattya*'s Three from making an approach. At least until she was settled with *Vasir*, Rallya corrected herself, and *Bhattya* could not wait that long. They would have to let her know, discreetly, that they were waiting to make an offer if she turned *Vasir* away. There was no doubt that she would welcome such an offer; a berth with *Bhattya* was a considerable prize. The problem would be getting Joshim to agree to the theft.

''It won't cost us anything to talk to the stranger,'' Vidar was saying. ''Until we broadcast the fact that we're considering Seconds for promotion, we'll have nobody else to talk to.''

''And if we do, we'll be inundated,'' Rallya predicted sourly. ''Every Second in the zone will be haunting the Guildhall trying to catch our eye. Or crowding us out of our own web-room, visiting their long-lost acquaintances and being boot-licking polite in the hope of impressing us.''

''Nobody who knows your reputation will be licking your boots, Rallya,'' Vidar promised her. ''Not unless they've finished with their teeth.''

Rallya snorted unwillingly. ''I'd still be happier with a qualified First,'' she insisted. ''We haven't explored all the possibilities yet.''

Joshim sighed and gave her the look that meant: I know what you're thinking and the answer is no.

Rallya scowled and shrugged unrepentantly.. ''You didn't have so many principles when I stole you from *Samchaya*,'' she accused him. ''Go on, then, ask the pretty boy if we can talk to him.'' As *Bhattya*'s Webmaster, it was Joshim's right to make the first approach to any webber they chose to court. "Anything rather than spend the evening being bullied by you two.

"Now I know I'm getting old," she muttered as Joshim left the table. "Ten years ago I'd never have given in so easily."

"You're only trying to lull us into thinking you've given up on Lina," Vidar said cheerfully.

"She's still the best prospect we have," Rallya muttered rebelliously. "Better than an over-pretty Second." She hooked one foot around a spare seat at a neighboring table and pulled it into position next to her. "Emperors, the child can't be more than twenty-five."

"Thirty," the stranger said, arriving behind her in time to hear. He spoke Empire Standard with a soft accent and a tinge of amusement, as if his age had been mistaken before and he was used to it.

"Commander Rallya, Captain Vidar, this is Second Officer Rafell. Rafe." As Joshim made the introductions, Rafe nodded the appropriate greetings.

"We're glad you could join us. Sit down, please," Vidar invited. "May we buy you a drink?"

"Thank you, but no." Rafe took the seat that Rallya had procured for him and waited with a hint of wariness for the next move. A webber being courted by a Three was temporarily their equal, although most webbers were cautious enough not to take advantage of that fact. Still, to refuse a drink was unusually cautious.

"Do you drink?" Rallya asked curiously.

"Yes, ma'am, but not when I'm hoping for some web-time in the near future," he explained.

"On the station waiting list?" Joshim asked.

"Yes, sir."

"Take the drink," Joshim advised. "Half the station's web is out of action—current leakage into the monitor circuits. The rest is fully occupied running the station. Every shipless webber in the zone is on the waiting list. The average wait is five days."

"Then a glass of veyu will do no harm," Rafe conceded.

"May I have a word, Joshim?" The interruption came from Amsur, the Guildhall Webmaster.

"Can it wait?" Joshim asked.

"No. It will only take a few minutes. I'm sure Second Officer Rafell will excuse you," Amsur insisted.

"Of course." Rafe tilted his head in polite permission for Joshim to leave. "Webmaster Amsur would not interrupt without good reason."

As Amsur led Joshim out of hearing, Rafe took the veyu that Vidar passed to him and set it down untouched. Rallya studied his wrists and neck. His web-bands were grey tarket hide, which was a good sign: any webber worth the name bought the best bands they could afford. Tarket was expensive: a set of bands like that cost fifty days' pay for a Second; but it was comfortable, long-lasting and the best protection there was.

"Whose work?" she asked, indicating the pattern tooled into the bands.

"Mosir," Rafe shrugged dismissively. "A conceit."

"An expensive conceit," Rallya commented sharply, doubling her estimate of how much the bands had cost. "Aristo?" she guessed.

Rafe shrugged again. "Maybe," he said carelessly, glancing across to where Amsur and Joshim were parting. "Shall we wait for the Webmaster?"

Nobody could accuse this one of boot-licking, Rallya thought in slight amusement. He must be an aristo, she decided, or he would have denied it. Very few of them became webbers; they had too many ties to family and Empire, too much to lose by swearing the Guild Oath. If they were not content with being decorative members of their Emperor's court, they joined his personal guard or bought a commission in his army. They might end up dead that way, but for an aristo, anything was preferable to serving the wrong Emperor in the wrong Empire. She remembered the second Oath marker on Rafe's sleeve and wondered which high-bred family in the New Empire had suffered the dishonor of a son's defection.

Joshim slipped back into his seat. "Sorry about that," he offered Rafe. Rallya heard the change of attitude in his voice and looked a question at him which was ignored.

"No doubt Amsur had some useful information for you." Rafe was smiling slightly. "Shall I leave now?"

"It would be helpful," Joshim said carefully. "We need to discuss this between ourselves."

"Discuss what?" Vidar asked, as baffled as Rallya.

"You'll find it far more comfortable if you talk about it

behind my back." Rafe stood up. "And so will I." He bowed formally to them all. "Webmaster Joshim, there's no need to inform me of your decision. I can guess it."

"What did Amsur tell you about him?" Rallya demanded as Rafe left the rec-room.

"He's an Oath-breaker," Joshim said baldly.

"Emperors!" Vidar exclaimed. "Is Amsur sure? You'd have to be insane to break your Oath, knowing the penalty."

"You'd have to be something special to get to Second afterwards," Joshim suggested. He drank from the beer in front of him. "Amsur says his record is excellent."

"Apart from the obvious blemish," Rallya reminded him drily. "And whoever promoted him did him no favors. As a junior, he'd have a chance of getting a berth. Not a good berth, but he'd be webbing. As an officer, he's got no chance. There'll always be somebody as good as him who isn't an Oath-breaker."

"He's here under the hundred day rule," Joshim confirmed. "Came in from Jeram today. If he doesn't find a berth here he'll never web again."

"I wonder why he did it," Vidar muttered.

"That's something he doesn't even know himself," Rallya pointed out. "Not if identity-wipe is everything it's said to be. He can make the same guesses as us, though."

"You think he is an aristo?" Vidar asked.

"Was," Rallya corrected. "It's the only answer that fits. Death before dishonor, and if death isn't possible, identity-wipe." She made a noise of disgust. "They shouldn't be allowed to take the Oath at all."

"He abided by the letter of the Oath," Joshim remarked. "It allows the choice: to switch allegiance between the Emperors or to accept identity-wipe. Strictly, he shouldn't be called an Oath-breaker."

"Logic chopping," Rallya snapped. "He broke the spirit of the Oath. That's what matters." She looked at Joshim suspiciously. "You can't want to continue courting him?" she asked in disbelief.

"I'd like to look at his record," Joshim said mildly. "We're not so overrun with prospective Firsts that we can afford to ignore him, and our orders will be arriving soon."

"I am not courting an Oath-breaker," Rallya said flatly. She pushed her seat away from the table, knowing better than to argue with Joshim when he was suffering from a surfeit of softheartedness; it was impossible to win, and there were easier ways to get what she wanted. "I promised Yessim I'd make a fifth at drag," she lied. "We'll talk about it tomorrow."

*   *   *

The out-side observation gallery was deserted; Rafe had his choice of viewing panels. He halted at random in front of one, hardly seeing the star-field it showed him. Out was currently sun-ward, a view without interest, which was why he had chosen to come here rather than the popular in-side gallery with its view of the gas giant above which the station hung.

A wise man would have been in his cabin, sleeping, without any of the problems that made it impossible for Rafe to sleep. A wise man would know when to give up, would not be wasting his time looking for a berth that did not exist. A wise man would be planning a future out of the web. A wise man... Rafe laughed at himself. A wise man would not have made the decision that he had made ten years ago.

Tonight had been a mistake as well. *Bhattya* was a Name; there had never been any chance that they would consider him once they knew. He should have declined their invitation, rather than risk their anger and the harm it could do him if they broadcast his guilt. He shrugged mentally. If not them, somebody else would do it. Amsur would always be ready with his words of warning: an excellent record, but you ought to know... Rafe had been through it all at Jeram and at Somir.

He dropped into a seat and put his feet up on the railing between it and the viewing panel. An old cargoship was easing out of dock, pregnant with fuel, pushing a string of pods in front of it. As its steering vanes spread ready for the ponderous wallow out to the jump point, Rafe's arms twitched in sympathy. He stilled them with an effort. Five days, Webmaster Joshim had said, and that was the average wait for web-time. How much longer would it be for an Oath-breaker?

Footsteps on the spiral staircase warned him that somebody was coming up to the gallery. He hoped that they were looking for solitude, as he was. He slumped lower in his seat to make it clear he wanted no company.

The footsteps reached the top and paused, replaced by a soft laugh. "I thought you'd run for the obvious bolt-hole."

Commander Rallya. At least his luck was consistent, Rafe thought bitterly. "I was about to leave, ma'am," he said, getting to his feet.

"No, you weren't." She came around the curve of the gallery. "Sit down."

Rafe sat; any instruction from a Commander was an order, unless they were courting you. If she wanted him seated, this was unlikely to be the standard tongue-lashing, starting with his presumption in accepting *Bhattya*'s invitation and finishing with his unworthiness for any berth on any ship. Either she planned to indulge her curiosity about him, or she expected him to bed with her in the hope of being rewarded with a berth. He grinned cynically; probably she intended to combine the two.

"What's amusing you?" she asked.

"You." Rafe abandoned caution. Whatever he said or did now would anger her; let it be deliberate. "To save you time and effort, ma'am: I don't know why I broke my Oath and I choose not to speculate; and I'm a webber, not a whore."

To his surprise, she laughed. "I couldn't be courting you?" she challenged.

"No, ma'am, you couldn't. You're playing with me."

She shook her head. "No, I'm not. I will admit to being curious." She turned her back on him and watched the cargoship pulling away from the station. "Not about why you broke your Oath. That's obvious. About how you got to Second, and why you're shipless." She swung around to face him again. "You're causing me a slight problem. You can help me solve it."

Rafe shrugged. "I can't solve my own problems, ma'am," he said frankly. "I doubt I can help with yours."

"You won't help yourself by being impudent," she said sharply.

"I won't help myself by lying down to be walked over."

"Have you ever tried it?" she asked with raised eyebrows. "No, you haven't."

She leaned back on the rail, hands on either side of her. Even relaxed, she seemed to have a rod of steel up her spine. The Emperors only knew how old she was: her hair had probably been gray before Rafe was born; and how long she had been in the web. Longer than anybody else alive, that was certain, and with no plans to retire. Long enough to be sure of getting her own way in everything. Rafe took pleasure in the thought that he had nothing to lose by thwarting her. She was waiting for him to speak. Let her wait.

"If anything gets you a berth, it will be your nerve," she told him after a long silence. "But not with *Bhattya*."

"You don't have to convince me of that," Rafe told her calmly. He grinned suddenly. "Who do you have to convince?"

"Cocky little scut," she accused him. "I don't frighten you one bit, do I? I ought to."

"Any damage you can do me, you've already decided to do."

"What about any good I can do you?"

Rafe laughed, gestured to the cargoship behind her. "If I'm good, will you get me a berth aboard that?"

"Would you rather have no berth at all?" she challenged.

Rafe closed his eyes briefly, brought up hard against the facts. "No, ma'am. I'd settle for a berth aboard anything."

"I thought as much." She looked him over, like a trader examining a bad bargain. "What was your last ship?"

"Exploration. *Avannya*. Somir Zone."

"*Avannya*." She repeated it thoughtfully. "Didn't you hit an EMP-mine last year? Lost your Three and half the web-room?"

"Yes," Rafe said unwillingly. "We were lucky to get home at all."

"Luck wasn't enough, from what I heard." She stared at him speculatively. "Her Second got an honor for bringing her home."

"Ludicrous, isn't it? All I did was save my own neck, and incidentally a few others, but they call me a hero and give me a badge to prove it."

"You don't wear it."

"Against all the regulations, no. Why embarrass people or confuse their prejudices? I can hardly be an Oath-breaker and a hero, can I?"

"What do you want to be?"

"A webber." Rafe snorted. "For as long as I'm allowed to be." He leaned his head back and looked up at the ceiling. "Tell me what you want from me, ma'am, and go away. I'm tired, I'm irritable, and the last thing I want is to end up on a charge of insubordination. That would be the perfect end to a perfect career, and I am reaching the end of my patience." He could feel a tic starting in his cheek. "I can't imagine what I can do or say to make myself more unacceptable than I already am, but if you tell me, I'll do it. For the peace and quiet," he added. "Not for any meaningless promise of a berth on an antiquated cargoship."

"How long since you last had some web-time?" she asked abruptly.

Rafe cursed the tic, embarrassed that she had noticed, angry that she had mentioned it. "What does it matter? Soon enough they'll be deactivating my web."

"How long?" she insisted.

"Forty days," he admitted bitterly. "Nobody is going to waste capacity on an Oath-breaker with no future."

"They didn't allow you in the web on the way from Jeram?" She sounded genuinely surprised.

"They didn't allow me in the web-room. Didn't want me corrupting the apprentices." Rafe closed his eyes. "Go away," he repeated rudely.

"Come to *Bhattya* tomorrow. We've capacity to spare," she offered unexpectedly.

"No, thank you, ma'am," he said stiffly.

"No conditions," she promised. She went without waiting for a reply, to Rafe's relief.

MEMBER IDENTIFICATION:

NE-P9000-42775 Rafell
DATE AND PLACE
  OF ORIGIN   Not recorded; date estimated 5013
DATE OF OATH   Not recorded; date estimated 5032

HISTORY:
082/5033 Central zone
    Identity-wiped to enforce the Member's Oath
265/5033 Somir zone: Web qualification
    Junior
280/5033 Somir zone: Assignment
    Junior, OE-S83491725-2 Surveyship *Avannya*
292/5037 Somir zone: Web qualification
    Senior (distinction)
297/5037 Somir zone: Promotion
    Third, OE-S83491725-2 Surveyship *Avannya*
325/5040 Somir zone: Promotion
    Second, OE-S83491725-2 Surveyship *Avannya*
107/5042 Somir zone: Promotion
    (Brevet) First, OE-S83491725-2 Surveyship *Avannya*

173/ 5043:
ACHIL ZONE, OLD EMPIRE

Rallya cursed automatically as she shifted from her right side to
her left. The ache crept up on her every night, but if she asked

the station surgeon for something to ease it, there would be the inevitable conversation about retiring. She only ached where she had been injured before they perfected regen; anybody would, eight or eighty, but the surgeons refused to believe it. Faffing fools had none of them been born back before they perfected regen. Probably thought nobody could survive a broken bone without it.

She squinted at the time. Second hour. Fadir would have started preparing breakfast in the web-room. She rolled off her bed and went to shower, setting the water to warm. As she soaped herself, she wondered whether the Oath-breaker would turn up for the web-time she had offered him. He would be a fool not to, after forty days without and with the prospect of a five-day wait for station time. As big a fool as she had been to make the offer. The sensible thing would have been to get him moved to the head of Amsur's waiting list.

She would tell Joshim about it over breakfast, in front of witnesses so that he could not immediately reopen the argument. Dressing, she ran through a mental list of ships in dock that had vacancies for a Second. Joshim would know better than she did but she could not ask his advice, and she had to find a berth for Rafe before *Chennya* came in or they would lose Lina to *Vasir* through Joshim's stubbornness. *Masma* owed her a favor, but not a large enough favor to take Rafe because of it. Maybe somebody would take him in return for a favor in the future?

Fadir had breakfast ready when she entered the web-room. Half a year more and his apprenticeship would be over. She would miss him, mostly for his habit of rising before her. *Bhattya* would acquire a new apprentice, a scared sixteen-year-old to take Rasil's place as the youngest and most ignorant, and Fadir would take the Oath and be given his web. He would make a useful junior but he would never reach senior rank; only one in ten did and it was obvious early on which ones they would be.

She was still scowling at that thought when Joshim came in, yawning. Eight years and she had never seen him truly awake until after breakfast, except in a crisis. She passed him a mug of alcad without a word and waited until he had drunk half of it.

"I offered somebody some web-time last night," she said casually. "He hasn't had any for forty days. I didn't think he should wait any longer."

"Anybody I know?"

"We bought him a drink last night."

"Rafe?"

"Don't jump to conclusions," Rallya warned. "He's entitled to web-time like anybody else, that's all."

Joshim looked unconvinced but could not pursue it in front of Fadir. "What time is he coming?"

"He didn't say he was."

"I'll need to have a look at his record," Joshim said hopefully.

"I doubt there's a queue for it."

Joshim gave her a sharp look. Rallya made a small gesture of apology. As a last resort, letting it slip in *Bhattya*'s web-room that Rafe was an Oath-breaker would force Joshim to give up; it would be impossible for Rafe to control juniors who knew. However, Rallya would rather succeed without antagonizing Joshim. He could hardly object if she found the child a berth, but he would be furious if she spread the truth about him around the zone and mentioning it in front of Fadir would do just that.

She would have to be careful whom she did mention it to, she realized. There were seniors of command rank who would broadcast it as far as any junior. *Masma*'s Captain, for example. She struck them off her mental list. Emperors, she was getting old! One accursed Second should not be causing her so much trouble.

"Still want the web for a workout this afternoon?" Joshim checked, putting his empty mug aside and stretching lazily.

"Yes." Rallya crossed to the notice board and examined the web schedule displayed there, then altered it to bring forward the time of her tactics workout. Anybody who neglected to check the schedule this morning deserved the standing penalty for missing a workout: three days confined to ship.

Stepping back, she almost fell over Fadir, craning to see what she had done.

"Make sure they pay the going rate for the warning," she told him, enjoying the blush that he could never quite control.

"Yes, ma'am. I mean, no, ma'am, I don't charge. I mean, no, ma'am, I won't warn them."

"Fadir, not only are you distinctly unenterprising, you are also a lousy liar. After two years with *Bhattya*, you should have been cured of at least one of those problems."

"Yes, ma'am. May I be excused, ma'am?"

"Yes, Fadir. I would like nothing better than to see the back of you. And there'll be three days confined to ship for you for every person you do warn.''

''Yes, ma'am.'' He contrived to bow and slink out at the same time.

''How does he expect you to find out if he disobeys?'' Vidar wondered, coming in as Fadir left.

''She's telepathic,'' Joshim said crisply. ''Fadir and Rasil reached that conclusion long ago.''

Rallya chuckled. ''Useful if I were.'' She poured herself another alcad. ''Vidar, are you waving that flimsy around for effect, or did you intend to show it to us?''

Vidar handed her the output from the messager. ''Orders,'' he said happily. ''With an expedite flash.''

Rallya read through them quickly. ''Back to Aramas,'' she said thoughtfully, handing the flimsy on to Joshim. ''The Outsider incursions must be getting worse.''

Joshim nodded agreement. ''How long before you have the new mass sensors in, Vidar?'' he asked.

''They'll be in by this time tomorrow,'' Vidar promised. ''If I have to steal them from the Stores, they'll be in.''

Almost more than anybody else, Vidar was eager to return to an active zone. There, his task of maintaining the ship in peak condition was made easier by the cooperation of a Storekeeper with the same priorities: get the patrolships back on duty with the minimum delay; complete the formalities later, if ever, when things were quieter. Here in Achil, Vidar and Second Officer Jualla had been forced to battle with the Storekeeper for every item of equipment, in spite of the fact that *Bhattya* had been assigned to the zone specifically for refitting.

Rallya frowned suddenly. Once Vidar had installed the new mass sensors, the only obstacle to *Bhattya*'s departure was their lack of a First, and the expedite flash made it a matter of urgency to find one. By the look on Joshim's face, he was having the same thought.

''I'll be off-ship most of the morning,'' she announced hurriedly.

''When are we going to talk about our First?'' Joshim asked, refusing to be put off.

''Vidar will be busy most of the morning, and so will you,'' Rallya temporized. ''You may as well take the opportunity to supervise Rafe's web-time. Save checking him out later if we do decide to consider him.'' As she had intended, the suggestion disarmed Joshim. ''Then we can talk about it after my workout.''

"You're up to something," Joshim said suspiciously.

"Nothing you could possibly object to," Rallya promised. "Why don't you call Rafe and make sure he's coming?"

* * *

Amsur was right, Joshim decided as he finished the last flimsy of the printout: Rafe's record was excellent. Only one ship in the ten years since he came across the Disputed Zone, and that was a first-class surveyship, *Avannya*. Promoted to Third after four years as a junior, to Second three years ago and last year a brevet promotion to First, now lapsed. Rapid progress by anybody's standards, and probably deserved: like patrolships, surveyships could not afford to carry dead mass at any level in the web-room. Nor could they afford to discard obvious talent because of a single line in his record—082/5033: Identity-wiped to enforce the Member's Oath. Even Rallya would have to admit that, Joshim thought hopefully.

Or had she admitted it already, by offering Rafe web-time? No, if she had changed her mind about him, she would have said so openly. Without an explanation, of course. Rallya never saw any need to explain herself, or to apologize for her actions. If she wanted to invite somebody into *Bhattya*'s web, she would, conveniently forgetting that only Joshim, as Webmaster, had that right.

Joshim sighed. He had not made that point at breakfast, as he had not made hundreds of similar points in the eight years since he joined *Bhattya*, because it was rarely worth the effort to argue with Rallya. Especially not when her hip was troubling her. The surgeons talked about the inevitable effects of age, suggested drugs that would keep her out of the web, and were surprised when she would not listen to them. Rallya refused to acknowledge the pain that drove her out of bed in the mornings, would have raised blue hell if Joshim dared mention that her performance in the web was not what it had been eight years ago, and continued to behave as if she owned *Bhattya* and would do so forever.

Blue hell would be a tame description for what would happen if she found out what Joshim was looking for in their new First. Yes, *Bhattya* without Rallya was unthinkable, but it was going to happen. In five years' time, by the rate at which her web-reflexes were deteriorating, and the Emperors only knew if she realized it was happening. Joshim dreaded the day when he had to tell her that he could not allow her in the web, but he intended to have a First ready to step into the Commander's place when it happened. A First trained by Rallya; there was nothing wrong with her devious, unprincipled, knife-sharp brain. Her tactical skill had brought *Bhattya* safely through forty years of action; Joshim was going to ensure that she left a fitting legacy, a successor who would make it easier for her to leave, somebody she liked and was prepared to trust with the ship that had been her life.

Chennya's Lina would be ready for command rank too soon. She would move on again within two years; she had a record of ship hopping. Somebody like Rafe would be ideal, newly promoted to First but with obvious potential. The trick would be to get Rallya to take him as her protégé. Without being seen to have anything to do with it. Joshim smiled ruefully. At least not until Rallya had too much invested in Rafe to be prepared to waste it.

All this was assuming that Rafe wanted to be a patrolship Commander; that was one thing that remained to be established. His record showed no specialization in ship systems or the web, which suggested that he had no inclination towards Captaincy or Webmastery, but he had no patrolship experience, which was a pity, and he was too young to have gained any in the New Empire before he came across. He could hardly have had his web for a year when he was captured. Could anybody so young have such entrenched loyalties that they would refuse to switch their allegiance from the New Emperor to the Old? Joshim dismissed the question with an impatient shake of his head: obviously they could.

His audio-messager beeped in his ear; Fadir's voice came through as soon as he acknowledged the call.

"Second Officer Rafell is here, sir."

"Bring him up to the web-room, please."

Joshim smiled indulgently at the excitement in Fadir's voice. The Senior Apprentice had his own ideas about the reason for Rafe's presence: if he was here for web-time, he must be the new First; *Bhattya*'s web was so finely tuned that no stranger would be allowed in. For Fadir's sake, Joshim hoped he kept his ideas to himself while Rallya was about or she would chew him up and spit him out in extremely small pieces.

"In here, sir." Fadir opened the web-room door and stepped aside deferentially for his companion.

"Thank you, Fadir." Rafe's face twitched into a tired grin as

Fadir bowed his way out. "I hadn't the heart to tell him he was wasting his time trying to impress me," he commented as he made his own belated bow.

Or the energy, Joshim judged as Rafe straightened up. Curse it, all the classic signs of web-cramp had been there last night: the rigid control of voice and movement, the unnatural tension masquerading as alertness, the dark circles of sleepless nights under the eyes, the untouched drink. How had he not recognized them?

"Which ship brought you from Jeram?" he asked angrily.

"Does it matter?" Rafe made a gesture of dismissal. "They're hardly unique in the way they feel about me."

"Which ship?" Joshim insisted.

"*Deretya*," Rafe said wearily.

"Have you registered a complaint with the Guildhall?"

"No, sir. It would attract too much attention."

Joshim nodded understanding, not liking it. Rafe's position was too precarious to risk claiming the rights that other webbers could take for granted. However, that need not prevent Joshim from having a few sharp words with *Deretya*'s Webmaster.

"We'll go straight up to the web," he said briskly, unlocking the door to the riser with his palm.

Relief showed in Rafe's eyes, as if he had expected Joshim to change his mind, even so late. He covered it quickly with long grey lashes, made a visible effort to steady his breathing and followed Joshim into the riser.

"Did you particularly want to wet-web?" Joshim asked as he stepped out at the top.

"Whatever is most convenient for you, sir."

Rafe was looking around hungrily as he answered. *Bhattya*'s web was big, even for a patrolship: twenty wet-web places and another four dry, all of them currently idle. Joshim never managed to view it without a pleasing rush of pride. To Rafe, it must look like heaven, after forty days of enforced abstinence; he was twitching in anticipation.

"We'll use these." Joshim indicated the nearest pair of dry places. Wet-webbing was more satisfying, allowing total immersion in the web without the requirement for a core of body control, but it took longer to prepare for and Rafe needed to be in the web without delay.

"What size web did *Avannya* have?" Joshim asked curiously, starting to prepare his place.

"Ten wet, two dry. We ran with eight in the web normally,

ten when jumping into a strange system for the first time."
Rafe rubbed at his wrists unconsciously and moved to prepare
the other place.

"*Bhattya* runs with twelve in the web. Eighteen in an alert,
including six on filtered standby," Joshim told him. "We're
thirty-six in the web-room, plus the apprentices."

"*Avannya* wasn't rigged for filtered standby. There'd never
been the need. You don't expect EMP-mines in abandoned
systems," Rafe said bitterly. "Especially not in the jump
point." He laid the bunch of web-contacts down on the couch
in front of him and hesitated. "I have to warn you, sir," he
said nervously. "I haven't had any web-time in forty days. I'm
going to be clumsy. There's a risk that I'll unbalance your
web." The words came out as if it was the last thing he wanted
to say. It probably was, Joshim thought approvingly: all the
more credit for saying it.

"I appreciate the warning, but you can't be any clumsier
than a junior in their first berth," he said easily. "This web has
coped with hundreds of those."

"My extension is greater than any juniors in their first berth,"
Rafe insisted. "It might be safer if I waited for station time."

"If I need to, I won't have any problems limiting you."
Joshim finished his preparations. "If I thought there was any
danger to my web, you wouldn't be here." He walked round to
Rafe's side and picked up the neglected bunch of web-contacts.
"Happy with these?"

"Yes, sir."

"Then hook in." He made it an order.

Rafe unfastened his wrist-bands and removed them, putting
them in easy reach on the ledge at the head of his couch.
Predictably, the contacts underneath were dull from disuse. He
took cleaner from the ledge and swabbed them gently. His
hands were shaking.

"My neck-contact will need cleaning," he apologized.

Joshim took the bottle of cleaner from him. Rafe unfastened
the band at his throat and put that with the others. He tipped his
head forward and pulled the curly strands of grey and brown
hair out of the way.

"Nice contact," Joshim commented. "You didn't have many
problems growing your web in."

"I don't remember, sir," Rafe said, sharp with embarrass-
ment. It was one thing to ask a web-mate to clean your

neck-contact for you, another to ask a strange Webmaster. He flinched as Joshim applied the cleaner and pulled away after a few seconds.

"Yes, that should be clean enough." Joshim closed the bottle and replaced it on the ledge. "What system of signals are you happiest with? *Bhattya* uses extended tens, but that's peculiar to patrolships."

Rafe frowned, then shook his head decisively. "The condition I'm in, standard fives may be beyond me, sir." He grinned, but it was obviously forced.

"Standard fives, then." Joshim gestured for Rafe to lie down on the couch. "Hook in, and I'll run a calibration sequence for you."

"Thank you sir."

Rafe strapped the signal-contacts into place on his wrists, face-to-face with his own contacts. He adjusted them slightly to get the position right and checked his judgment by the readout on the monitor screen beside the couch. Lying down, he twisted comfortably onto his side before strapping the control-contact into place at the back of his neck. The accurate positioning of that was more critical and took longer, but eventually he was satisfied.

"Ready, sir."

Joshim triggered the standard calibration sequence and watched the readouts with interest. Reflex speed and extension at the top end of the spectrum; range and control less good, but that would be the result of the web-cramp. Nodding his satisfaction, he made a few adjustments to the settings of Rafe's links.

"We have two hours before anybody else needs the web," he remarked. "I'll signal when your time's up."

As Joshim hooked himself into the web, the configuration displayed on the monitor beside his couch changed to show the new key-position and his links activated automatically, the contacts warming invitingly. He opened the paths from the web to his brain and closed the non-essential paths from brain to body, leaving himself a view of the monitor and his speech and hearing.

"Ready for activation, Rafe?" he called, when he had reached his compromise between the demands of caution and the space that Rafe would need to stretch away his cramp, and imposed the corresponding limits on the web.

"Ready, sir."

Rafe had obviously been alert for the moment that his

contacts became active. He surged into the web eagerly, extending until he reached the edges of the space available and holding himself there for long seconds of clear relief before pulling back and moderating his strength. The monitor showed that there had been more overlap between body control and web control during that surge than was wise, but less than Joshim had anticipated. He relaxed into passivity, content that any danger to Rafe and to the web was over in those initial uncontrolled moments, and settled himself more comfortably on his couch to observe.

Rafe was already working each of his circuits individually, methodically stretching the cramps out of his nerves. After thirty minutes of precise level and range-control exercises, he moved onto pairs and higher combinations, working up to the complete sequence of Senior qualifiers. He ran through those twice, once with his eyes open to monitor his performance.

[Good] Joshim signaled as Rafe finished. [Time up]

There were ten minutes left of the time that he had promised but Rafe had already pushed himself further than he ought. Without any apparent ill-effects, it was true, but web-cramp was unpredictable. Joshim wished he had thought to say that *Bhattya* had enough spare capacity for Rafe to return every day if he wished. It was an omission he would correct as soon as this session was over.

[Acknowledged. Disengaging] Rafe made the switch from web to body almost as soon as he signaled, a smooth switch this time, without unnecessary overlap. "Disengaged, sir," he confirmed.

Joshim deactivated Rafe's links and disengaged from the web himself, stretching pleasurably as he returned to full body control. Rafe had moved while he was in the web, sprawling on his stomach with his hands trailing over the edge of the couch. He looked more amused than embarrassed by his lapse, sitting up slowly and crossing his legs in front of him while he verified on the monitor screen that his links were inactive.

"Let me check your contacts before you put your bands on," Joshim requested, detaching his own links and slipping the web-contacts into their housing. Nobody could work so hard after so long out of the web and not suffer web-burn.

"No need, sir," Rafe protested confidently, unstrapping the control-contact from his neck and spoiling the effect by wincing. He removed the signal-contacts from his wrists more carefully and waited obediently for Joshim to inspect the damage.

"Not too bad, considering you were determined to cram six hours' work into two," Joshim reproved him, rummaging on the ledge for some salve. "Wrists." Rafe held them out meekly and he anointed the reddened skin around the contacts. "Tip your head forward." He brushed the curls out of the way and treated the larger burn on the neck. "Tomorrow, you do exactly what I tell you. No more and no less," he said sternly as he applied the ointment. Rafe started to turn his head. "Keep still. You skipped breakfast, I assume?"

"Yes, sir."

"Then we'll go and find out what the apprentices have concocted for lunch." He patted the curls gently back into place, put the salve away and handed Rafe his bands one at a time. "After two years, Fadir shows signs of mastering the cook-unit."

"Do I have to listen to the rest of his life-story?" Rafe asked plaintively, uncrossing his legs and slipping down from the couch.

"Not in company," Joshim promised. "He'll just worship you from afar."

Rafe snorted cynically. "Not for long," he predicted. "Not if Commander Rallya is there."

"What did she say to you last night?" Joshim asked sharply.

Rafe shook his head. "Nothing," he claimed, tugging at his tunic to straighten it. "Just the offer of web-time, for which I'm grateful." He tilted his head and grinned impishly, stripping another five years from his apparent age. "Shall we go and make Fadir happy?"

* * *

Rallya glared at Rafe as he stepped out of the riser behind Joshim. His web-time had been well-spent; he was relaxed and smiling at something Joshim had said on the way down from the web. Joshim too looked pleased with his morning, which was more than Rallya could say about hers. Yes, there were ships in dock that needed a Second, but no one she cared to approach with details of Rafe's history. No, she had not explicitly promised to find him a berth, but she had implied that she could and he had openly doubted it.

And while she had been wasting her time, Rafe had been impressing Joshim. Not deliberately—she would grant him that— but it was obvious from the light in Joshim's eyes that he had been impressed. Obvious to every webber in the web-room, by the speculative looks that were flying about. And as for Fadir, mooning around over a pretty face and a well-turned backside . . .

"Fadir, if you don't remember to breathe soon, you'll faint," she told him sharply.

"There speaks the voice of experience," Rafe commented.

Even Fadir forgot to blush in the stunned silence that followed. Rallya opened her mouth and closed it again. "I never actually fainted," she said eventually. "But only because somebody else reminded me to breathe." She looked Rafe up and down slowly. "Of course, the provocation wasn't quite as intense," she added.

"Of course, ma'am," Rafe agreed seriously, taking the mug of alcad that Joshim handed him and raising it in salute.

Rallya returned the salute with a single eyebrow. "Did you enjoy your introduction to *Bhattya*'s web?" she asked sweetly.

"Thank you, ma'am, yes. I'm grateful for the opportunity."

"Good. Good." She turned to Vidar, who had finally stopped choking silently. "Is Jualla going to be free for my tactics workout, or do you need her to finish installing the mass sensors?" she inquired.

"I need her," Vidar said firmly.

"Then you shall have her," Rallya said happily. "It will give Rafe another opportunity to enjoy *Bhattya*'s web. You can join my workout, can't you Rafe?"

Joshim made a warning noise but Rafe smiled cheerfully. "It will be a delight, ma'am," he claimed.

"It will," Rallya agreed readily, refilling her mug and beaming at the web-room in general. "A delight."

Rallya stepped out of the riser and looked happily around the web. Ten of the wet-web places were filling with shub, ready for the workout. All that was missing were the eight juniors and Rafe, and by the sounds coming out of the changing-room, they were well on the way to being ready too.

Somebody came out of the riser behind her; she knew without looking that it was Joshim.

"I may not pass him fit," he said flatly. "He burnt himself this morning."

"That's what happens when you play with fire," Rallya

remarked. "Don't worry. I'll be gentle with him. Don't you want to know what he's like at tactics?"

"You'll be lacking your usual advantage," Joshim commented. "He isn't afraid of you."

"I'd noticed. Insolence as the last refuge of the desperate," Rallya jibed.

"Tell me that if he beats you," Joshim challenged.

"If he beats me, I'll take him as First," Rallya said confidently. "Staying to watch it happen?"

"It's too crowded down below," Joshim confirmed. "If anybody else wants to watch the monitor screen, they'll have to sit in Jualla's lap. On top of Rasil."

Rallya chuckled. "Time I was changing. Wouldn't do to be late for my own workout."

The changing-room was its usual tangle of bare skin, pale and dark, brown, yellow, and red. Rafe was an even hazlenut brown, with a light dusting of grey and brown body hair. Near-human blood in there somewhere, Rallya decided. All sorts of skeletons in his aristo family's cupboard. And if Fadir was allowed in here, he would definitely faint. She swatted Lilimya out of her way and started to strip.

"Two teams," she announced as she pulled her tunic over her head. "Lilimya, Rasmallya, Churi, Ajir: you're in Rafe's team. The rest of you, with me." Joshim could not accuse her of being unfair; she had given him the pick of the bunch. "Rafe, we use extended tens. You do know them?" She flung her breeches in the direction of the hook behind him.

"If I don't, I soon will."

Rafe caught the breeches one-handed and hung them up. His hair was tied in a short bunch of curls on top of his head. Rallya pinned up her own plaits and shook her head to be sure they were secure.

"Want a few minutes in the web alone with your team?" she offered.

"I wouldn't get them in a real battle situation," Rafe said easily. "But ask me again afterwards," he said over his shoulder on his way out.

When Rallya emerged into the web-room, Joshim was checking Rafe's contacts and muttering something that sounded suspiciously like advice. Rallya ignored it; she could afford to be generous.

Vidar had suspended work on the mass sensors to be present.

"Anybody making a book on the outcome?" Rallya called across to him.

"Why? You want to bet next year's pay?" he answered.

Joshim finished his inspection and nodded his consent for Rafe to web. There had been no real chance that he would refuse; he knew as well as Rallya that the encounter would not last long enough to do any real damage. Except to Rafe's pride.

She gestured to the members of her team that she wanted a conference and quickly assigned them their roles. From the corner of her eyes, she saw Rafe doing the same. That was probably what Joshim's advice had been about: a summary of the strengths and weaknesses of webbers Rafe had only just met. The young scut should have taken her offer of time in the web with them. So, you wouldn't get it in a real battle situation, Rallya scoffed. In a real battle situation, you take every advantage you can.

She stepped up to the nearest wet-web position and checked the level of the shub. High enough to support her.

"Webmaster's permission?" she called as a courtesy to Joshim.

"Granted." He stepped through the circle of wet-web places to take his position at the central monitor.

Rallya tucked her web-bands into the niche below the rim of her chosen position and dangled her feet in the shub while she positioned her links. It was colder than she liked, but she would not complain to Joshim; her fault, for not checking it earlier. A glance at the screen to check her links before climbing down the ladder into the shub and triggering her ready-light, then the wait for Joshim to activate her links.

She was wondering if he would dare to active Rafe before her when her contacts warmed, catching her off balance. She recovered quickly and flared out through the web, easily identifying her team and Rafe's, and locating the single unfamiliar presence. She kept a fraction of her attention on her team, enough to be sure they were following instructions and keeping the opposition too busy to help Rafe. The rest she focused on him, not attacking, just waiting pointedly for him to try something before she jumped on him and cut him out of the web.

Lilimya and the others were acting without coordination, just managing to retain their places and no threat to their opponents. Disappointing; even without a leader, Rallya would have expected better. Even as she thought that, Caruya was separated from the web without warning, leaving Rallya's team without its strongest member and Lilimya free to help Ajir. The pair of them ejected Khisa before Rallya could help her and then they turned to help Rasmallya and Churi.

Furious, Rallya lashed out at Rafe and found nothing except a resonance construct. Almost simultaneously, Shayoni and Magred lost their uneven struggles, leaving Rallya alone to face Rafe's team and an invisible Rafe. Curse you, she told him silently, digging herself into the heart of the web. Come to me if you want to finish this, or we'll be here until eternity.

Lilimya and the others were holding back. My usual advantage still holds against them, Joshim, she mocked herself, setting herself to locate Rafe in the web. Forty years against a few hours? There was no place he could hide from her, not now that she was looking for him. The construct had been good, and it had won him the first round, but not the battle. Never the battle.

Churi was getting nervous. Good. Good. Soon he would start signaling for reassurance, for instructions, and then she would know where Rafe was. She had only to dispose of him and the others would crumble. Come on, Churi. Commander Rallya is going to lose her temper and throw you out of the web soon. Do you remember how it feels to be thrown out of the web by Commander Rallya? Why not ask pretty boy what he wants you to do next? Churi, if you don't do something soon, I'm going to jump on you so hard you'll end up in tomorrow. Pretty boy won't watch while it happens. If he'll stand up for Fadir, he'll stand up for you.

She pounced. She came up hard against a solidity that was not Churi. Lilimya and the others were piling into her before she could retreat, including Churi who oozed out of the signal circuits with uncharacteristic determination. Emperors, two slick tricks in one workout was two too many! She was maybe going to lose, but she was going to take pretty boy out of the web with her. She grabbed for his core circuits and pushed as much power as she could through them, determined to break his grip on the web before Lilimya and the others forced her out. He resisted her for a moment, then crumpled frighteningly fast. Only then did she remember his web-cramp and try to cushion his way out of the web, but it was too late. Lilimya and the others drove her out as Rafe disappeared.

She dragged herself out of the shub and tore her links away without bothering to check that they were inactive. Joshim was already bending over Rafe's position, pulling him out with the aid of Rallya's dejected team. Just conscious and breathing, Rallya saw with relief.

"Jualla's on her way with your drug-pack," Vidar reported, leaving the central console to join Joshim.

"What's wrong?" Lilimya climbed out of the shub with a smile on her face that faded quickly as she saw the cluster around Rafe.

"Go get dressed," Rallya said without ceremony. "All of you." She swiped at the excess shub still clinging to her and pulled her web-bands out of the niche, strapping them on as she crossed the circle.

"You didn't have to jump on him so hard," Joshim accused, looking up for a moment when she halted beside Rafe.

"I'm sorry. I forgot your web-cramp." Rallya addressed Rafe directly. The youngster was pale and still twitching involuntarily, but he was in no danger.

"So did I." He grinned wearily. "A pity. Now we'll never know who would have won."

Rallya crumpled up the last flimsy and flung it in the general direction of the others littering one corner of the Three's small rest-room.

"He's got no patrolship experience at all," she complained to Vidar.

"Didn't seem to worry him this afternoon," he said maliciously. "Do you want this last mug of alcad or will you leave it for Joshim?"

"I'll have it. If Joshim wants some, he can fetch it from the web-room."

Rallya dragged herself out of her seat and emptied the pot. The first time in forty years that she had been thrown out of a web and every part of her seemed to know it. At least Rafe was feeling as bad, she comforted herself, and he deserved to. Nobody but a fool went into a tactics workout with web-cramp. Still, he had done well, considering that he had wasted the last ten years in a surveyship.

Joshim came through from the web-room. "Sorry I've been so long," he said, lifting the empty pot and putting it down again with a shrug.

"Web check out all right?" Vidar asked him. "There was some unusually rough play in it this afternoon."

"Which will not be repeated in future," Joshim said firmly.

"No point in having a workout if it doesn't hurt to lose," Rallya muttered. "Keeps people sharp." She sat carefully back in her seat.

"I noticed," Joshim said drily. "Rafe looks like death warmed up. And so do some of the other participants."

Rallya stared him down, defying him to name anybody else. Or to mention the careless promise she had made before the workout.

"Where is Rafe?" Vidar asked.

"He left nearly two hours ago." Joshim looked unhappy about it. "His nervous system checked out within the normal limits for everything—just. I couldn't justify ordering him to stay."

"Since when have we had to justify orders to Seconds?" Rallya challenged.

"Since they started being able to think for themselves."

"And there's no doubt that Rafe can do that," Vidar commented. "And he's good in the web, Joshim. As good as they come. You could turn him into a Webmaster in a few years' time."

"That's what I was thinking," Joshim agreed.

"You can't be serious," Rallya protested. "He's a born Commander."

"Two clever tricks don't prove anything. He was lucky, that's all. He'd never beat you like that twice."

"Luck like that you earn. And in a real combat situation, once is enough," Rallya insisted. "Anyway, he didn't beat me. The outcome was inconclusive. If I hadn't gone soft on him, I could still have won." *And the next time we tangle, I will,* she promised herself.

"I still think I could make a Webmaster out of him," Joshim said stubbornly.

"We can sort that out later," Rallya decreed. "How soon can we get him promoted to First?"

"Amsur will brevet him immediately, if we ask," Joshim predicted.

"Will his record cause any problems getting it made substantive?" Vidar asked.

"With *Bhattya*'s recommendation?" Rallya scoffed. "No problems at all. Joshim, how soon can you see Amsur?"

"Oughtn't I ask Rafe first if he wants the berth?"

"Emperors, of course he wants the berth! What do you think he's been doing here all day, if not working his bumps off trying to impress us?'' Rallya said in exasperation. ''Still, if it will make you happy to ask him first, ask him. And ask him which he wants to be: a Commander or a Webmaster,'' she called after Joshim's retreating back. ''I'll bet twenty days' pay I know the answer.''

* * *

Rafe poured himself a third glass of jack and drank from it without tasting it. Sleepers would be a safer way of achieving the oblivion he sought—alcohol on top of web-cramp was a fool's trick—but sleepers had to be obtained from the station surgeon at the cost of a question-and-answer session to which Rafe refused to submit. And with his web in its current overstretched state, he was more likely to be prescribed mild painkillers and a homily, neither of which would be of any help for his real problem.

He smiled sardonically. There was no help for his real problem, which was why he was running away from it inside a bottle of jack. After ten years, he thought angrily, there should be no more surprises. No drowning inrush of knowledge, no return of skills that he had no memory of possessing. All that should have been over in the first confusing year after he woke without any awareness of who he was, with only the knowledge of what he was—a webber—and of what he had chosen to have done to himself.

And yet there were still surprises, moments when he turned a corner inside himself and found: complete recall of the extended tens system of web signals, and the certainty that he had once used it regularly, but no memory of learning the system, nor of the circumstances in which he had used it. He emptied the glass in his hand and refilled it. There were no memories of anything that had once made him a person, only the things that made him a webber. And if he failed to find a berth in the next ninety-nine days, that too would be taken away from him.

The door alert sounded. He cursed. There was nobody in Achil zone to whom he wanted to speak. There was nobody in any zone in either Empire to whom he wanted to speak. Get gone, he wished the unknown visitor. Get gone and leave me to get drunk.

The alert sounded again. Rafe pushed himself to his feet and went to answer it. If he did not, his visitor would only come back later, when he would be even less able to deal with whoever it was.

"What?" he demanded as the door slid open at his touch. "What, sir?" he corrected himself belatedly as he recognized his visitor.

Joshim looked at him in silence. "You ought to be in bed," he said at last.

Rafe shrugged. "Yes." He leaned against the wall by the door, more drunk than he had realized. "Is that all, sir?"

Joshim was sniffing the air. "Jack? In your state?" he questioned.

"Jack. In my state." Rafe stepped back into the room. "Want some? The bottle isn't empty yet."

"I should hope not." Joshim followed Rafe in, closing the door behind him. "How much have you had?"

Rafe picked up the bottle and squinted at the level. "This was full," he said, abandoning the effort. He sat down again and looked up at Joshim. A crick in the neck was preferable to collapsing in an untidy heap on the floor. "There's another glass somewhere," he said, picking up his own. "Help yourself."

Joshim shook his head. "No, thanks. And you've had enough," he said firmly.

"Doesn't that depend on how much enough is?" Rafe queried.

"Enough is when you can't stand up, or see straight."

"Enough is when you're unconscious," Rafe contradicted him. "General anaesthetic," he added, gesturing at the bottle. "That's the theory anyway. As usual, the practice has a very loose correspondence with the theory, but I expect them to converge eventually."

"When you're unconscious." Joshim plucked the glass out of Rafe's hand and set it down. "Do you do this often?"

"No." Rafe closed his eyes and watched the patterns of light spinning inside his eyelids. Better than watching Joshim watching him.

"So why tonight?"

"It hasn't been a good day." Rafe opened his eyes. "Sorry, sir. After the trouble you took over me today, I ought to be treating my web with more care than this, I know. But tonight, there isn't any alternative. I don't recommend that you stay and watch."

Joshim seated himself on the edge of the low table, so that his eyes were on a level with Rafe's. Green eyes, Rafe noted, a

cap of sleek black hair, and uniformly pale brown skin, at least
as much of the skin as Rafe had seen. A ring bearing the silver
web of a Webmaster traced through a green stone on one hand,
and a silver pendant with the linked circles of an Aruranist,
visible earlier today but now hidden inside a black jacket.

"Do you take the pendant off in the web?" Rafe asked.

"Yes. And the ring." Joshim was amused by the question.
"I have a tattoo of the circles—most Aruranists do—but not of
the web." He continued to watch Rafe speculatively. "Apart
from getting thrown so hard out of the web, I would have
thought today was a very good day. I don't know of anybody
else who's ever beaten Rallya in a workout."

"I didn't beat her. If she hadn't gone soft on me, she could
still have won."

Joshim smiled. "That's the second time I've been told that
this evening. It was still a creditable performance."

"Surprisingly so," Rafe said bitterly. "Especially to me."

"Because of your web-cramp?"

"Not because of my faffing web-cramp!" Rafe reached for
his drink, evading Joshim's attempt to prevent him. "Until
today, sir, I had no idea I knew extended tens. Until today, I
had no idea I could create a resonance construct. Or mimic
somebody else in the web. Or hide somebody else in the signal
circuits." He gulped at the drink, emptying the glass before
Joshim could take it off him again. "Now I know I can do all
those things, but I don't know what else I know, or how I
learned, or who taught me. And if I go to sleep now, I shall
spend the night chasing nonexistent memories around my
dreams and beating myself against the walls inside my head."
He flung the glass against the wall beyond Joshim. It bounced
off and rolled across the floor. "And there isn't anybody to
blame except myself, and I'm never going to know why I was
stupid enough to break my Oath!"

He stopped and laughed self-consciously. "And I ache," he
admitted. "I feel as if somebody knocked me down and walked
all over me." He put his head on one side and looked at the
out-of-focus Webmaster. "You didn't come here to listen to me
whining, or to watch me drinking."

"No. I came to offer you a berth as *Bhattya*'s First."

Rafe swore incredulously, inadequately expressing the sickness in the pit of his stomach. "My luck could be used as a
metric for consistency," he muttered, stumbling to his feet to

retrieve the glass. "You wouldn't like to go away and pretend you haven't seen me like this?"

"No."

"I didn't think so." Rafe froze as his web twinged warning of an imminent spasm. "You could at least look the other way while I throw up," he said carefully.

"If I do that, you'll never reach the san."

Rafe found himself supported to the san, and after his stomach had rejected the alcohol with which he had flooded it, to the bed. He rolled onto his side, away from Joshim's efforts to remove his boots.

"Go away," he urged. "Take the bottle with you if it makes you happy, just go."

Joshim finished removing his boots. "I'm going to fetch something to sober you up," he said. "Your web is in no shape to cope with what you're doing to it."

"Why bother? It isn't your responsibility." Rafe turned miserably onto his stomach.

"We'll talk about that when you're sober."

"Hell, you are going to sober me up," Rafe said in disbelief, seeing the drug-pack with which Joshim returned.

"Yes." Joshim set the pack down on the table and came to look at Rafe where he was curled up in the san. "Sick again?"

"It seemed a good idea to stay here. Saves me having to clean up after myself later."

"That may be the first sensible thought you've had all evening. Think you can get to the bed? With help, of course. I'm not going to treat you in there."

Once Rafe was safely on the bed, Joshim opened the pack and took out a drug-mask and canister. "Deep breaths," he said, sitting beside Rafe on the bed and slipping the mask over his face.

Rafe obeyed, uncomfortably aware by now that the strictures about alcohol and web-cramp were fully justified. Joshim strapped a blood monitor to his arm; he flinched as the probe bit.

"Finish the canister," Joshim said, studying the readout. "There's still enough alcohol in your system to knock out half a web-room. Emperors only know how you stayed on your feet so long."

"Near-human blood," Rafe informed him through the mask. "Inconvenient when I'm trying to drink myself senseless."

"Shut up and breathe," Joshim told him.

Rafe closed his eyes and concentrated on pulling the drug into his lungs. As the alcohol was neutralized, it left behind an emotional numbness that he welcomed. Anything rather than think about the chance he had thrown away tonight.

"Enough," Joshim decided at last, lifting the mask off Rafe's face.

"Thank you, sir." Rafe sat up and hugged his knees. "That was good of you."

"It was also the one and only time I will do that for you," Joshim said grimly. "The next time you try to kill yourself with a bottle of jack, I'll leave you to it."

"I wasn't trying to kill myself," Rafe said flatly. "I can't. That's part of the conditioning that goes with identity-wipe. There isn't any way I can voluntarily deprive the Guild of my services. I have to wait to be thrown out." He shivered and started to remove the blood monitor from his arm.

"Leave that," Joshim ordered. "I'm going to give you a pain-killer."

"You wouldn't have a sleeper to spare?" Rafe asked hopefully.

"You can't take one tonight. Your system can't handle it."

"It can. Another effect of my near-human blood." Rafe grimaced. "Though I can't prove it."

"Your medical record . . ."

"Is incomplete, for obvious reasons. It notes that I'm a hybrid, without giving details." Rafe shrugged. "Forget I asked. I'll have to sleep without help sooner or later. Why not tonight?"

"If you're going to be *Bhattya*'s First, I shall want a full metabolic workup for you," Joshim commented. "Until then, I'll take your word about the sleeper."

"Is the offer still open?" Rafe asked disbelievingly.

"Yes. On the condition that this does not happen again." Joshim handed him a small cup of liquid. "Drink that." He took the cup away when Rafe had finished, rinsed it out and shut it in the drug-pack. "Lie flat."

Rafe obeyed, feeling the drug starting to work. "How in hell did you persuade Commander Rallya to accept me?" he asked sleepily.

Joshim laughed. "One day I may answer that. Go to sleep."

From the Old Empire Guild Bulletin, 200/5043

In Aramas zone, ship losses to the unidentified Outsiders continue. Convoys are being instituted on the routes of greatest risk, and extra patrolships assigned to the zone. At the request of the Guild Council, the Emperor Julur has dismissed Drevir Lord Rhamar as head of the team of diplomats and historians attempting to make contact with the Outsiders, and appointed Madjaya Lady Gremor, noted for her successful contact with the Lam-ti-ranog system (now Dasnar zone).

Report by Palace Security Chief Braniya to the Emperor Julur

In the matter of your particular interest, personnel changes in the Aramas zone will take effect shortly; a preliminary report on the new situation is attached. Investigations into recent events are continuing.

205/ 5043:
ARAMAS ZONE, OLD EMPIRE

"Glad to be back, Rallya?" As he spoke, Noromi, Commander of *Meremir*, looked around the conference room in disgust.

"Emperors, we'll never get this lot sorted out. I doubt one of them has run in a convoy before."

"They'll learn," Rallya told him. She did not envy Noromi his task as Convoy Commander, in spite of the apparent authority it gave him over the other patrolships. He was welcome to the tiresome business of keeping the cargoships in some semblance of order and mediating between cargoship Threes who all thought they deserved special treatment at each other's expense. Far better to have *Bhattya*'s role, only loosely attached to the convoy and free to pursue Outsiders while Noromi chivvied the convoy to safety.

"They won't learn. Not until we've lost one of them," Noromi predicted sourly. He glowered at the group of cargoship reps, congregated for mutual protection on the side of the room nearest the door. "Pity we can't pick which one."

"I don't see Jomisa here," Rallya commented, changing the subject before Noromi could tell her which of the cargoships had the distinction of being the first to annoy him.

"She got promoted into a Second's berth on *Sarasya*. Just before they went for a refit. The blond is her replacement." Noromi pointed carelessly towards the back of the room, where the patrolship seniors, brought along to gain experience of strategy conferences, had gathered. "Talking to the half-size First."

"Rafe," Rallya informed him.

"Yours?" Noromi turned for a longer look. "Much experience?"

"Enough," Rallya said vaguely. Enough to force her to a draw in the web twice since their initial encounter, but she was not going to admit that to Noromi. Enough to cope with the heavy load of tactical case studies that she had set him and to come back with unexpectedly perceptive analyses of them. He had served in a patrolship before he was identity-wiped, that was certain, and a patrolship with a Commander who had singled him out for special training.

"You must introduce me," Noromi decided.

"I'll add you to the list."

Noromi grunted and turned to watch the door again. "Here's Maisa at last," he grumbled. "You'd think she'd be on time for her own conference."

Maisa looked understandably harried. She was the wrong person to be Zone Commander in a zone where Outsider incursions were a serious threat to shipping; she should be

sitting out the last few years of her career in a backwater.
Rallya scowled. There were enough Commanders whose webs
had failed for whom the Guild could not find any job. She
wondered whose favours Maisa had called in. And whether she
was regretting it now.

It was a big convoy—four patrolships and eleven cargo—and
it took a while for Maisa to get the silence she was waiting for.
Rallya glanced back at Rafe, lounging against the back wall
with his hands in his pockets and every appearance of having
seen it all before. He acknowledged her glance with a tiny tilt
of his head: still here, ma'am. It would be a waste of time to
question him later, she decided sourly; he was not missing a
thing that was going on around him.

Maisa shuffled her notes for the last time and plunged into
her prepared speech. Rallya leaned back in her seat. There was
nothing new to her in what Maisa was saying, only a rehash of
the current situation. Outsiders of unknown origin . . . historians
making every effort at identification . . . diplomats attempting
peaceful contact . . . convoy system for your protection . . . Rallya
yawned ostentatiously. If there was one thing Maisa could do,
it was take a blatant hint. She skipped hurriedly to the end of
her notes, introduced Noromi and excused herself, duty done.

Noromi took the cargoship reps through a rapid review of the
convoy rules and running order before allowing them the
pretense of debating the decisions already taken. No cargoship
carried a trained Commander; whichever member of a Three
came closest to the necessary skills was deputized to fill the
role when needed. Rallya could see equal numbers of Webmasters,
Cargomasters and Captains, and every one of them convinced
that they had something useful to say. At least it was an
opportunity to identify the troublemakers and the steady few
who would not panic in an Outsider attack.

There was one Captain to whom it would be worth talking;
she had survived Outsider attacks on her last two runs along the
convoy's route. When the conference had straggled to an end,
Rallya rose with the intention of intercepting her but was
delayed by a Webmaster hoping for an apprentice's berth with
Bhattya for a protégé of hers. By the time Rallya had extricated
herself, she expected to find her quarry gone and was surprised
to see the woman lingering near Rafe, waiting for an opportunity
to talk to him when Noromi moved on.

"Captain Sajan, I'm Commander Rallya. Can we talk? I'd like more details about the Outsider ships that attacked you."

"Gladly, if you'll wait for me..." She gestured at Rafe, who had disposed of Noromi and was waiting for Rallya.

"Rafe is with me. Is it a private matter, or will you join both of us for a drink?"

"A drink will be welcome, after this waste of time." Sajan waved a hand around the emptying room.

"Not a complete waste, surely, ma'am," Rafe commented. "Commander Maisa's summary of the situation here was very informative."

Rallya looked at him suspiciously. Sajan gave a short laugh.

"With your looks, and a sense of humor like that, you must be related to Yuellin," she snorted.

"I'm afraid the name isn't familiar, ma'am." Rafe did not change expression. Never play cards with him for money, Rallya cautioned herself, watching with interest to see how he dealt with this.

"You were born in the New Empire?" Sajan pointed to the twin Oath marks on Rafe's sleeve and to a similar pair on her own tunic breast.

"Yes, ma'am." Rafe smiled apologetically. "But I'm a chance-child. I don't know my parentage."

"You could be his brother, the resemblance is so close. Or his son. You're young enough, and he could have fathered you before he got his web." Sajan snorted again. "Although he isn't a man for women. I should know. I tried hard enough when we were serving together, before he made Commander on *Janasayan*. That was fifteen years ago, of course. Surprised he isn't on the Guild Council by now. One of the youngest Commanders ever. Didn't look old enough to have a web, let alone a Commander's berth."

"Sounds like you have a lot in common with him, Rafe," Rallya suggested slyly. "Is it impossible that you're his son?"

"Not impossible, ma'am, merely improbable." There was a hard edge of anger on his voice, unmissable evidence of a temper; Rallya wondered what it would take to make him lose it.

"If you ever cross the Zone again, ask him," Sajan suggested. "Yuellin Lord Buhklir. Tell him I sent you." She squeezed Rafe's shoulder and Rallya found herself holding her breath. "Who knows? You might turn out to be the Buhklir heir. Wouldn't that be something for a chance-child?"

"Yes, ma'am, it would." Rafe removed himself from Sajan's grip as if by accident and turned to Rallya. "Will you excuse me? I promised the Webmaster I'd take the afternoon training session with the apprentices today."

A lie, and he knew that Rallya knew it. Rallya nodded permission and Rafe bowed his farewell. Captain Sajan looked disappointed; she had obviously hoped to reminisce with him at length about her aristo acquaintance in the New Empire. Rafe would have to be careful to avoid her in future, Rallya thought. There would be few webbers as intolerant of an Oath-breaker—aristo's son or not—as one who had themselves crossed the Disputed Zone.

Still, she had answered the obvious questions about Rafe's past. Chance-child, hell; he was the beloved son and heir of Yuellin Lord Buhklir, and the recipient of all the care and attention that an aristo could arrange. Buhklir had probably supervised the lad's apprenticeship himself, then made sure that he was assigned to a ship with a Commander who could be relied upon to continue his special treatment. Rallya grinned nastily. Relied upon to continue his special treatment, but not to keep him safe in the right Empire.

Or was Rafe's crossing of the Disputed Zone not the result of a mistake by his Commander but arranged as a deliberate curb on his father? It had happened before: an aristo who put loyalty to Empire before loyalty to Guild, rising to a high position and needing to be reminded of the full meaning of the Oath. The only thing that an aristo put before Empire was family; what better reminder than a son in the other Empire? No aristo would argue so eagerly for lethal combat in the Zone if their own son was facing them across it.

Rallya pressed her lips together, irritated by the sour taste in her mouth. A pity if the son felt compelled to be identity-wiped, but the welfare of the Guild came before the welfare of any individual member; Rafe had acknowledged as much when he took his Oath. If he wanted to complain that he had been badly treated—and he would have to work out for himself what had happened; Rallya would not help him—let him complain to his father.

Or to the Emperors, Rallya corrected herself savagely. The Immortal Emperors, who would only be content when they had drawn the Guild fully into the endless and aimless war between them. When they measured their losses in the Zone in maimed and dead bodies, not transferred Oaths. When the Guild's autonomy was shattered and the fleet permanently divided between the Empires. When they were released from the Oaths that bound them to the Guild as tightly as the Guild was bound to them, the only constraint that had ever been placed upon them and held. One webber subjected to identity-wipe would not trouble *their* consciences; the Guild could not afford to be less ruthless in its fight to survive. If Rafe had a complaint to make, let him make it to the Emperors.

"Let's find that drink," Rallya told Sajan abruptly. "I want to know everything you noticed about those Outsider ships."

*   *   *

"Commander back?" Joshim asked, finding Rafe grabbing a very late lunch alone in the web-room.

"No, sir. I left her talking with one of the cargoship Captains. Gathering information on Outsider capabilities."

"Conference go well?"

"Yes, sir. Or, I assume so," Rafe said lightly. "There was no violence done during the debate, and everybody seemed to leave it with their expectations met." He stood up and slid his empty plate into the cleanser. "Do you want me to take the training session with the apprentices this afternoon?"

"Vidar is taking it." Joshim looked at Rafe narrowly. It was odd that Rallya had not kept him with her. "You can supervise Churi and Magred in the web, if you would. Signaling practice. Wet-web with them, if you like." He glanced at the web schedule. "They're down for three hours, but cut it to two. We've a new junior arriving this afternoon and I want him in the web as soon as possible."

"I thought we had our full complement," Rafe commented.

"So did I, but I've just received notification that it's been increased by one and he's arriving this afternoon."

Joshim tried to keep the irritation out of his voice and failed. It was not that he objected to the increase, only to the timing of it, the day before they were due to leave with the convoy. A newcomer always disturbed the established patterns in a web; it had taken several days to assimilate even somebody as skilled as Rafe, and that had been on the milk-run from Achil to Aramas.

"Stay in the web when you've finished with Churi and Magred," he decided. "You can help me evaluate him. If he isn't good enough, we aren't taking him." He checked the time. "Go and have a look at his record. It's on the table in the rest-room. Shall I bring you some alcad through? I'm making some for myself anyway."

"Thanks, yes."

Rafe had finished reading when Joshim sat his alcad down in front of him.

"You haven't read this yourself yet, sir?" he queried.

"No. Why?"

"I know him. He was with *Avannya*."

"And?" Joshim prompted.

Rafe leaned back in his seat and crossed his ankles. "Elanis is competent, but lazy. He never gives 100 percent when he thinks 50 will be enough." He wrinkled his nose. "It wouldn't matter except that his judgment is poor. He always thinks 50 will be enough."

Joshim leafed through the record. "He was with *Avannya* for six years," he noted. "Could you afford to carry him?"

"We couldn't get rid of him." Rafe shrugged. "He's got influence somewhere. The Three tried twice to get him reassigned but he clung like a limpet. It was a surprise when he moved on voluntarily." He scowled. "Two days before our last trip, into a cushy berth on a passenger carrier. I'm surprised he left it."

"Maybe he found somebody with more influence that he has," Joshim suggested. "You recommend we don't take him?"

"Not if you can avoid it." Rafe leaned forward and picked up his alcad. "If you can't avoid it, you can always put him in the Commander's team. That would encourage him to move on again."

"I heard that," Rallya said from the doorway behind Joshim.

"You were meant to, ma'am." Rafe stood up with his alcad. "If you'll excuse me, I have some work to do."

"The apprentices' training session?" Rallya asked.

"No, ma'am."

"You surprise me." Rallya stepped out of Rafe's way. "You should have come with us for that drink. Captain Sajan was full of useful information."

"Be careful, ma'am," Rafe warned. "Much sharper and you'll cut yourself."

"I'll bear it in mind, son," Rallya promised.

Rafe turned in the doorway to stare at her. "I may not know whose son I am, ma'am, but I do know whose son I'm not."

The anger in his voice was plain and unexpected; until that

moment Joshim had thought this was just another of the mock battles that gave the web-room such pleasure. Rallya too was taken aback; she paused for a fraction of a second before responding.

"I'll bear that in mind too, Rafe."

He turned on his heel and left. Rallya watched him leave, then gave a little nod as if she had learned something worth knowing. "Who am I going to encourage to leave?" she asked.

"What in hell was that about?" Joshim demanded. Emperors, if Rallya had not backed down...

"Answer my question and I'll answer yours."

"A new junior. Elanis. Used to be on *Avannya*." He held out the record to her. "Arriving this afternoon."

"Another ghost from Rafe's past," Rallya mused. "Must be his day for them."

"Another?"

"There was a Captain at the conference who knew his father. Apparently the likeness is startling." She chuckled. "Yes, I know. I shouldn't have pushed him so hard. But the results were interesting, weren't they?"

You old fraud. You were as surprised as I was, Joshim accused her silently. "It would have been even more interesting if he'd hit you," he growled.

"Shall I call him back? You can hold his tunic." Rallya took the record that Joshim was still holding and dropped it on the table. "What's wrong with him? Besides the fact that Rafe doesn't like him?"

Joshim made himself swallow his first answer. Rallya had never made him lose his temper and she would not do so now. "He's lazy. And he relies on influence instead of ability," he said levelly.

"Aristo?" Rallya demanded.

"Look for yourself." Joshim stood up. "Rafe will be working with me for the rest of the day."

"To protect him from me?" Rallya asked in amusement.

"To protect you from him," Joshim flung back, and walked out leaving Rallya still looking for a response.

*   *   *

Rafe sat on the rim of his web-position, listening to Churi and Magred talking in the changing-room about him. They had already agreed that he was a darling in the web-room but a stickler in the web; now they were discussing whose lover he would become and when. Magred's opinion was that it had already happened, with Joshim, and Churi favored the Commander, at some indeterminate point in the future. Very indeterminate and far future, Rafe felt like telling him; he contented himself with a yelled reminder that the Webmaster would be arriving soon. There was a sudden silence, followed shortly afterwards by the fully clothed emergence of two very junior juniors wondering how much, if anything, he had overheard. He smiled at them, sphinx-like, and let them go still wondering.

The shub beneath his feet was warm and inviting. He wished he could slip back in, to wait for Joshim and Elanis, but it would be a bad example to set: apparently webbing alone. He swung around through ninety degrees and stretched out along the edge of the web, closing his eyes and relying on his ears to warn him of somebody coming up the riser.

Yuellin Lord Buhklir. The name woke no echo, nor did he expect it to; if it had, he would have distrusted it as wishful thinking. His father, or brother, or merely somebody who shared his particular genetic mix: it did not matter. As Rafell, he had no connection with the man and he never would. If some belly-kick of fate took him back into the New Empire, he would not have any memory of the encounter with Sajan; he would be identity-wiped again. Insurance against an Oath-breaker deliberately recrossing the Disputed Zone. Effective insurance.

He sighed, wondering what the Commander had learned from Sajan, and when he would find out. Not about the Outsiders: the safety of *Bhattya* might depend on his, or somebody else's, correct interpretation of that information; Rallya was too good a Commander not to know that. But anything she had learned about Buhklir, she would keep to herself until she found a use for it, and that use would be against Rafe. Emperors knew how she had amused herself before he had joined *Bhattya*. Was there a forty-year-long succession of webbers with whom she had played like a cat with small prey, or was he unique, because she thought he was uniquely vulnerable?

He had given her reason to question that earlier, and it was too late to doubt the wisdom or otherwise of that moment of anger. He smiled, briefly amused that she might think he had been upset by what Sajan had revealed, angered by her method rather than her intent. She would learn eventually. I will not lie down to be walked over, he promised her silently. Because others saw fit to play God with my life, that does not give you the right. I am not your toy, nor a pawn to prove your power. Push me too hard and it will become very clear. Did you think I was angry today? You have never seen me angry, Commander.

He took a deep breath. In ten years he had never lost his temper any further than he had with Rallya, and that only rarely. How then did he know that he could, and that it was something for others to fear? Nothing but skills and impersonal knowledge survived identity-wipe; it could not be personal memory that told him. More wishful thinking? Or a near-human race-memory? He shrugged. Another thing he would never know, and he could not fret over every one of those, or even over any of them. If he did, he would spend his life in a bottle of jack.

A whisper of air blowing across his damp skin told him the riser was in use. He sat up as Joshim stepped out, smiling a greeting which Rafe returned.

"Sorry to keep you waiting." Joshim moved aside for Elanis. "You two know each other."

"Yes, it's a reunion." Elanis looked around avidly. "I'm impressed. It makes *Avannya* look tiny, doesn't it, Rafe?" he commented.

"The changing-room is through here." Joshim steered him in the right direction and out of sight. Rafe got to his feet and moved to prepare one of the dry-web positions; Joshim would want a calibration sequence first. He had just finished when Elanis reappeared.

"The Webmaster said you're to do a calibration sequence," the junior announced.

"The Webmaster asked if you'd do a calibration sequence, please," Joshim called out.

Elanis glared as he removed his web-bands. "Are you a real First this time, or is it still brevet?" he asked more quietly.

"Does it make a difference?" Rafe asked mildly. "And whichever it is, you still ought to check those contacts before you use them."

"I assumed you had." He made a perfunctory check. "You haven't changed much, have you?"

"That's reassuring to know." You cannot like everyone you web with, Rafe told himself strictly, starting the calibration sequence. You only need to trust them. It was unfortunate that Elanis did not inspire trust either.

Elanis' performance in the web had not improved in the

near-year since Rafe had last worked with him. It took Joshim less than an hour to reach an assessment of his abilities, and only five minutes to tell it to him afterwards. Rafe lingered out of hearing until Joshim had finished, and Elanis had dressed hastily and departed. He had enough experience of Elanis's character to know that he would blame Rafe for Joshim's opinion, just as he had blamed Rafe for every unfavorable opinion of him since Rafe had been promoted into the Third's berth that Elanis had expected to get; Rafe had no intention of being the target for his immediate spite.

The Webmaster was taking a leisurely shower when Rafe finally went through the shower-room.

"Was he the Webmaster's lover on *Avannya*?" he asked, moving aside for Rafe.

"No." Rafe grinned maliciously. "Although he wanted to be, for the privileges he thought it would get him. He wasn't anybody's lover, not for very long. Things he learned across the pillow were all around the web-room the following day."

"You speak from experience?"

"No. Observation. That's another of the things he has against me."

Joshim laughed. "I suspect he's planning his way into my bed. Any advice on how to avoid it?"

Rafe took the tie out of his hair and shook the curls down. "I suspect he'd be lucky to make it through the cabin door."

"True. Although it isn't so difficult for the right person."

Rafe stepped into the spray to give himself time to think. There had been enough warning of this in the speculative looks that Joshim had been giving him since he joined the ship. He ought to have a response prepared; what he had was a hollowness between heart and groin, both of which were responding without words. He was not a virgin; there had been nights of curiosity and comfort with other webbers, but always single nights, sharing nothing except the hours of pleasure. There had never been any commitment, no exchange of pasts and promise of futures, because Rafe had no past that he dared to offer. But with Joshim, who already knew? The prospect unexpectedly frightened him.

"Is this such a surprise, Rafe?" Joshim set his hands lightly on Rafe's shoulders and bent forward to kiss him. Rafe had a moment of déjà vu that shook him as much as his physical reaction—green eyes beneath black hair, parted lips bending to kiss him. He trembled. Joshim released him at once and stepped back.

"Sorry, Rafe. I thought . . ."

Rafe took his hands and pulled him back under the spray, standing on tiptoe with his hands on Joshim's hips to reach his mouth. They kissed, broke apart for breath, and kissed again as fiercely. Joshim called a halt at last, holding Rafe firmly at arm's length with one hand and switching off the spray with the other.

"Dry, dressed, and down to my cabin? As Webmaster, I have to set a good example, and what will happen in this shower if we don't leave it soon is not something I want the juniors to emulate."

*   *   *

Rafe was a playful lover, his lips laughing as often as kissing and in as many ways, but now he was lying beside Joshim in the prolonged, easy silence that had followed their first loving, his face against Joshim's shoulder, one leg bent over Joshim's thigh. Joshim traced a mischievous finger along his back. Rafe sighed in unabashed pleasure and turned his head just enough to nip the lobe of Joshim's ear. Joshim moved without haste until he could see Rafe's face and stroke the fine sheen of silky grey hair on his belly that merged into the diamond of brown curls at his groin. Rafe gasped and rolled onto his back, reaching urgently for Joshim. Joshim held his wrists gently and ran his tongue up the sensitive under-surface of each arm before releasing them and setting his tongue to trace descending circles through the grey down of Rafe's belly. Rafe moaned in eager anticipation and Joshim paused to look up at his face.

"Did you say something?" he teased.

Rafe said something that showed scant respect for Joshim's rank. Joshim tutted and settled himself lower between Rafe's thighs. Playful and delightfully noisy, he amended as Rafe answered to his lips and tongue. The final yell would have woken the whole ship were it not for the soundproofing of the cabins.

He lay with his head on Rafe's thighs afterwards, listening to his breathing move into the even cadence of sleep. Rafe had a rare gift for knowing when words were needed, and when silence was right; he was a comfortable person to be silent with, and if he fell asleep without words, it was because he trusted Joshim to know what might have been said.

He had a gift too for enjoying himself, for drawing every drop of pleasure out of a moment before moving to the next. Joshim smiled at the memory. There had been no haste when they closed the cabin door behind them. A slow undressing, each savouring the initial revelation of the other's body outside the discipline of the web, exploring with the eyes before they touched. A gentle embrace, kissing with none of their earlier urgency, moving to the bed, searching for the words and the caresses that brought response, building a language to be shared between them: "This?" "Yes." "And this?" "Oh, please, yes!"

Joshim slipped off the bed, careful not to disturb the sleeper, and said his evening prayers in front of the Arura in the niche behind his desk. Late, but then they often were, and he could not believe in a deity who required stopwatch accuracy, anymore than he really believed in a deity who would hear his prayers. Prayer was a reaffirmation of belief; the Arura was a visible symbol of that belief; a deity, or thousands of them, were only other symbols, necessary because his mind was too limited to comprehend the reality behind them. How many reincarnations would it take before he progressed beyond the need for those particular symbols? He stroked the curve of the Arura, thinking that he would keep one even when he no longer needed it, amused by his sudden, unusual introspection. There is a reason for every question, but not necessarily an answer, he reminded himself as he lay down beside Rafe to sleep.

*   *   *

A face. A succession of faces, or were they all the same face? They flashed in and out of focus, mouthing snatches of speech that were sounds, not words. Rafe tried desperately to cling to one of them, any one of them, to hear what was said, to see the face clearly. The effort drove the dream away and he was lying in the dark with nothing left.

A dim light came on, making him blink, and there was a face looking down on him. He struggled to put a name to it, knowing that he knew one, not knowing what it was. He squeezed his eyes shut and swore in frustration.

"Rafe?"

The voice triggered memory. Joshim. Rafe opened his eyes again and tried his own voice. "Sorry. Nightmare." He sat up and rested his chin on his knees. "Did I wake you?"

"Yes." It was not a complaint. Joshim put his arm across Rafe's shoulders and squeezed briefly. "Tell me?"

Rafe shrugged. "I wish I could. There isn't anything to tell. Nothing I can remember," he added sardonically.

"Your father?" Joshim guessed.

"The Commander told you?"

"She mentioned it."

"There's no proof that he is my father. Or anything else to me. And if you'd asked me before I went to sleep, I would have said it didn't bother me at all." Rafe smiled with difficulty. "Obviously, I would have been wrong. Something must have triggered that nightmare."

"How often do you have them?"

"Not often, now." Rafe sighed. "Immediately after I was wiped, they came every night. Now, it's once or twice a year, with the occasional bad patch." He rubbed his cheek against the hand on his shoulder. "You're honored. You're only the second person who's ever been woken by one."

"Oh? What sort of company am I in?"

"One of *Avannya*'s juniors. She was in the web when we hit the EMP-mine."

"I'm sorry. Was she special to you?"

"We only spent the one night together. She was a nice kid, though." Rafe shook his head in remembered grief. "About Churi's age, and as plump. Working her way through every cabin in the ship, the way they do when they've just got their webs. Making up for lost time as an apprentice and eager to find out about the fringe benefits of their new nervous system. Hell, the way I probably behaved when I first got my web."

"Churi been in your bed yet?" Joshim teased deliberately.

"No." Rafe accepted the diversion gratefully, determined to enlarge on it. "He thinks the Commander is in possession, or will be soon. Magred has better powers of observation. She was backing you." He turned to face Joshim completely, slipping one arm around his waist and tracing the linked circles of the tattoo on his left breast with the fingers of the other hand. "Ready to go back to sleep?"

"You have another idea?"

Rafe grinned mischievously and straddled Joshim. "I do," he promised deep in his throat. "Lie there and I'll show you."

Conversation at the office of
Councillor Danriya Lady Carher

"The agent is in place, with explicit instructions to cover every contingency. If all goes well, the problem will be solved by the end of the year."

"You said that last year too."

"This time the matter will be handled by the agent in person. He is in no doubt about the consequences of another failure."

227/5043:
ARAMAS ZONE, OLD EMPIRE

Rallya dropped into the seat that Elanis had just vacated in front of the web-monitor, perfectly aware that he had only risen to collect a cup of alcad. The monitor showed no unusual activity, just two web-teams in the last hour of another uneventful shift. Vidar was nominally in the key-position, with Rafe as second, but they had switched roles for this shift. Good practice for both teams, and halfway to the convoy's destination without incident, everybody needed a little variety to keep them sharp.

The small screen to one side of the web-monitor showed a mass-scan of the convoy, the cargoships as fat, lumbering blips and the patrolships as smaller blips tied to the speed of the cargoships by invisible chains. The cargoships were complacent; Noromi spent his whole time exhorting them to make better speed, without results. Having passed safely through the system's major jump point, the obvious place for an Outsider attack, the cargoship Threes had given a collective sigh of relief and dropped their speed, to settle happily around the optimum of their mass-speed cost curves for the run down to the settlements on the inner planets.

Only Sajan, aboard *Tariya*, was showing any sense, and in her position at the back end of the convoy, she was handicapped in her attempts to gain speed by the ships in front, who wailed to Noromi whenever *Tariya* ran up their tails. In Noromi's place, Rallya would have used Sajan to force the others to increase speed, instead of giving her a warning about convoy formation whenever the wails became too loud. In fact, she had offered *Bhattya*'s services to perform the same function; a patrolship creeping inexorably up your rear end was a powerful incentive to accelerate. The hell with Noromi's veto; if things did not improve soon, she would do it anyway.

The view on the small screen altered as Rafe focused on the large cluster of asteroids in the trojan point of one of the system's gas giants, altered again to scan to the limits of *Bhattya*'s sensors. He learned well, Rallya thought approvingly. Aware of the obvious, but not concentrating on it to the exclusion of other possibilities. The asteroids would make a good hiding place for one or two raiders. Noromi was aware of that and had positioned both of the other patrolships to cover it. *Bhattya*, above the plane that held asteroids and convoy, was equally well placed to meet an attack from the asteroids or from the three other sectors within her reach.

Rallya narrowed her eyes as she calculated how well placed they were. They had gradually moved out from the position she had left them in at the end of her shift, three hours ago. Accident, or Rafe thinking ahead? The latter, she conceded grudgingly. As she watched, he continued to flick between the long-range scan and the asteroids.

"Rafe showing off again?" Elanis said quietly from behind her seat. He had learned not to make such comments for everyone to hear—Joshim had reduced him to incoherence with a few well-chosen words the first time that he did so—but he continued to make them to Rallya in private, taking her sparring with Rafe as encouragement.

"Trying to emulate his father," Rallya suggested. Rafe had not mentioned Sajan's information since that day, made no attempt to discover what Rallya knew. It would be interesting to see how he reacted to this pestilent aristo apparently knowing more than he did, and she could rely on Elanis to use what she told him.

"His father?" Elanis rose to the bait beautifully.

"Some aristo in the New Empire. Commander Buhklir. Sajan, aboard *Tariya*, knew him before he came across the Zone." Rallya smiled happily. "Did you know he was an aristo, too?"

"He's never mentioned his past," Elanis said stiffly. "No doubt he's an unacknowledged son."

"Ask him," Rallya suggested. "If he is, that's another advantage he has over you. Looks, skill, intelligence, and he isn't an aristo. What more could anybody ask for?"

Elanis fell silent, lacking the wit to respond in any way that would not be insubordinate. Rallya had not yet forgiven Joshim for moving Churi from her team into Rafe's and replacing him with a lazy lump of bone and blubber; the first opening that Elanis gave her, he would be off *Bhattya*. Joshim had filed a request to transfer him the day after he arrived, but Rallya would not rely upon the goodwill of some assignment clerk. She would push him into insubordination sooner or later; he did not have Rafe's fine judgment of where the line lay. She grinned, admitting to herself that the line for Rafe was not in the same place as it was for everybody else. She had not had so much fun with her clothes on in years, and she would not hamper Rafe with rules.

Rafe's main view had changed again, picking out a lone asteroid above and to one side of the convoy. Rallya stiffened as he tightened the focus and switched to a large scale mass-contour chart. Yes, that discrepancy would be a raider, well hidden and waiting to pick off the tail-end ship of the convoy with a tight tractor-beam before a preset jump; that was how she would do it in their place.

As she pushed herself out of her seat, the primary alert sounded and she swore. No time to get into the web; Vidar would have to handle it alone. No, not Vidar, Rafe. The teams could not switch roles now, not without wasting seconds that would let the raider escape. As she sat down again, still cursing, Rafe started the tight turn that would take *Bhattya* after the raider.

Joshim displaced Lilimya from the seat beside Rallya, blatantly disregarding the alert; he had not been in the web-room when it sounded, should have stayed where he was. The raider was moving away from the asteroid, trying to get out of its mass shadow in order to jump. A beautiful ship, built for speed and stealth. Rallya cursed the historians, for their failure to identify the source of such a ship, and the diplomats, for their repeated failure to make peaceful contact. If they could do their jobs properly, there would be no need for this.

Rafe had calculated the turn beautifully, second-guessing the direction that the raider would choose to escape. The only questions were the timing and the range of the raider's weapons. Rafe did not have the shields up, could not put them up before the turn was complete without risking the loss of the steering vanes. If they completed their turn before they were within the raider's range, and if the raider was unable to jump before they were within *Bhattya*'s range . . . Rallya ran the calculations in her head and came up with a question mark.

"If Rafe snaps one of the vanes, Vidar will be furious," she remarked for the benefit of her audience. Rasil tittered until Fadir hushed him.

They were coming out of the turn now, the vanes that had been flattened against the hull straightening, restoring the spherical symmetry of the drive field. Vidar's team were easing into control of more and more functions, careful not to disturb the working of Rafe's team but relieving them of background tasks and allowing them to concentrate on weapons, shields, and timing. Rallya sustained the effort necessary not to hold her breath until Rafe raised the shields.

He did it later than she would have done, perhaps making his own balance between the slight loss of speed and the increased safety, and perhaps catching the first signs of the raider preparing to fire: the temperature increases along their hull, the minor adjustments in orientation. When the raider did fire, he resisted the temptation to fire back immediately, letting the shields take the battering they were designed to take, using the time to decrease the range. Yes, Rallya urged. They must stop firing and lower their shields before they jump. Wait for that moment, when there is nothing to confuse your aim, neither their fire nor the backwash of your own, and nothing to protect them except the favor of their gods.

He waited, as if he could hear her, and at the moment that the raider prepared to jump, he fired. One shot, as if he would do it neatly or not at all. A square hit, and where there had been a shining hull, there was a spreading mess of metal. Fadir gave a whoop of triumph.

"Fadir, go calculate how many crew that ship could carry." Rallya snarled the order without taking her attention from the screens. Rafe had switched again to long-range scan. Emperors, as if he had done this hundreds of times before, Rallya thought disbelievingly. He should have been reacting like Fadir, exulting in his victory, not immediately wary of another attack. How in hell was he managing to do everything so right?

"I'll take my team up," Joshim decided, standing up. "We can be ready to relieve them as soon as Rafe gives the signal."

Rallya grunted agreement. "I'll bleep Jualla and her team, send them up too." The messenger alarm was flashing insistently. "Congratulations from our Convoy Commander and his grateful charges," she predicted. "Wonderful how fast they've all started to move now."

"Rafe down?" Rallya asked Vidar as he entered the rest-room.

"Yes. In the web-room, drinking alcad." Vidar chuckled. "I'm surprised you weren't out there to jump on him as soon as he came down."

"Why should I want to do that?"

"I can't imagine. He didn't do a thing wrong, but that doesn't usually stop you." Vidar was in a high good humor.

Rallya ignored the jibe, knowing when Vidar was teasing. "And now he's basking in applause from everyone who knows no better," she predicted.

Vidar shook his head. "He stopped that just as soon as it started. Asked Churi how many people he'd helped to kill today. Everybody else took the hint. Except Elanis. He accused Rafe of being an Outie sympathizer. Got most upset when Rafe reminded him that *his* family had been Outies three generations ago. Called Rafe an upstart chance-child whose only talent was for bending his back in the Webmaster's bed." Vidar had obviously relished the confrontation, was repeating it word for word.

"So you put him on a charge?" Rallya said hopefully.

Vidar shook his head. "Wasn't necessary," he said gleefully. "Rafe apologized for beating him into Joshim's bed and wished him better luck with you. Elanis was laughed out of the web-room."

Rallya grinned broadly. "With his tail tucked firmly between his legs and likely to stay there."

She stretched gently, reflecting that the seats in the rest-room got lower every time that she sat in one, and more difficult to get up from. So Rafe was sharing Joshim's bed, was he? That took a lot of doing. Joshim was too good a Webmaster to have a string of casual liaisons in the web-room, the way that Vidar did; nor did he do what a lot of Webmasters did, regularly taking every member of the web-room to bed as part of the process of monitoring their physical and emotional states. In fact, to Rallya's certain knowledge, Joshim had only shared a bed aboard *Bhattya* with herself or with Vidar, and that infrequently. Although she had often teased him about it, she had to admit that it saved a lot of trouble in the web-room; his judgment had never been questioned on the grounds of pique or favoritism, and, in eight years, nobody had brought a problem to herself or to Vidar that should have been taken to Joshim first.

"Just as well you didn't put Elanis on a charge," she told Vidar. "He'd have yelled favoritism so loud they'd hear it in Imperial." She frowned suddenly. "Did you know about Joshim and Rafe?"

"No."

"Which makes it the only pairing aboard this ship that you haven't known about since the day it happened," Rallya concluded.

"True, but neither of them is the sort to post the news on the notice board."

"That doesn't usually inconvenience you too much." Rallya pressed her lips together. "If you didn't know, how did Elanis?"

"Lucky guess? Maybe Rafe makes a habit of it."

"Don't be stupid," Rallya said irritably. "If you don't know Rafe well enough to know that isn't true, you should know Joshim well enough to know he'd recognize somebody like that."

"I've never known him when he was in love," Vidar pointed out. 'He could be as stupid as the rest of us in that state."

"Speak for yourself. And if he is in love, you'd better start worrying. Rafe will be ready for a Commander's berth within a few years. Any guesses what Joshim will do then?"

Vidar whistled. "We could lose him."

"We probably will," Rallya said gloomily. There were not many established Threes who would consider an Oath-breaker as Commander, but the Guild might give a new ship to an established Webmaster with a reputation like Joshim's and a new Commander with Rallya's recommendation . . . She would give Rafe that recommendation, she admitted; he was too good for her to withhold it. And if she did withhold it, they would still lose Joshim. Hell's teeth though: if Rafe thought that his relationship with Joshim would win him any concessions from Rallya while he was aboard this ship, he was going to get a nasty shock.

*   *   *

It was not hard to guess who was knocking at his cabin door, Rafe thought wearily; he was only surprised it had taken her so long to arrive.

"Come in, ma'am," he called, turning to face the door but not standing to greet her.

She halted just inside the door and stood with her hands on her hips, surveying the room. "Pleased with yourself?" she challenged.

"Should I be?"

She picked up the reck nearest to her on the desk, looked at the label, tossed it back. "You didn't make many mistakes today."

What would you say, ma'am, if I told you that I made no mistakes at all? That everything I did was the right thing, at the right time, for the right reasons? And that it was all there in my memory: juggling speed against safety, judging the moment to raise the shields, the moment to fire. Even my web remembered the sensation of being in control of a ship's web during combat!

Rafe controlled another wave of nausea. He was not really remembering those things; it was the identity-wipe playing tricks with him again. He had witnessed another person in a similar situation; was not allowed to remember that person; could only recall what he had seen as though it was something he had done himself. They had explained it to him when he was still asking for explanations, in the early days. Maybe if he had asked them, they would have explained why he could remember how it *felt*. And why it made him sick to think about it.

He realized that Rallya was watching him closely, as if she could see his thoughts written on his face.

"Did you come to tell me about the mistakes I did make?" he asked with an effort.

"No." She tried the edge of the bed and sat down. "There were things that I might have done differently, but the result is what matters." She looked at him measuringly. "Will you be able to do it again? Or do you not like the thought that you killed twenty people today?"

"The time to worry is when I stop not liking it."

"Did Buhklir teach you that?"

Rafe's stomach lurched another warning. "I worked it out

for myself." He jammed his hands in his tunic pockets. "Was that all you came to ask, ma'am?"

"No." Rallya stood up and crossed the room to look down at him. "You're shaking," she remarked, lifting his chin with a single finger. "Reaction to combat? Or to thinking about your father?"

Rafe pulled away. "None of your business."

"None of your business, ma'am." She replaced her hand under his chin, turning his face up to the light. "And if it's reaction to combat, it is my business."

"If you don't let go of me, I shall be sick over you. Ma'am."

"Nonsense." She released him anyway. "You've got too much pride, and the self-control to support it."

And I have been sick so many times since escaping from the web-room that my stomach is empty, Rafe thought ruefully; the only thing I have left in it is the urge to be sick. "There was something else you wanted to ask," he prompted.

"I came for your thoughts about that raider," she said, taking the empty chair. "Did you notice anything that isn't on record?"

"Their cannon range." Rafe seized the change of subject. "The estimates I've seen were 20 percent too low."

Rallya nodded agreement. "Must have been a third of their mass just powering those cannon," she commented. "And if they were intending to carry another ship through jump with them, they'd need another third for the tractors. Not a lot left for drive, is there? Either they had no margin for error, or they came from somewhere just one or two jumps away."

"They may not have intended to hold the ship with tractors during jump," Rafe speculated. "If they cast a wide enough jump-field, they could carry it through in their wake. That would have allowed them to get away with half the power for their tractors."

"They'd have to be hellishly confident about their jump capabilities. Get that stunt wrong and you lose yourself for good."

"The F'sair used it regularly," Rafe pointed out. "Took a lot of ships before the cargoships learned to flick their own jump-field on to turn the jump wild. That stopped the raids within half a year. For the F'sair, dying in battle is a lucky death: their gods carry them straight to heaven; but if they get lost during jump, their gods can't ever find them and they're condemned to hell." He balled his fists in his pockets, forcing fingernails into palms, a futile effort to drive away the vivid images of the interior of a F'sair warship, of a meal shared with a F'sair war-leader. Impossible. Imagination, not memory, he told himself desperately.

"Useless set of gods they've got," Rallya commented. "I doubt our Outsiders share the same ones, but the thought about the wild jumps is worth passing on. Buhklir had you taught well." She raised both eyebrows. "Did you know that you turn a fetching shade of grey whenever I mention his name?"

"I'm glad you find it amusing, ma'am," Rafe managed.

"Interesting, not amusing," she corrected him. "Is it part of the conditioning that goes with identity-wipe?"

Rafe shrugged. "I presume so, ma'am, although I haven't experienced it before."

"You haven't had any knowledge about your past before," she pointed out. "And it has to be something that operates very infrequently, or you'd be useless as a webber." She rose to her feet. "You'd better get some sleep. You look like death, and you're due back in the web in five hours." She grinned. "I'll send Joshim down, shall I? In his capacity as ship's surgeon, of course. The shape you're in, you'll have no other use for him."

*   *   *

"Into bed with you," Joshim said firmly, as soon as a paper-colored Rafe closed the door behind him.

Rafe gave him a tight smile. "What for? We both know I won't sleep. Or only long enough to wake up yelling."

"Bed," Joshim repeated. "This is your Webmaster speaking." He gave Rafe a gentle push in the right direction. "Is it just nausea?"

"What did the Commander say?"

"That I should come and hold your hand while you threw up." Joshim frowned. "Are you fit to web your next shift?"

"If I'm not, the Commander has got a lot to do with it," Rafe said sourly.

"I was assuming that." Joshim put both hands on Rafe's shoulders and pushed him down to sit on the bed. "What else is wrong beside the nausea?"

"It's quite enough on its own," Rafe admitted, resting his head against Joshim's forearm. "You'd think they could come up with some more dignified way of reinforcing the identity-wipe," he complained. "At least they had the sense to put a delay mechanism in. If this had hit me during combat . . ." He shivered.

"Was that the trigger?" Joshim asked, alarmed.

"Yes," Rafe said miserably.

Joshim took a deep breath. Rallya had attributed it to her reference to Buhklir. If it had been the encounter with the raider, the experience of being in the web during combat . . . He had a clear vision of *Bhattya* as a sphere of debris spreading in the wake of the convoy because of a lapse in Rafe's concentration or in his web control. As Webmaster, Joshim thought unhappily, he might have to bar Rafe from the web for this. As Rafe's lover . . . that had to be a secondary consideration, he chided himself.

"All right," he told Rafe steadily. "Lie down. I'll go and fetch my drug-pack. We'll get rid of your sickness and then we'll talk."

He stopped on his way, to ask Jualla to switch shifts with Rafe: four more hours to solve this. She agreed readily, and offered to ask her team and Rafe's if they were willing to make a change permanent. Elanis's news was travelling fast, Joshim thought wryly. Jualla had been in the web during the argument in the web-room, but she had already heard about it. A permanent change would put Joshim and Rafe on the same shift pattern, give them more time out of the web together. He thanked Jualla and gave her permission to ask.

Am ampoule broken under his nostrils gave Rafe relief from his symptoms. As he regained his normal color, Joshim wished there was as easy a cure for their cause.

"Jualla has swapped shifts with you," he said, sitting down across the room from the bed. If he sat beside Rafe, it would be harder to maintain the separation between Webmaster and lover, too great a temptation to take Rafe in his arms and comfort him. He already knew that comfort was not enough; he had comforted Rafe every time that he woke from a nightmare, and the nightmares still continued. He had to offer something more specific than comfort: a solution, or an attempt at a solution. It was his responsibility, both as a Webmaster and as somebody who cared very much about Rafe.

"When did this start?" he asked. "Exactly."

Rafe grimaced. "I was fine until I disengaged. Then I was almost sick in the shub."

"You're sure it isn't just the stress of combat?" Joshim asked hopefully.

"I'm sure." Rafe sat up and characteristically hugged his knees. "You're worried about allowing me in the web again."

"Yes," Joshim admitted. "While there's a chance that this will happen again, I'm worried about allowing you in the web."

"There's always that chance," Rafe said heavily.

"Not if we find a way to prevent it," Joshim pointed out.

"What? You can't give me any drugs to suppress the sickness while I'm in the web. If you did, the conditioning would only express itself another way."

"Then we work on the cause and not the symptoms." Joshim said calmly.

Rafe laughed harshly. "What are you going to do? Undo the conditioning? Restore my memory? Hell, Joshim, if it were possible, do you think I'd have waited this long?" His voice was rising.

"Have you ever tried?"

"No." Rafe let out a long sigh. "I wouldn't know how to start. Or what damage it might do." He looked away, looked back again. "Sorry I shouted. I'm just scared."

"What are you scared of?"

"Having my mind messed around any more. Losing my web. Losing you. Finding out who I used to be. It's a comprehensive list, isn't it?"

"Why shouldn't it be? And I don't have a definite answer, Rafe, only an idea that might work, if you want to try it."

"What is it?"

"An Aruranist technique. You know that we believe in reincarnation?" Rafe nodded. "It's important to us, remembering as many of our previous lives as we can, so that we don't waste the current one covering old ground. I could teach you the methods we use to remember."

"Working on the theory that, if they work across multiple reincarnations, they might work across identity-wipe?" Rafe asked doubtfully.

"I'm not promising," Joshim warned.

"I know you're not. And I'm not saying I believe in reincarnation, but..." Rafe shrugged jerkily. "How many do you remember?"

"Three. That isn't many. There's a woman in Jasan who remembers twenty-eight."

"And you remember them all clearly?"

"No. The first one is hazy, just snatches of detail. One day

I'll improve it." Joshim laughed softly. "Although I've been saying that for years. I suspect I remember enough not to want to remember anymore. I don't like her very much."

"Her?"

"Yes. I was a woman last time too. A priestess in a temple outside the Empires. Salu'i'kamai. The Hand of the Goddess is on the Earth," he translated.

"With my luck, I'll end up with a complete memory of a previous life as a night-soil porter on Rasasara, and nothing else," Rafe muttered. "You know we'll be violating our Oaths if we do this?"

"Yes." Joshim wondered exactly when he had realized. At the time he had first wondered whether the recall techniques would work for Rafe, he decided, and that had been nights ago, watching Rafe fall into the uneasy sleep that followed yet another nightmare. It was suddenly absurd that he was planning to break his Oath while sitting as far as he could from the man from whom he would do so. He went to Rafe's side and took his hands.

"If it works, you can't go back to being who you were," he warned.

"Not without getting us both wiped," Rafe agreed grimly. "And I don't want to go back. All I want is to be able to live comfortably inside my own head." He squeezed Joshim's hands hard. "You're crazy to even think about this," he said fiercely. "I won't let you involve yourself."

"It's too late to stop me." Joshim traced Rafe's cheekbone with a kiss. "And I don't let anybody make my choices for me."

"I won't let you break your Oath for me," Rafe insisted. "Emperors, Joshim, I may be called an Oath-breaker but I haven't broken my Oath yet and I never will!"

"Would it be Oath-breaking?" Joshim queried. "You're not the person you were ten years ago. Even if you remember who you were, you won't be that person. You've no intention of bolting back across the Disputed Zone. What harm will it do if you remember who you were?"

Rafe shook his head firmly. "I don't know, Joshim, but . . . If we did this, how could we ever know again what was Oath-breaking and what wasn't? If I'd sworn false allegiance to the Old Emperor ten years ago, then contrived to cross the Disputed Zone again, would that have been Oath-breaking? Or would it have been all right, because nobody knew I'd sworn falsely, because no harm had been done?

"And if we can justify this to ourselves, what will we be able to justify next? And how could we object if the Guild changed its interpretation of the Oath it swore to us? If the Emperors changed their interpretation of the Oaths they've sworn to the Guild? Those Oaths are too important, Joshim. If we break our Oaths, we can't hold them to theirs. And if we can't hold them to theirs, they'll plunge the Twin Empires into full-scale war. We have to keep our Oaths, Joshim. We haven't any choice."

Joshim took Rafe's hands in his again, raised each one in turn to kiss it. The vehemence of Rafe's reaction had shaken him, left him ashamed of the ease with which he had proposed that they break their Oaths.

"When you put it like that, we don't have any choice, do we?" he agreed reluctantly. "It shouldn't have been necessary for you to convince me of it."

"Convince you? I was convincing myself," Rafe said bitterly. "Hell, Joshim, do you think I'm not tempted? Do you think I don't dream about waking up one morning and knowing who I am? But if I break my Oath now, I might as well have broken it ten years ago and spared myself all this!" He made an angry gesture. "You'd better bar me from the web. I'm a danger to everybody else in it, and that's Oath-breaking as well."

"Stop taking the Webmaster's decisions for him," Joshim said, deliberately lightly. "You can stay in the web on two conditions. One: you don't take the key-position. Two: you disengage if you suspect your conditioning is beginning to operate. Agreed?"

"Agreed." There was only dull resignation in Rafe's voice. "I'd better get some sleep. Can I have a sleeper?"

"I'll get you one."

There was nothing else he could offer Rafe at the moment, Joshim realized, watching him take the drug. A few hours of unbroken sleep, and Rafe's place in the web, and Joshim was not certain that he had made that decision solely as a Webmaster. This was why you never involved yourself in the web-room, he reminded himself: you always doubted your own ability to make decisions about the people you love, rightly doubted it. He ruffled the sleeping head fondly. It was too late to pull back now, even if he had wanted to.

From the Gazetteer of
the Old Empire, revised 5030

Jalset's World (Aramas Zone): a lightly settled agricultural world, sole source of the recreational drug blissdream; a typical frontier backwater, with no features of physical, biological, or cultural interest. Passage can be obtained on cargoships departing from Aramas station.

251/ 5043:
ARAMAS ZONE, OLD EMPIRE

Rallya breathed in the spice-ridden air of Jalset's World and gagged.

"How the hell does anybody live in this?" she demanded.

Lilimya grinned. "The dirtsiders will probably tell you they couldn't live anywhere else, ma'am."

Rallya shaded her eyes to watch *Bhattya*'s shuttle lift off with the returning liberty party, then turned to address the party that had come down with her.

"You've got ten hours," she reminded them. "If you can find anything to do with them down here—you could spit from one side of this town to the other. Keep out of trouble, and if you can't keep out of trouble, don't bring it back to the ship. The Webmaster has better things to do with his time than treat the local variety of sexbug—ask Rafe if you don't believe me." She glanced around the inattentive faces: they had heard it all before, even Fadir, and were impatient to be on their way. "Go

---

on, vanish,'' she urged them. "Anybody who isn't back here in good time for the shuttle will forfeit their next ten liberties.''

The town was overflowing with liberty parties, the dirtsiders making the most of the influx of fresh money by doubling their normal prices. Rallya took a desultory look through one of the small shops: nothing she had not seen before on maybe a hundred other worlds. Sixty years, two or three different worlds every year. Yes, call it a hundred, and none of them in any way memorable. Friends on half a dozen of them, retired webbers who had found a world they liked, or claimed to like. Ex-friends. Once they were forced to retire, there was always the loss of everything they had had in common, the unspoken jealousy in the look they gave her web-bands: why has *she* still got her web? And always her relief at the end of a visit, the escape from a reminder of her inevitable future.

She shook herself irritably, stood with hands on hips in the middle of the main street and glared along it. The best cure for morbid thoughts was a drink, and at least this dirtball did not have restrictive drinking laws. For the hundredth time, she wondered why she had bothered to accompany a liberty party, and answered herself: it was simply good sense to have one of the Three on hand if anybody got into real trouble. Not that anybody from *Bhattya* would dare get into real trouble, but there was always a first time.

She chose one of the quieter bars, found that she could eat there too and ordered a meal. The food tasted heavily of the local spices but was better than she had expected. From her seat on the verandah, she could see all the activity along the main street. She ordered another beer—also better than she expected—and lifted her feet onto the rail around the verandah. With another nine hours to kill, there was no need to hurry anywhere.

One of the dirtsiders drifted over to join her, wanting to know if the tales about webbers were true without actually saying as much. A nice-looking lad, about a third of Rallya's age. She considered accepting his offer, to fill an hour or so, then decided against it. He would find somebody to tumble with: there were enough webbers in town. Maybe Lilimya: she was renowned for being generous to the curious. Rallya told him she was old enough to be his grandmother and pointed him in the direction of the most brightly lit bar, amusing herself by being gentle with him. There were plenty of dirtsiders she had dismissed red-faced with the question: does your mother know you're out?

"Excuse me, ma'am. Have you seen Captain Sajan?"

Hajolir, Rallya remembered with an effort, Sajan's Third. She had met him briefly back on Aramas station. A tall man, tall enough to give her a pain in the neck and the sun in her eyes if she looked up to him.

"Didn't know she was dirtside," she answered.

"She came down with the rest of us eleven hours ago, but we were due to return an hour ago and she hasn't turned up for the shuttle."

"Is that unusual?"

"Yes, ma'am. Very."

"Might she be sleeping off a drunk? Or too busy in the local joy-house to notice the time?" Rallya suggested the two most common reasons for overstaying a liberty, although Sajan had not seemed that irresponsible a woman.

"We've checked the joy-house. She hasn't been there. And we're checking all the bars now," Hajolir said. "The last time anybody saw her was eight hours ago. That was in one of the shops on the north edge of town, looking at cloth."

Rallya frowned. "Shopkeeper see her leave?"

"She says so. And that's the respectable side of town, the dirtsiders tell me."

Hajolir had obviously run out of ideas, was hoping for guidance. Rallya swore and dropped her feet to the ground.

"If she turns up drunk, or tumbling, Hajolir, I'll have your ears to make my next wrist-bands. And hers to make the neck-band," she threatened. "This is not how I planned to spend my liberty. Go find every webber able to stand, including the ones who are currently horizontal. I want them here within thirty minutes. Refer any arguments to me." She glanced at the position of the sun. "We've two hours left of good light—we'll sweep the town. Every street, every alleyway, every public building." She watched him dash off, relieved that the responsibility for finding Sajan was no longer his. "Hell, if my liberty is going to be ruined, so is everybody else's," she muttered angrily.

Thirty minutes later there was a crowd of webbers blocking the main street and an irate leader of the local peace-force complaining that Rallya was not going through the right channels. Rallya spared him enough time to inform him that Sajan was a webber; that the right channels were the webbers waiting for instructions; and that he could either shut up and keep out of the way, or make some constructive suggestions about what might have happened to Sajan in his town. He made a few more noises of protest, then suggested that they start their sweep on the west side of town, which was not quite as respectable as the rest.

It was forty minutes before Lilimya's group found Sajan's body. She had been dragged to the end of an alley and covered with the refuse from the eating-house that backed onto it from the main street. She had been stabbed once in the back, the knife nowhere close by, and robbed of everything she had been carrying. Naturally, nobody in the eating-house had seen anything or heard anything. Naturally, the leader of the peace-force was aghast that a webber had been murdered, would make every effort to bring the killer to justice. Rallya cut through his platitudes, told him curtly that the other members of Sajan's Three would be in touch to make arrangements for disposal of the body and left him to mouth his apologies to Hajolir, who had no choice but to stay.

Back in the bar, she bought herself a drink of Jalset's firewater, then one for Lilimya, who wandered up with Fadir in tow and no inclination to drift on. The main street was full of webbers in angry groups. Rallya watched them carefully, alert for any sign that they might vent their anger on local people or property. It would not be the first time it happened.

"Lilimya, go back to the shuttleground and call Commander Noromi," she ordered. "Tell him that I said to cancel all liberty throughout the convoy and recall existing liberty parties at once. Fadir, you stay here, in case I need a runner. Or are you too drunk to run?"

"No, ma'am," he said indignantly.

"Good. What are you waiting for, Lilimya?"

"On my way, ma'am!"

Rallya watched her go. "Fifteen minutes, then we'll spread the good news," she told Fadir absently. "Do you want a beer?"

"No, thank you, ma'am."

"Have one anyway. It might stop you fidgeting." She bought the beer from a anxious-looking owner. "Don't worry," she told him drily. "Yours is the safest bar on the street, with me in it." It did not seem to reassure him.

"Do you think there will be trouble, ma'am?" Fadir asked nervously.

"There already has been," Rallya reminded him. "Emperors, if you've got enough sense to stay out of dark alleys with strangers—and I'm assuming you have—then Sajan should have known better too!"

It was not only the waste of it that angered Rallya, it was the stupidity. Sajan was a veteran, with as much experience as the party of webbers who had found her body all taken together. It was sheer negligence to let a dirtsider kill her so easily.

"It didn't look as if she'd put up a fight, did it, ma'am?" Fadir ventured.

Rallya looked at him sharply; she had not realized he had seen the body. It explained why he was so pale. "Difficult to put up a fight when you've been stabbed in the back," she commented.

Fadir flushed. "Yes, ma'am, but . . ."

"Go on. I've nothing better to do with my ears than listen to you."

"Wouldn't she have known better than to let somebody come up behind her like that?"

Rallya shrugged. "Yes. If she had been sober. If she hadn't been distracted by somebody else. If she hadn't been with somebody she thought she could trust." She finished her drink, gestured at Fadir's untouched beer. "If you want that, drink up before we round everybody up and get them out of here."

She watched him drink, realizing that for Fadir, Jalset's World would be memorable, the place he had seen his first dead body. It was faintly annoying that she could not remember where she had had the same experience, and that she suspected she would forget about Jalset's World as easily.

"You've done all right today, Fadir," she told him roughly. "Don't spoil it by growing roots in that seat."

Conversation at Peace-force Headquarters, Jalset's World

"You know it has to be another webber, and I know it has to be another webber, but we'll never get the Convoy Commander to agree. According to him, there isn't a single member of the Guild who'd give another webber a bloody nose, let alone stab one in the back. Their precious Oath doesn't allow it."

"Why are we wasting our time worrying about it? If the murderer is aboard one of the ships, that's the Guild's problem, not ours."

"We have to arrest somebody, to keep the Guild happy. Especially now, with this damned Outsider trouble. If they decide to stop the convoys..."

"They can't. Half the Imperial Court uses blissdream."

"They'd find something to replace it quickly enough, and if they didn't, the Guild wouldn't care. Listen, we didn't arrest Chalir until the day after the webber was killed, did we?"

"No."

"Talk to him. Persuade him to confess to killing the webber as well as his partner, and concoct a believable story to pass on to the Convoy Commander."

"What do I offer Chalir?"

"Whatever it takes."

254/5043:
ARAMAS ZONE, OLD EMPIRE

Joshim hid a smile as Churi ran out of words and resorted to enthusiastic but imprecise gestures to complete his answer.

"You've worked hard at that since your last assessment," he said instead.

"Yes, sir. Although I didn't really understand it until Rafe explained about compound feedback. Once I understood that, the rest was simple. Well, easier," Churi corrected himself. "It wasn't that Rafe's explanation was better than yours," he added, belatedly remembering the two hours that Joshim had spent explaining the same subject to him. "It just made more sense to me."

Joshim did smile at that. "Have you explored the mathematics of it yet?" he asked.

"No, sir. Rafe said I should concentrate on getting the ideas right first."

"When you're ready to try the maths, tell me and I'll start you off. Or ask Rafe, if you want."

"I'll do that, sir."

Churi had moved forward to the edge of his seat in nervous anticipation of Joshim's verdict. A Webmaster's assessment was always an ordeal for a junior in training, and particularly so when they had done badly in their last assessment, as Churi had. A consistently poor performance could cost a junior their berth aboard *Bhattya*, or in an extreme case their web. A webber had to have an instinctive understanding of the way the web worked, of its possibilities and limitations, of the consequences of their actions within it. Without that instinct, they might think when there was no time to think, or act when action was the worst choice they could make. Few webbers were born with the instinct, but all of them had to acquire it or lose their place in the web, and Joshim was the final judge aboard *Bhattya* of who had it and who did not.

"You've made good progress this quarter-year." Joshim said encouragingly. "Especially since you've learned that there are no shortcuts."

Churi relaxed visibly. "Yes, sir. I think it's because Rafe has helped me a lot, particularly when we're in the web."

Rafe had plenty of time to spare in the web, Joshim thought unhappily as Churi left, time he would not have if he were allowed to take the key-position again. That decision would have to be reviewed soon, before Rafe's brevet promotion was made substantive; no ship could have a First—or any senior—barred from the key-position. And without any new evidence, Joshim did not know how he could reverse his decision.

It did not help that Rafe would not discuss the matter. He had referred to it once—obliquely—since Joshim had imposed the restriction, when he asked for permission to fit some training sessions into their shared web-shift, the training sessions which had helped Churi so much. The irony was that it took a high degree of web-skill to combine the number two position in the web with a teaching role without disturbing the work of the active team. By giving permission, Joshim was showing a rare level of confidence in Rafe, and deflecting questions from the rest of the web-room about the restriction placed upon him. Which was probably one reason why Rafe had suggested it.

Salu'i'kamai would never have had this problem, Joshim thought ruefully. She would have followed her gut feeling, certain that it was the voice of her Goddess prompting her; no conflicts for her between duty and desire. A direct link to a deity was an advantage best appreciated when it had been lost; prayers, to which the answers were unclear or unrecognized, were a poor substitute which so far had produced no solution to Joshim's dilemma. Or if they had, it was not the solution that Joshim hoped for and so he had not seen it. That was another problem with prayers: it was permissible to pray for what you wanted, but what you got was what the gods wanted, and there was no guarantee that the two would coincide. And if the gods had no interest in your problem, you got nothing, not even an indication that it was yours alone to deal with.

The door alert sounded, reminding Joshim of another problem, one which had been wished on him by the assignment clerks and—as far as he knew—not by any higher authority. Elanis was punctual to the second, not out of simple good manners but from his policy of investing the exact minimum of effort necessary to escape criticism from his seniors. He had been given ample time to realize that it was not an approach that would be tolerated about *Bhattya*; he had failed to change it, so now he was due for a warning. Unless he produced an acceptable explanation, Joshim reminded himself scrupulously.

"You wanted to see me, sir." Elanis bowed as he stepped through the door.

"Yes. Sit down, please." Formality was the right note for this interview; Elanis would respect nothing else.

"Thank you." Elanis sat back in the chair, either not nervous or hiding it well.

"I talk to every new member of the web-room after they've had some time to settle in, about their work and their adjustment to a new ship. Most Webmasters do, so you'll have been through similar interviews before."

"Yes, sir."

"Are you satisfied with your work in the web?" Elanis's chance to make his excuses, if he had any.

"Yes, sir, quite satisfied."

"You're not aware that there have been complaints about it?"

"No, sir. May I ask who has complained, and on what grounds?"

"Several members of the web-room have expressed doubts about your commitment, both in the web and out of it. I believe that they discussed the problem with you before coming to me because they were unhappy with your response."

Elanis shrugged. "I'm not accustomed to being criticized by juniors with less experience than me."

"They may have less experience, but they're entitled to an opinion about your performance, and to more respect from you than they received," Joshim said sharply. "Their opinion is shared by the two seniors who web with you regularly, and confirmed by my own observations. Your work is not satisfactory."

"In what respect?"

"You're lazy, you're inconsiderate, and you overestimate yourself," Joshim told him bluntly. "You expose the rest of your web-shift to needless risk."

"My previous Webmasters had no complaints," Elanis said stiffly.

"I can see that from your record." See it, but not understand it, Joshim added silently. "*Bhattya*'s requirements are more stringent that the requirements of a surveyship or a passenger carrier. If you feel unable to meet them, you should consider a transfer to a less demanding berth."

"Is this a formal warning?"

"Yes." Joshim had not intended to make it formal, but it

was plain that an informal warning would have no effect. "You have the right to enter a defense into your record, if you wish."

"If a formal warning goes into my record, I shall certainly enter a defense," Elanis said calmly. "Although it would be better for both of us if neither entry were made. And for Rafe."

"In the face of statements from every member of *Bhattya*'s web-room who has complained about you, an accusation of undue influence is not going to be much of a defense for you, or a problem for Rafe and me," Joshim said softly. "You have the right to know that I will be entering an account of this conversation in your record, in support of my existing request for your transfer out of my web-room. I am also giving you formal warning that, if there is no lasting improvement in your work starting with your next web-shift, you will be barred from my web for willful negligence."

"You would certainly regret that," Elanis said smoothly. "I have friends who would make sure that you did."

"You could be pillow-friend to the entire Guild Council without gaining enough influence to get a Webmaster removed from their ship," Joshim said scornfully.

"Enter that warning in my record, or bar me from the web, and you'll never be anything but the Webmaster of a passed-over patrolship," Elanis sneered. "No Guildhall berth when your web starts to fail you. No future at all."

"The warning stands," Joshim told him icily. "You may enter your defense when you wish. I suggest you also submit a request for a voluntary move, if you do not want your record sullied with a compulsory transfer. And if your work does not improve immediately, the charge of willful negligence will also be entered and you will be barred from the web."

"You *will* regret this," Elanis promised.

"You may go now."

So that was the explanation for Elanis's blameless record, Joshim thought angrily as the door closed. Influence, or the threat of it. Rafe had suggested as much when he commented on *Avannya*'s failure to get rid of the lazy aristo. How close to retirement from the web had *Avannya*'s Webmaster been, and how intent on getting a Guildhall berth? Close enough to worry about Elanis's threats, probably, and close enough to dread a future outside the Guild.

Joshim called Elanis's record onto his screen and started to word the new entry. The record of their conversation had to be

made at once, while his memory of it was still fresh, and to
defer the warning, even for a few hours, would be seen by
Elanis as a sign of weakness. He was determined that the
arrogant junior would not have the pleasure of even a few
seconds mistaken triumph.

One thing influence could not achieve was the alteration of a
webber's record; once made, Joshim's entry would haunt Elanis
until he retired. It would not stop him getting a berth as a
junior; only a judgment that he was totally unfit to web could
do that. However, it would make it difficult for him to get a
prime berth and impossible to gain promotion to senior. Unless,
of course, he set his friends to work on the problem, but if he
had enough influence to get himself a senior's berth, he would
already have done so. It was doubtful that there was enough
influence anywhere in the Twin Empires to get Elanis promoted
to senior, Joshim decided cynically.

The door alert sounded again, quickly followed by Vidar's head
around the door, his red hair still damp from his shift in the web.

"Busy?"

Joshim shook his head. "Just let me finish this." He added
his identity-code and stored the record, remembering to grant
temporary access to Elanis so that he could enter his defense.

"A good morning, from the way Churi is grinning from ear
to ear," Vidar commented, dropping into the empty chair and
putting his feet up on Joshim's desk.

"He did well, and so did Magred."

"But not Elanis?"

"Have a look at his record."

"I've been watching you update it."

Joshim was not surprised. An observer from outside *Bhattya*'s
web-room might be fooled by Vidar's pretense to be interested
only in sex and ship systems, but there was nothing that went
on in the web-room that he did not make his business. And
nothing that he and Rallya would not bet on.

"Who won?" he asked.

Vidar laughed. "I did. Rallya said you'd think you had to be
gentle with him because Rafe doesn't like him. I'm looking
forward to collecting when she comes back from the escort
Commanders' conference."

Joshim grunted irritably. "She deserves to lose if she doesn't
know me better than that."

"True." Vidar dropped his feet off the desk. "It's a pity you didn't make a reck of the interview."

"You think I'll need one?" Joshim asked in surprise.

"I'd be happier if you had one."

"Elanis probably thinks bedding one member of the Guild Council once counts as influence," Joshim said drily.

"You aren't worried?"

"However much influence he's got, I'm safe until I retire from the web. Or until the other members of *Bhattya*'s Three throw me out," Joshim teased.

"Which I won't do, and Rallya won't do, and Rallya's successor won't do," Vidar prophesied slyly.

"Rallya will be with us for years yet."

"How many years? I may be Captain and not Webmaster, but I can tell when somebody's reflexes are slowing. She isn't the webber she was ten years ago, Joshim."

"None of us are."

"But you're thinking ahead to Rallya's replacement," Vidar guessed. "Why else were you so choosy about our new First? You'd never been so difficult to please before."

"Pure lust?" Joshim suggested.

Vidar made a rude noise. "That came later."

Joshim knew that Vidar would press until he got the answer he was certain was there. "The thought of Rallya's retirement did cross my mind. I haven't discussed it with her though," he warned.

"So how long?"

"Five years," Joshim said reluctantly. Vidar had the information and the experience to work it out for himself. "That's my best guess. I can't be more accurate without doing a full recalibration."

"And you can't do that without telling her why, and the resultant explosion would breach the hull," Vidar said sympathetically. "Have you heard the rumors that she won't get a station post?"

"Yes, before I joined *Bhattya*. Rumors that she won't get a station post, that *Bhattya* is down on somebody's hate-list, that nobody from *Bhattya*'s Three has ever risen higher." Joshim shrugged. "If it's true, she must have made some powerful enemies. Forty years is a long time to keep a vendetta going."

"Would Rallya make any other kind of enemy?" Vidar said in amusement.

"Well, if I'm damned already, it's one more reason not to be scared of Elanis." Joshim frowned, remembering something the junior had said. "He's certainly heard the rumors. Called *Bhattya* a passed-over patrolship."

Vidar stroked his moustache with one finger thoughtfully. "We could be," he remarked. "Only one assignment to the Disputed Zone in forty years? Never assigned to the Imperial Zone? With our reputation, we could expect a few of the prestige assignments to come our way."

Joshim raised his eyebrows. "Do you want to fight in the Disputed Zone?" he challenged. "Or to do ceremonial escort duty for the Old Emperor's favourite aristos?"

"No more than you do. Which is why I approve of your choice of Rallya's replacement." Vidar smiled widely. "Nobody is going to give an Oath-breaker any prestige assignments. Just the hard and necessary jobs, the ones we get now."

"You're making a lot of assumptions," Joshim warned.

"Justified assumptions," Vidar said smugly. "You can't convince me that you don't want Rafe as our next Commander. I've no objections, and he'll never get a better offer. The only question is whether Elanis can stop the Council from ratifying his promotion to Commander."

Joshim scowled. "He didn't threaten Rafe, not after the initial accusation of undue influence."

"Doesn't know how vulnerable Rafe is," Vidar suggested. "If he finds out . . ."

"The Council has never refused to ratify a promotion into a Three," Joshim pointed out. "Blue hell would break out if they did. The autonomy of each Three is one of the foundations of the Guild. Nobody is going to jeopardize that for the sake of Elanis's spite. And if Elanis has any influence worth having, what's he doing aboard a passed-over patrolship anyway?"

"I wonder if Rallya made the same sort of misjudgment when she made her enemies," Vidar commented.

"Knowing Rallya, she knew exactly what she was doing and went ahead out of sheer stubbornness."

Vidar put his head back and laughed. "Maybe. Going to ask her advice about protecting your back, and Rafe's?"

"Without mentioning that I'm worried about Rafe's promotion to Commander?"

"Difficult," Vidar conceded. "Does Rafe know you've got his career planned for him?"

"We haven't discussed it."

"He's no fool. He'll have guessed," Vidar predicted.

"His brevet rank has to be made substantive before anything else can happen," Joshim said heavily.

"Elanis won't have time to prevent that," Vidar objected. "The approval will be ready by the time we get back to Aramas. All it will need is our signatures."

"True."

Vidar looked quizzically at Joshim. "What's the problem?"

Joshim sighed. "The problem is, I don't know if there is a problem."

"But you think there may be. Any connection with swapping Rafe's web-shift and keeping him out of the key-position?" Vidar asked shrewdly.

"Yes." Joshim hesitated, knowing he had to ask but not wanting to hear the wrong answer, which was why he had not asked before. "Tell me, when you were in the web with him while we were in combat with that raider, did you notice anything odd?"

"About Rafe's performance? Apart from the fact that he handled himself like a veteran, no."

"No sign that his concentration was disturbed?"

Vidar shook his head. "Not a thing, and I was watching him damned closely. It's not too comforting, going into combat with somebody in the key-position who's never been in combat before." He frowned. "Had he been in combat before?"

"It's possible," Joshim said cautiously. "After he came out of the shub, he was as sick as a first-timer through jump. It might have been caused by the conditioning that goes with identity-wipe."

"Whatever it was didn't hit him until he came out of the web," Vidar said positively. "I was monitoring him so closely I was almost inside him. Emperors, I was monitoring him so closely I probably *was* inside him," he said sheepishly.

Joshim tutted automatic disapproval. Shadowing somebody in the web so closely that you experienced everything they felt and did was dangerous. At best, it could damage their control. At worst, with the potential that it introduced for circular feedback, it could cause permanent burn-out of both webbers involved.

"I don't think he registered that I was doing it," Vidar volunteered. "And I'm not good enough to shadow perfectly. If I didn't disturb him, nothing else would."

"I hope not." Joshim chewed his lip. Vidar's comments were encouraging, but they were not conclusive.

"If he were any other First who'd never been in a patrolship before, you'd be watching him carefully but you'd let him take the key-position," Vidar said reasonably. "Especially when he's sharing a web-shift with you. There's nobody better qualified to take control if anything does go wrong. And he's one of the best webbers in *Bhattya*'s web-room. Almost as good as you or Rallya. He's wasted as a permanent number two."

"I know," Joshim acknowledged. Rafe's skill in the web was a delight. He did not have Rallya's innate talent, which made her such a poor teacher and a demanding key because she subconsciously expected others to find webbing as easy as she did. Rafe's skill was learned, and polished carefully and continually; he knew how to pass it on, and how to use it to get the best from others. It was rare to find that in somebody with only ten years' experience, and a crime to waste it, but...

"You won't get a definite answer by keeping him out of the key-position," Vidar pointed out. "You'll always be wondering."

"So I should let him take the key-position and wait for him to fold in the middle of combat?" Joshim argued. "Just to get a definite answer?"

Vidar tugged at his earring. "You're not restricting Rallya, and you know that now deterioration has started, there's always a chance that her web will fail without warning during combat. If you're worried about Rafe, shouldn't you be equally worried about Rallya?" he countered.

"The chance of sudden web failure in Rallya's current condition is negligible."

"You can't be sure of that until you do a full recalibration."

"If there had been any major change, Rallya would have mentioned it. She may be willful, but she isn't irresponsible."

Vidar conceded the truth of that with a gesture that made his collection of gold bracelets clink together. "I still think you're wrong about Rafe," he insisted. "Even if there is a risk, wouldn't it have been greatest the first time he was in combat? He survived that, and he's aware of the danger now. It can only get safer."

"Not if the conditioning is set to get stronger if it's ignored."

"If they wanted him to keep out of combat, they would have conditioned him against taking a berth on a patrolship, not faffed around making him a liability in the web if he did." Vidar shook his head in mock despair. "You can't even be sure it was the conditioning that made him sick. When I was a junior, we had a Commander of ten years' standing who still threw up every time he came out of the web after combat. Nobody dreamed of barring him from the key-position."

When he was exasperated, Vidar had a lot in common with Rallya, Joshim realized fondly. But not so much that he thought he could make the Webmaster's decisions for him, thank the gods.

"I'll decide one way or the other before we start on the in-bound run," he promised.

"No, you won't. You might change your mind and let him back into the key-position, but you won't make a decision."

"Would you explain to me the difference between making a decision and changing my mind?"

"If you change your mind, it will be for the wrong reasons and you won't be able to stop worrying about it. If you make a decision . . ."

". . . it will be for the right reasons and I'll be happy with it?" Joshim concluded. "Well, if that's the difference, I'm not in a position to make a decision. Only to change my mind."

Vidar shook his head firmly. "You shouldn't try so hard to be the perfect Webmaster," he said, not unsympathetically.

"Maybe not." Joshim twisted his ring around his finger. "It would be simpler if I were just his Webmaster. Loving him as well . . . I can't keep the two things separate."

"Don't try," Vidar said crisply. "It doesn't work. You can't be a Webmaster without being influenced by your personal feelings. Your instincts about people are as accurate as any measurement of their performance that you can make."

"Even if I care about somebody so much that I dare not trust my judgment about him?"

"Your judgment about Rafe is fine. What's wrong is your judgment about yourself. You think that you're being objective about Rafe, but you aren't. You're letting your fear of being biased in his favor push you too far in the opposite direction, into a choice you know is wrong." Vidar leaned forward. "Admit it, Joshim. If you really believed that he was an unacceptable risk in combat, he wouldn't be in the web at all, would he?"

Joshim hesitated. "Probably not," he conceded at last.

"So why didn't you ban him from the web?" Vidar insisted.

Joshim glared across his desk. "Because it wasn't necessary," he admitted. "And because I didn't want to," he added defiantly.

"If it was necessary, would you have done it?"

"Yes. I would."

That answer, unexpectedly easy, freed a tangle of doubts. Making it and knowing it to be true, Joshim could look clearly at the decision he had made about Rafe and recognize that it had been a mistake. Not just for all the reasons that Vidar had argued, but also for the simpler and more important reason that he had not made it as Webmaster, as he had deceived himself that he had. He had made it as Rafe's lover, swayed by Rafe's distress and by his own guilt about the Oath-breaking that he had proposed into doing something—anything—to ease the tension between them. Something that made him feel that he had not abandoned his duty as Webmaster, so long as he did not examine it too closely.

No wonder the gods had not responded to his prayers: he had been asking for a solution to the wrong problem, to a problem that only existed in his head. Or had they responded, by whispering in Vidar's ear? Joshim smiled at the thought of the reaction he would get if he asked Vidar whether he had received any divine guidance recently.

"At least I'm not the only fool involved," he realized ruefully. "Rafe would have argued the ears off any other Webmaster over this, but he hasn't said a word about it to me."

Vidar sat back contentedly. "Too honorable to take advantage of his position in your bed?" he teased.

"And in my affections," Joshim corrected good-naturedly.

Too honorable to risk talking me into another form of Oath-breaking, letting him in the key-position against my better judgment, he added privately. That was not a subject he could discuss with Vidar, in spite of the friendship they shared, but it was something he had to discuss with Rafe, now that Vidar had bullied him into seeing sense.

"Thanks, Vidar," he said quietly.

"Buy me a drink when we're dirtside." Vidar grinned. "Bring Rafe along. He can buy me one too."

'Ah, Rafe." Noromi welcomed him to *Meremir*'s web-room with a curt nod. "Rallya not with you?"

"She's outside, talking with Commander Erelna, sir."

"Expects us all to wait for her, I suppose," Noromi complained. "Find her difficult to work with, do you?"

"Not particularly, sir."

"Not likely to say if you did, in your position." Noromi chuckled knowingly. "Ought to congratulate you on your success against that raider. Mostly the result of luck, of course, but still a creditable effort." He patted Rafe's shoulder.

Rafe contrived a brief smile and moved out of easy range of another pat. "I don't underestimate the value of luck, sir."

"Don't overestimate it either," Noromi warned. "It's no substitute for hard work and thorough planning."

"No, sir, but it's often the thing that makes the hard work worthwhile."

"Rallya told you that, I suppose?" Noromi shook his head disapprovingly. "Take my advice, Rafe. Don't believe everything she tells you. Just because she relies on luck doesn't mean you can do the same. Hard work and proper training, that's what it takes to get anywhere."

"I couldn't hope for better training than I'm receiving from Commander Rallya," Rafe said bluntly. The clumsiness of the approach was an insult and the envy behind it irritated him. "At least she knows the difference between luck and skill," he added unkindly.

"One fluke success doesn't make you a Commander," Noromi said, offended. "You'd do well to remember that instead of aping Rallya's arrogance."

There were worse things to ape, Rafe decided as Noromi stalked off. Like a pedestrian Commander who could not make a direct approach to a First that he wanted to poach from another ship. Noromi should never have been given overall responsibility for the convoy; Rafe had learned that from the conference at Aramas. It was a formula for missed opportunities, for slavish adherence to the tactics that Noromi had personally proven successful. He was not incompetent, Rafe conceded honestly, but he lacked initiative.

Rallya was the obvious candidate for Convoy Commander, which was one reason why Noromi was jealous of her, but she would have refused the job if it had been offered, and her reputation was so formidable that Commander Maisa would not dare order her to take it. Rallya would refuse Commander Maisa's job if it were offered, Rafe decided as she entered the web-room and paused to greet Noromi. Too much routine work involved and too many people to deal with who were not webbers, people who had to be coaxed instead of bullied.

"Noromi informs me that you're impertinent," Rallya announced as she joined Rafe.

"I expect so, ma'am. I'm surprised that he's so eager for me to join *Meremir*."

"Blinded by your more obvious attractions," she said scornfully. "Or hasn't heard about your dubious past yet. How does it feel to be in demand for once?"

"It's your reflected glory that makes the difference," Rafe retaliated.

Rallya laughed. "Sit down and bask in it," she advised, relaxing into the nearest seat and closing her eyes. "Wake me up when the farce is over."

Noromi's uninspired plans for the in-bound run, a reprise of the out-bound run but in the opposite direction, aroused Rafe's old intolerance of a task performed barely adequately. It had been wise to keep all the patrolships with the convoy when the cargoships were heavily loaded and unable to move fast, but now that they were capable of some speed, it was wasteful to repeat the tactic. Even *Bhattya*'s limited roving commission was only confirmed by Noromi as a bow to the inevitable.

Rallya sat throughout with closed eyes, as if intolerably bored with the proceedings. Clearly, she had no more intention of arguing with Noromi than had either of the other Commanders present, but at least they had the excuse of lack of seniority. Wake me up, she had decreed; in a flood of devilment, Rafe resolved to do exactly that.

"Any questions?" Noromi asked ritually at the end of his presentation.

"Yes, sir," Rafe said, violating the convention that the Commanders' shadows never spoke.

Noromi was disconcerted, but signaled for Rafe to continue.

"I'm not quite sure what the point of it all is, sir," Rafe said. Peripherally, he saw Rallya sit further down in her seat. No support from her then, but no interference either.

"The point?" Noromi repeated. "The point is obvious." He moved to cancel the displays he had created.

"Not to me, sir," Rafe said imperturbably.

"The point," Noromi said acidly, "is to deliver the cargoships safely to Aramas station. I would have thought that was obvious to a half-wit."

"I see, sir. Is that all, sir?"

"All? Isn't that enough?"

"Aren't our orders to ensure safe delivery of the convoy *and* to gather intelligence about the Outsiders?"

Noromi choked. "You're impertinent," he accused repetitively.

"Probably, sir," Rafe agreed cheerfully. "You haven't answered my question."

Noromi looked around for support, received none from Rallya or from the other Commanders, and was forced to fall back on his own resources to regain control of the meeting.

"Before you reach command rank, which is extremely unlikely on the basis of today's dismal showing, you will realize that orders are rarely meant to be interpreted literally," he told Rafe sententiously. "Until then, your best course of action is to remain silent and learn from your betters."

"Then you'll explain your interpretation, sir?"

Noromi sought inspiration from the bulkhead above him, and received it.

"Perhaps you'd like to explain yours," he suggested maliciously. "And the way it should be put it into practice." He made a grandiloquent gesture of invitation. "The meeting is yours."

"Thank you, sir," Rafe said happily.

"Some people never learn," Rallya commented, opening her eyes for the first time.

Rafe wiped Noromi's displays, leaving only the plot of the direct route back to Aramas. Turning to face his audience, he wondered for a moment whether he was about to make a fool of himself. It was a familiar uncertainty and he grinned, the grin which always persuaded his audience of his confidence. An internal alarm flickered and he muted it hastily, helped by the blatant expectation of his coming failure on Noromi's face.

His ideas took shape as he transferred them to the displays, his uncertainty and the nagging of his conditioning fading as he did so. He laid down the simple elements first, the measures to ensure the safety of the convoy. The aim of the Outsiders was to steal ships, not destroy them, so group the cargoships in a fast, tight formation. Their combined mass shadow would be protection against a ship being snatched without warning in the wake of a raider's jump; a tractor beam would have to be used to drag them free first.

The patrolships were at their slowest and most vulnerable in a turn, so keep them at the rear of the convoy, poised to run down on a raider approaching from any direction. The raider's need to use a tractor beam would grant the time the patrolships required.

The cargoships were lightly armed but not shielded, so order them not to open fire unless fired upon, nor to attempt to block a raider's escape route. Under no circumstances were they to break formation or reduce speed without permission.

The patrolships were not to fire upon a raider unless a cargoship would otherwise be lost. A damaged patrolship was a greater danger to the convoy's safety than a fleeing raider. If a raider was about to jump alone, let it go. If possible, ride on its wake, take a full spectrum sensor recording of its arrival point and jump back at once through the same hole before it faded. The maneuver was not compulsory, Rafe stressed drily; it was an option open to a ship with the right team in the web. It would be useful to know where the raiders jumped to, but not at the risk of losing a patrolship.

The point of greatest danger would be the jump from the Jalset system into the Aramas system; two patrolships would go ahead to secure the arrival point. But they would not travel with the convoy. Once the cargoships were taking their share of the responsibility for their own safety, two patrolships would form an adequate escort from Jalset's World to the departure point. The other two would be free to carry out the second part of their orders: to gather intelligence about the Outsiders.

The Jalset system's nearest neighbor was an uninhabited binary system. Uninhabited, and with the multiplicity of major jump points that any binary system had; an ideal system for the raiders to route through. Two patrolships would leave within a planetary day to seed that system with recording drones, set to monitor jump flares, before jumping on to Aramas. The drones would be collected during the next convoy's turnaround. If the raiders were passing that way, the recordings would reveal it, the first pointer for the diplomats and the historians to the origin of the Outsiders. If the records were blank, then the drones could be reused in another system.

It would have been too insulting to Noromi to ask for questions at the end of the presentation, too likely to undo any good that had been done. Instead, Rafe gave the audience a hesitant, expecting-to-be-corrected look and waited for their reaction. Equally tactfully—or, on Rallya's part, maliciously—the other Commanders waited for Noromi to speak first.

"There's a lot you haven't considered," he said grudgingly. "How would you persuade the cargoships to agree to their share, for example?"

"It would have to be explained to them by the right person." Rafe told him. "Somebody they already trust with their safety."

"He means, not by an upstart First," Rallya said helpfully. Her face was expressionless but Rafe suspected she was enjoying herself.

"I should think not," Noromi grunted. He stood up and studied the displays closely. "Your manners leave a lot to be desired, young man," he pronounced, "but you've done quite well for a first attempt. The idea about jumping after the raiders is too risky, of course. The kind of crazy idea we all have when we're young. But there are elements of this we may be able to use."

*   *   *

Rallya glared at the list on her screen: texts from her library that Rafe had accessed since joining *Bhattya*, and not one of them dealt with convoy tactics. Wherever he had learned the basis of today's performance, it had not been there.

It was not, she reflected irritably, that he had come up with anything of startling originality. The organization of a convoy with a limited escort was standard enough, and the seeding of the binary system with recording drones was an obvious use of a spare patrolship or two. The interest lay in the way he had put it together, jumping from the facts that the raiders had never destroyed a cargoship to the conclusion that the convoy would be as safe with two escorts as it was with four, and using that to create the spare patrolships that Maisa perpetually lacked.

And it had taken real skill, she credited him jealously, to trap Noromi into allowing him to speak. It was not a ploy that would work twice, but as she had remarked to Joshim in another context, once was usually enough. It was certainly more success than Rallya had had in years with Noromi, who spent more energy in avoiding her opinions that he did in forming his own.

Inevitably, Rafe's plan had survived Noromi's review unscathed, and Noromi was disgustingly pleased with it. By the time the convoy returned to Aramas station, it would have become Noromi's plan and Rafe's name would not be mentioned in his report to Maisa. Rallya grinned wickedly, sorry that she would not be there when the rumor about Rafe's Oath-breaking reached Noromi.

It would be instructive to learn where that rumor had started. Rallya had had it from Erelna, Commander of *Corir*, just before the conference. Erelna had had it from a junior in her web-room, who had had it from an unknown junior from a cargoship during shared liberty time. There would be no tracing it back to its source, even if there was time to try before *Bhattya* left orbit.

It would also be instructive to learn if Rafe knew about it yet. He had chosen an opportune time to display his talent. Had that been luck, or the knowledge that he needed to shine? When the rumor reached *Bhattya*'s web-room, if it had not done so already, he would need every scrap of good will that he could muster. Emperors knew, seeding an uninhabited system with drones was only marginally less boring than convoy escort duty, but to arrive at that viewpoint took forty years of experience. Most of *Bhattya*'s web-room would be delighted with the news, and impressed to learn that Rafe was responsible.

Well-timed or not, there was something that bothered her about Rafe's performance at the conference, Rallya realized. Not the cynical asides to his audience, about the Court's urgent need for blissdream or the overwhelming gratitude that they might earn from the diplomats if things went well; every patrolship Commander shared that cynicism about the results of their work. Nor the smoothness with which he had presented a plan which there had been no time, no reason, to think through beforehand; Rallya had had plenty of examples of him thinking on his feet.

No, it was the sheer confidence with which he had led them through his ideas. Rallya could recognize fake confidence and she could recognize the real thing. This had been real, somebody sure of what they were saying, accustomed to being listened to and heeded. It was the understated confidence that only came with experience; as she had thought when he destroyed the raider, she was seeing more than raw talent in Rafe. It was an intriguing conundrum: how much could a junior with maybe a year's experience have learned, even from the most expert of teachers? And, since the answer was less than Rafe knew, how much experience had he had when they identity-wiped him?

Damn Sajan for getting herself killed before Rallya could ask her again about Buhklir. About how young he had looked when she knew him, and how young he might have looked ten years ago. Young enough to be taken for a junior just qualified? And was he so committed to the New Empire that he would make the choice that Rafe had made? If a Commander was identity-wiped, they would have to start again as a junior; in that situation, Rafe's youthful appearance could make a mistake about his age inevitable.

How old would Buhklir be now? Fifteen years ago, he had become the youngest Commander ever, so Sajan had claimed, or the youngest Commander in the New Empire. He might have been forty then, the same age as Rallya when she reached command level, but certainly no younger. That made him fifty-five now. Rallya scowled in disappointment. At fifty-five a web's growth was invariably complete, but at thirty it would still be maturing. Joshim would not have missed a discrepancy like that between Rafe's age and the state of his web. But everything fitted except the arithmetic, so damn Sajan again for getting herself killed; her timing could not have been worse.

Or better, Rallya thought suspiciously. If Rafe were Buhklir, how would his conditioning react to a prolonged encounter with somebody he knew in his previous life? The brief meeting at Aramas had shaken him badly, and Sajan would have sought him out again, on Jalset's World or at Aramas, to reminisce about the New Empire and to add him to her collection of aristos, or near-aristos. Even if Rafe were only Buhklir's son, would identity-wipe survive such a direct counter-stimulus? And what would be the result if he did regain his memory? Who would have an interest in ensuring that he did not?

Nobody, if the identity-wipe had been applied for Oath-breaking; if memory returned, it would be wiped again, with nobody a loser except Rafe. What if the identity-wipe had not been the result of Oath-breaking, but to hide something in Rafe's past? In those circumstances there would certainly be people interested in preventing a return of memory, Rallya thought grimly, people at the highest level in the Guild. Identity-wipe was so serious a step that it had to be sanctioned at Council level; to impose it on a webber for any reason except Oath-breaking was a betrayal of every Oath the Council members had taken. Discovery would destroy those implicated.

But, if it was vital to conceal something that Rafe knew, why run the risk of discovery by keeping him alive, even identity-wiped? Simpler and safer to kill him: no need to involve a psych-surgeon to perform the identity-wipe, no need to keep him under constant observation. The observer's identity was clear: Elanis, first on *Avannya* and now on *Bhattya*. Clear too that his instructions included murder if necessary; Rallya herself had told him that Sajan recognized Rafe, and Sajan had died at the first opportunity. Which brought Rallya full circle: if they were prepared to kill to keep the secret, why was Rafe still alive?

And, when Elanis had all the influence necessary to keep his berth on *Avannya* indefinitely, why had he left it so suddenly, just before an accident which should have led to the death of every webber aboard? Accident? Rallya snorted derisively. Nothing that happened around Rafe was an accident. Somebody *had* tried to kill him, somebody with more influence than Elanis's controllers. Somebody willing to sacrifice an entire web-room to be sure that he died. Rallya swore bitterly. *Avannya*, then Sajan. *Bhattya* next? There was a good reason to keep Elanis aboard, in spite of Joshim's protests. Whoever wanted Rafe dead did not consider Elanis expendable; his presence was protection of a kind, his departure a warning of imminent danger. Unless there was a reassessment of priorities and Elanis became expendable, but a patrolship—an alerted patrolship with Rallya aboard—was not the easy target that *Avannya* had been.

New Empire Guild politics, ten years ago? Rallya could not remember what had been going on, doubted that she had ever known. No reason to suppose it was any more attractive than Old Empire Guild politics, and she had a surfeit of that thirty-five years ago. Buhklir would have been a likely candidate for the Guild Council, Sajan had suggested. Was he in favor of partition, or against it? Whatever view he held, neither faction would have been forced to go to such extreme lengths to prevent his election. And if the reason lay only in the New Empire, how had help like Elanis been enlisted on this side of the Disputed Zone?

There were too many linkages missing to make sense of it yet, but too many elements of the picture present to doubt that there was a secret to be discovered. Rallya smiled contentedly. No mistakes this time, she promised herself. Handle it slowly and carefully, like the explosive it was, and detonate it where it would have the most impact: under the Guild Council. There would not be many with anything to hide who would survive the shock waves that would travel through the Guild. Especially not those who had accepted the offers that Rallya had turned down thirty-five years ago. The ones who had achieved power since then because Rallya had spoken out too soon, before she had the whole picture. The ones who would soon learn that thirty-five years was not too long to wait to win a war.

From introductory material for apprentices to the Guild of Webbers

...After induction, you will be assigned to the web-room of a ship for two years, where you will receive your initial training under the supervision of your ship's Three...

...Upon satisfactory completion of your apprenticeship, you will be granted a half-year's leave, which should normally be spent in your home environment. The purpose of this period is to enable you to consider the gravity of the Oath that you intend to take... Twenty percent of apprentices leave the Guild at this time...

...Once introduced, your web will take between one hundred and four hundred days to establish itself. The degree of discomfort experienced during establishment varies between individuals... You will already be aware that permanent sterility is a side-effect of establishment... Training starts again when establishment is complete...

...Once qualified as a probationary junior, you will normally be assigned to the web-room of a ship or station, and achieve full junior qualification within two years. Junior assignment is the responsibility of the Personnel Directorate, although your preferences and those of the Webmaster concerned are always taken into account...

...If you wish, you may go on to qualify as a senior, entitling you to accept the offer of a senior berth. Selection of a web-room's seniors is the responsibility of the Three involved, but subject to approval by the Personnel Directorate...

... You may also wish to train in one of the specializations open to you. These include: Captaincy (specializing in ship, station, and communication systems); Webmastery (specializing in personal, ship, and station webs); Cargomastery (specializing in the commercial aspects of the Guild's work); Surveymastery (specializing in interstellar navigation and exploration); and Command (specializing in peace work) ...

... Any senior may accept the offer of a place in a Three, thus achieving command rank. Selection of a new member of a Three is the responsibility of the existing members, subject to ratification by the Guild Council (see later). Each Three consists of: one Captain, one Webmaster, and one other specialist appropriate to the ship or station to be commanded ...

... You may apply at any time for a berth in one of the Guild's specialist Directorates (Personnel, Central Support, Systems, Webs, Survey, Commerce, Peace, and External Liaison). These berths are located at Guild Zone Stations, including Central, and at planet-based establishments, including both Imperial Worlds. Appointments to a Directorate are the responsibility of that Directorate, subject to approval by the Personnel Directorate; command rank is a prerequisite for the higher positions... The head of each Directorate is appointed by the Guild Council (see later) ...

... Anybody who has reached command rank is eligible for election to the Guild Council. Members of the Council are responsible for formulating Guild policy, and for making and enforcing Guild legislation; they are the Guild's supreme authority. The Central Support Directorate is the Council's executive arm... All Guild members who have reached command rank are eligible to vote for Council members...

... You will continue as a Guild member until your web performance drops below the acceptable level for ship and station control. This is the inevitable consequence of aging, and normally occurs at about sixty years old. At this time, your web will be deactivated, to avoid the slight risks associated with an active but unused web. You may then chose to apply for a specialist berth, or to retire with a Guild pension...

... You may be worried about the relationship between the Guild and the Twin Empires, particularly in view of the current conflict between the Emperors. Time spent in a web-room is the best way to dispel this concern, but a few words on the situation are appropriate here. As you know, the Guild is pledged equally to the people of both Empires and the majority of the Guild's work is unaffected by the division between Old and New... The Guild has an agreement with the Emperors over resource allocation in the Disputed Zone. Each Emperor may purchase as much Guild support as they wish for their combat forces, at prices determined by the Guild Council. Services that are provided by the Guild are limited to: interstellar transport of Empire forces (excluding intra-system transport in combat areas); strategic and tactical advice during operations involving Guild ships; and nonlethal combat between Guild ships assigned to opposing Empires... All Guild ships and personnel captured while supporting an Emperor's combat forces are reassigned in the opposing Empire. The cost of replacing such ships and personnel in the Empire from which they have been lost is recovered from the Emperor responsible; an equivalent sum is credited to the combat account of the opposing Emperor... This agreement can only be changed by unanimous consent of the Guild Council and both Emperors. The Guild may terminate the agreement unilaterally if Guild casualties are incurred in the Disputed Zone, or if Empire combat forces take any action that might result in Guild casualties; sanctions would also be applied against the Emperor responsible for any Guild casualties...

255/5043:
ARAMAS ZONE, OLD EMPIRE

Rafe paused by the Arura in the niche by Joshim's desk and touched it experimentally. It was smoother and a little warmer than he expected it to be, the curves fitting comfortably into his palm, but it gave him none of the comfort that Joshim drew from it. He smiled slightly, acknowledging that he had not expected that either, and sat cross-legged on the seat that Joshim's visitors used. It was better to sit quietly in the dark than to lie sleepless.

Had there been more than three hours before he was due on duty again, he would have taken a sleeper from the supply that Joshim kept by the bed for him. He did not want to be awake with nothing to do except listen to Joshim's even breathing and wonder how many more nights he would have in this cabin. It was frightening how easily he had come to need somebody else, frightening how much the idea of losing Joshim hurt. If he had known how tangled in each other they would get, would he have responded to Joshim's kiss, the first time? Probably yes. There was the pull of Joshim's eyes and smile, the sensation of déjà vu that had touched him then and every time since when he woke to see Joshim's face, the feeling of homecoming. A curious analogy for love for somebody to choose who had no home, he thought fleetingly, or no home that he could remember except the web-room of *Avannya*, long since broken up for scrap.

"Are you all right?"

Rafe had not heard Joshim leave the bed and come to stand behind him. He reached a hand back over his shoulder to squeeze Joshim's hand.

"Fine. It's too late to take a sleeper, that's all."

"Do you want company, or do you want to be alone?"

"I didn't want to wake you."

"That's not what I asked."

Rafe leaned his head against the back of the seat. "I don't want to be alone with the night-devils," he admitted.

Joshim rested his hands on Rafe's shoulders. "What sort of night-devils?" His fingers found the knot of muscles at the base of Rafe's neck and moved to ease them. Rafe sighed with the pleasure of it. "Sit forward a little and I can do this properly," Joshim suggested.

Rafe obeyed wordlessly, centering the weight of his head down the line of his back and curling his hands in his lap, losing himself in Joshim's massage. *A shaman once told me that, if I sat like this long enough, I would rise up and float. It was a pity that he never told me how long was long enough and I could never spare the time to learn . . .* As the voice in his head laughed, Rafe shuddered violently.

"A memory?" Joshim guessed.

"Yes."

"Want me to stop?"

Rafe shook his head. Joshim sensed the movement and resumed his gentle probing for the tension.

"They're coming more often while I'm awake," Rafe said softly. "Just a snatch of a voice, or a flash of a scene. No names. No links. Just broken pieces that will never fit together to make a whole."

"It frightens you."

"No, not frightens. That's too strong. Disturbs. Unsettles. I can't have what I want from my future, and I can't have what I had in my past, and I'm left juggling fragments of them both." Rafe sighed again. "Don't listen to me, Joshim. It's the night-devils talking."

Joshim's fingers moved along the line of Rafe's jaw and back again. "What do you want from your future?"

Rafe shrugged. "I'll have to settle for what I can get."

"Why not what you want?"

Rafe shook his head, refusing to answer aloud. *What I want is what I have now, only without the nightmares and the memories and the sickness and the doubts.* Joshim's fingers traced circles on his temples, drew lines out from the center of his forehead. Rafe wanted to freeze the moment in time, live secure in it forever, but he could not have that either.

"I was thinking about *Avannya* earlier," he told Joshim. "I spent my whole life in her web-room, or the ten years of which I'm allowed to make sense, but she never felt so much like home as *Bhattya* does."

Joshim traced a symmetrical pattern on Rafe's cheekbones. Rafe turned his head to kiss one set of fingertips. *I want to stay with you. It would be too painful to say it.*

"You're worrying about yesterday after the conference, aren't you?" Joshim suggested.

"After that bout of sickness, don't you think I should be?" Rafe asked tightly.

"No." Joshim set his hands on the back of the seat and turned it so that they faced each other in the darkness. "Are you worried about the cause of the nausea or its consequences?"

"Both." Rafe could not see Joshim's face, but it made talking about the problem no easier. "Not to mention the sheer misery of throwing up endlessly for an hour."

"If I'd thought to leave a supply of anti-nauseant with the sleepers, you wouldn't have had to wait for me to come out of the web," Joshim said guiltily.

"I hadn't planned to need any," Rafe joked. "If I'd kept quiet at the conference, I wouldn't have needed any. Next time I'll know better."

"Next time, I'll make sure it's available for you."

"If you want."

"No, Rafe," Joshim said sternly. "You're not going to avoid talking about it by caving in to everything I say."

"Then we'll talk about it," Rafe said angrily. "We'll talk about when you're going to ban me from *Bhattya*'s web altogether, and whether your recommendation—if you can give me one—is going to be enough to get me a berth on another ship. One that isn't a patrolship, so I don't get ripped apart by the impossible things I can do and the impossible things I remember. One where I don't have to watch you being torn between what you want to do and what you have to do, because of me."

"Is that what you want?"

"No, damn you! It isn't what I want! It's all I can have!"

Joshim said nothing. Rafe shut his eyes and concentrated on regaining enough control to speak calmly again. "Sorry, Joshim. I shouldn't have shouted at you. It isn't your fault, and it's making you as miserable as it's making me."

"Not quite. Not since I realized what a fool I was being." Joshim laid the back of his hand briefly along Rafe's cheek. "I panicked, you know. I didn't need to bar you from the key-position. If I'd just taken time to think, I'd have seen then what I saw yesterday. You're fine as long as you have something important to focus on, like webbing, or showing Noromi how things should be done. The backlash only hits you when you relax, when you stop holding it off. You can control it. You're controlling it already.''

Rafe chewed his lip, troubled. "It can't be that simple," he objected. "Why would they set it up at all if it's so easily beaten?"

"I don't think anybody set it up," Joshim said after a pause. "It is too easily beaten and too unspecific. As Vidar said, if they'd wanted to keep you out of combat, they'd have conditioned you against taking a berth on a patrolship."

"You've been talking about me to Vidar?" Rafe demanded.

"Vidar is a friend, and he could see I was worried about you. I would have talked to you if you'd let me."

Rafe had no answer to that. "If nobody set it up, why is it happening?" he asked instead.

"I think it's your normal physiological reaction to stress," Joshim said carefully. "Do you feel sick when you're nervous?"

"Sometimes, slightly, but this is different," Rafe argued.

"More extreme," Joshim conceded, "because the stress you're under in the web during combat, or facing a web-room full of sceptical Commanders, is compounded by your identity-wipe."

Rafe shook his head doubtfully. "It would be nice to believe it," he said slowly. "I'd rather be sick with nerves than as a direct result of somebody tampering with my mind, but . . . it's only wishful thinking Joshim. We both know that."

"Gods, Rafe! What do I have to do to convince you?" Joshim grabbed the Arura over Rafe's head, knelt at his feet and pressed it into his hands, retaining his own hold on it. "On my honor, on my life and on any lives I have to come, by all that is sacred to me, I swear that I believe it is safe for you to work in *Bhattya*'s web. In the key-position. In any damned position you choose. May I be cursed for all time if I have sworn falsely." He released the Arura and took Rafe's hands. "Is that enough?"

Rafe nodded mutely, then remembered that Joshim could not see him. "You're that certain?" he asked, shocked by the gravity of the oath that Joshim had given him, with its echo of the Webber's Oath and the binding of the Arura held between them.

"I'm that certain." Joshim brought Rafe's hands up to his lips and kissed the palms in turn. "Is it enough?"

Rafe leaned forward, put his arms around Joshim and rested

his cheek on his shoulder, his face to his throat. Joshim could not have sworn that oath if there had been any conflict within him, or any doubt. Was it so wrong to accept as truth the thing that you wanted to be true? Sometimes, the two had to coincide. If Rafe could prove it, by controlling the sickness, as Joshim suggested he could . . .

"How are you at teaching stress control?" he asked shakily.

Joshim laughed and hugged him hard. "A back-rub is the best way to start," he claimed. "Come to bed and I'll show you."

From the Constitution of the Guild of Webbers

...If the members of a web-room unanimously petition for the expulsion of one of their number, that request is binding upon their Three and upon the Personnel Directorate of the Guild...

268/5043: ARAMAS ZONE, OLD EMPIRE

"You could have more weight on that," Vidar suggested, examining the setting of Rafe's exercise bench.

"Only if I want to do myself permanent damage," Rafe objected. "Some of us are built for speed, not strength."

"All it takes is application." Vidar adjusted the empty bench to his liking and stretched out on it. "Did you find the fault in Khisa's monitor circuit?"

"No." Rafe secured his bench-weights and lay back for a brief rest. "I ran the full set of first level diagnostics on it, and on the adjacent circuits. Joshim's got them all in the workshop for further investigation."

Vidar grunted approval and started a warm-up sequence that made Rafe ache just watching. *Bhattya*'s Captain was as conscientious about keeping himself in top condition as he was about keeping the ship there. "Don't let me stop you," he urged Rafe.

Rafe anchored his feet under the bar at the end of his bench and did a slow sit-up with his hands behind his head, turning so that his left elbow touched his right knee and then stretching down towards his ankles before straightening out unhurriedly.

"Isn't this your sleep period?" Vidar asked curiously, finishing his warm-up and embarking on a series of leg-raises.

"As soon as I've finished here," Rafe agreed. There was no need for Vidar to know that he had already tried to sleep and failed, beaten by a vicious nightmare of endless underground tunnels. He had come to the gym to purge the lingering traces of the dream with physical activity, and to bring his body to a point where it would overrule his mind. He would rather do that than take a sleeper.

As he performed another sit-up, he speculated about the echo that Khisa had reported in her monitor circuit. It had only shown itself once, faintly, but no fault in the web was taken lightly; lives depended on the correct functioning of the electro-components that linked *Bhattya*'s webbers together and to the ship's systems. Only fools—and dirtsiders, who knew no better—were complacent about the safety of the web, about the nature of the knife-edge balance between performance and risk.

Hell's irresistible bargain, Rafe had heard a retired webber call his once-active web; a passport to soaring power which no sane person dared reach for. It was an apt analogy. In the web, your brain was linked to the body of the ship, your nerves carried sensations that nonwebbers would never know. You only had to loosen the chains of discipline a little to tap the web's full potential, to create new sensations, to explore new pathways through your extended body, a body that encompassed your companions in the web as their bodies now encompassed you.

And there was the danger: stray from the predefined pathways and you could not know what your web-mates would experience—pleasure, pain, or insanity because they could no longer interpret the behavior of the body that they shared? Even if you were alone in the web, experiments jeopardized your own sanity, your own grip on mundane reality. So, you worked to strict rules in a fully activated web, or played—as in Rallya's workouts—in a limited imitation, always aware of the tantalizing possibilities that were within reach but unattainable. Until eventually, even the possibilities were gone and you were confined forever within a body with a deactivated web.

The ten-minute jump alert sounded, jolting Rafe out of his

reverie. He reached up to check that his bench-weights were secure, lay back to await the jump and then changed his mind, sitting up and reached for his soft-shoes.

"Expecting trouble?" Vidar asked, securing his own bench-weights.

Rafe shook his head. "It's unlikely." He slipped the shoes on and stood up. "After *Avannya*, I prefer to see where I'm going as soon as I arrive," he confessed.

"The EMP-mine was sitting right in your jump point when you broke out, wasn't it?" Vidar asked sympathetically.

"Yes." They had hit it with every sensor wide open and the web full; *Avannya* could not have been more vulnerable if it had been planned, Rafe thought bitterly. It would have made no difference if he had been in the web-room to witness it, instead of working on a malfunctioning mapping drone, but it would be a long time before he felt comfortable going through jump out of range of the sensor displays.

The five-minute alert sounded as Rafe arrived in the web-room. Rallya's team and Lilimya's were in the web, Rallya in the key-position. The web-shifts had been rescheduled so that she would be there when they broke out into the strange system; it was a routine precaution. Most of the waking crew were gathering in the web-room, with nothing to do during jump except watch.

Joshim was not there and, looking at the monitor screen, Rafe identified the nimbus that was an occupied dry-web place. The Webmaster was taking no chances; if the fault Khisa had reported was symptomatic of a wider problem, the stress of the jump could trigger an imbalance that could only be corrected in time by the reflexes of somebody monitoring the web from within.

"Can't wait to see what's on the other side?" Jualla asked, joining Rafe at the back of the room. "Be a pity if there's nothing to see after the effort you expended to get us there."

"Wouldn't it?" Rafe agreed easily, ignoring the bite in Jualla's voice. Although she would not be ready for promotion for another year at least, *Bhattya*'s Second was still jealous of him for taking the berth that she had subconsciously thought of as hers. And for the relationship that he had with Rallya, he thought with gentle amusement. A relationship that Jualla would never achieve until she exchanged blind veneration for respect tinged with a healthy degree of impiety. The analysis made him feel unaccountably old.

The one-minute alert sounded as Vidar came in, fully dressed in contrast to Rafe's shorts and soft-shoes and with no sign of his exertions in the gym. Rafe continued to watch the displays around the main screen, noting the increased power coming from the drive, the vanes settling into quiescent sleekness against the hull, their increasing speed through inertial space.

"She really flies, doesn't she?" he said to nobody in particular.

"Yes, when there's nothing to hold her back," Jualla agreed proudly. "And she can punch a jump through anywhere."

The ten-second alert sounded. Rafe braced himself against the seat in front of him. Reality blurred, streaming into chaos, then refocused. As he blinked at the displays, waiting for his eyes to realize that reality had returned, he heard the repeated shriek of the primary alert.

"A ship!" Jualla exclaimed, her eyes adjusting an instant before Rafe's and identifying the distant shape.

Rallya had the shields up already, must have raised them the instant they emerged from jump without waiting for a reason, just as she had primed the weapons. It was the caution of a veteran who intended to grow older, Rafe reflected grimly, pushing his way through to the front of the observers in Vidar's wake. The displays were showing multiple views of the strange ship—mass-scans, light-scans, heat-scans—as Rallya gathered all the information she could.

"Only one," Rafe decided after a moment's scrutiny. They had emerged into a relatively empty region of space, with no close masses large enough to hide any other threats. The nearest star of the binary was a garish red circle beyond the stranger, its partner a smaller disk beyond that.

"Who's got comm control?" Vidar asked, sounding as frustrated as Rafe by his inability to influence events, by his forced reliance on others. No webber liked to be out of the web at a time like this; it was almost like being deaf and blind.

"Dathir." Jualla triggered the link that routed incoming messages to the web-room, was rewarded only by star noise as Dathir searched the frequencies for EM messages. She reduced the volume, continuing to study the screens avidly.

"We're slowing," she said after a moment.

"And changing course directly toward them," Rafe agreed. Rallya could not be intending an attack; she would not reduce speed if she was. The stranger was growing slowly in the screens as they approached, but showed no obvious reaction to their presence. Rafe frowned at the displays, trying to prize from them detail that the screen's resolution was too coarse to show him. What was Rallya's enhanced view showing her that he could not detect?

"It's a derelict," he announced, at last recognizing the significance of the nearly featureless heat pattern of their target.

"Are you sure?" Jualla said dubiously.

"He's right," Vidar said with confidence. "Rallya's taking us in for a rendezvous."

"Is it a Guild ship?" Rasmallya voiced the obvious question.

"Could be," Vidar said cautiously. "From this distance, I can't tell. Can anybody else?"

Nobody responded as they continued to watch the screen, looking for a clue to the derelict's origin or fate.

"Boarding party, sir?" Rafe asked the next obvious question.

"Yes." Vidar looked around, noting who was present. "You, me, Peretya, and Nikur," he decided. "Jualla, pick three more and be ready to come find us if we find trouble."

They rode across the gulf between *Bhattya* and the derelict on a drone; Rallya was too cautious to take them close enough to spin over on a line. As they approached, details of the wreck which had been reported by those in the web became visible to the naked eye: the Guild insignia above the name *Hadra*, familiar from the list of cargoships lost in the zone; the short gash in her side, seemingly cut to gain access to her interior; the curious tarnish on the surface of her hull. Heat damage, Vidar had suggested as the cause of the discoloration, and Rafe had not disagreed, because he had nothing concrete with which to support an instinct that said otherwise.

"Only the one opening in the hull, Vidar reported over the comm for the benefit of the listeners aboard *Bhattya* as the drone completed a careful circle of the ship, examining the side that had been hidden until then. "No sign that the E-boats were launched."

Rafe grimaced inside his airsuit at the implications of that. Corpses inside, unless the crew had been taken prisoner. He was not sure which was a kinder fate to wish for them, not knowing what use the Outsiders would find for prisoners.

"We'll go in the obvious way," Vidar decreed.

They anchored the drone to the hull a few lengths from the opening. Rafe attached one end of the guideline from his belt to a ring-bolt on the drone.

"I'll fix the other end inside," he promised, setting out carefully across the smooth surface.

The heat-curdled edges of the opening showed how it had been made. Rafe examined them closely, noting where the sharp edges had been made safe. Those responsible had been no happier about breathing vacuum than he would be.

Shining a beam around inside revealed an engineering space through which a pathway had been cleared. Rafe pushed a cutter from his belt through the entrance, aiming it into the center of the space. It moved under his impetus alone, confirming what he had suspected. There was no gravity field operating inside the cargoship.

"Going in now," he reported. "There's machinery just inside which will make a good anchor."

He snagged his cutter from where it drifted as he passed, then unfastened the guideline from his belt and tied it around one stanchion of a storage rack, tugging hard to be sure it was secure.

"Come on in," he invited the others.

"Nikur, you come with me to the engineering and cargo levels," Vidar decided when they were all inside. "Rafe, you and Peri cover the cabin and command areas." He flicked his beam at the open hatchway that led to the rest of the ship. "We'll meet back here in two hours. Progress reports every thirty minutes."

Outside the hatchway, a short length of corridor led to a riser shaft. Vidar sprayed a color splash on the riser wall opposite, a marker for their exit. Rafe oriented himself from the now-dead lights on the corridor ceiling, shone his beam towards the unseen top of the riser.

"We'll start at the top and work down," he told Peri, switching to the private channel between them. "Web, web-room, rest-room, comms-room. Carry away anything we can, visi-reck the rest."

They used the rungs of the emergency ladder to boost themselves along. Rafe counted levels as they passed them, knowing that Peri was doing the same, a precaution against getting lost in the darkness in a strange ship. The restricted view that his beam gave him made the riser walls ahead press in upon him and he knew that, if he looked back, the unlit shaft behind would look like a chasm. Even knowing that he could not fall if he released the ladder, he still preferred not to look back to where Peri followed a few rungs behind.

"Four," he called, halting at the last opening as his beam showed the top of the shaft above them.

"Four," Peri agreed. "I'll mark it."

Rafe shone his beam through the opening while she did so. It showed him a wall of blank screens opposite. "Web-room," he announced, widening the beam and increasing its power until only the corners of the room remained dark. "And three dead," he added harshly.

They were drifting free, one with a spherical halo of long fair hair that Rafe had a misplaced urged to stroke away from the face it obscured. He pulled himself through the doorway, heard Peri curse under her breath as she followed.

"Let's establish the cause of death," Rafe said flatly, using the backs of the web-room seats to control his crossing of the room. The woman with the long hair was nearest, her tunic identifying her as *Hadra*'s Cargomaster. Rafe caught her arm, which was stiff with the brittle cold of space, and tugged her into one of the seats, making a mental apology to her for the indignity of it.

Behind the hair, her face was middle-aged, drained of personality by death but frozen in surprise. As Rafe gave in to himself and smoothed her hair gently, his gloved fingers found what the floating hair had hidden: a wound on her scalp on the top of her head. He looked closely and recoiled in revulsion. A hole had been driven down from the top of her head, deep into the brain.

"Not decompression, nor asphyxia," Peri was saying as she examined another of the bodies. "No visible wounds..."

"Check the top of the head," Rafe suggested grimly.

"Gods and Emperors!" Peri exclaimed after a moment's silence. "His head..."

"This one too," Rafe told her.

"Why kill them that way?" Peri demanded.

"They were dead when it happened," Rafe decided, checking the third body and finding the same grotesque wound, the same lack of any other discernible cause of death. "There's no evidence of bleeding. Either this is some kind of ritual mutilation or..."

He broke off as an obscene idea suggested itself. The Outsiders were taking samples of brain tissue. Webber's brain tissue, carrying in it web-seed, the virus that created webbers. Gods, Rafe thought angrily, they might not even be Outsiders, who were unlikely to know the reason for a webber's enhanced nervous system. But there were certainly people within the Twin Empires who knew, and who resented the Guild's monopoly of the advantages it brought. Could the raiders be coming from inside the Empires?

"Report, Rafe?" Vidar came through on the common channel.

Rafe switched to the same channel. "We're in the web-room," he responded cautiously. His unproven suspicions were no subject for discussion on an open channel with the whole of *Bhattya*'s web-room listening in. "There are three dead here, all with head wounds."

"We have two dead, also with head wounds," Vidar said, the tone of his voice making it clear that he had reached the same horrifying conclusion about the wounds as Rafe had. "There's nothing missing from the cargo-holds. The seals hadn't even been disturbed until we broke them," he added, putting the matter beyond doubt. "We're going on to the engineering section now."

"We're on our way up to the web," Rafe replied. He switched back to the private link to Peri. "I'll get the log first."

In the rest-room, he went immediately to the door to the secure space beyond. It was still locked, to his intense relief, and there was no other way in. The R-K-D kept inside had not been taken. The raiders knew about web-seed, but they did not know about the drug that was needed to help the seed establish itself in the body of a new host. As he sealed the log inside a storage pocket on the outside of his airsuit, he wondered how long it would take them to learn that they only had part of the secret.

There were four dead in the web, tethered in their wet-web places by their web-contacts, surrounded by drifting globules of freeze-dried shub. Rafe checked them each in turn, finding what he expected to find.

"I've got the web-reck," Peri announced. "That should tell us something about the scum that did this when we replay it."

Rafe assented automatically as he disengaged the web-contacts from what had once been a young man. The skin around the contacts was blistered; the contacts themselves were blackened. Looking at the damage, Rafe was almost reminded of something, something he had seen before if only he could remember where and when, something locked away from him ten years ago. Blackened web-contacts, and the tarnish on the hull . . .

"Input overload?" Peri said in puzzlement, seeing what he had found. "The safety circuits should have operated long before that sort of damage happened."

"I don't know." Rafe gave up trawling his memory, knowing it was useless. "The autopsy will tell, when we get them back to Aramas." He looked around sadly, knowing they could not take all the dead back with them. "We'll take this one and the woman from the web-room," he decreed. "The others will have to wait for the salvage tug."

*   *   *

"Web-seed," Rallya said consideringly. "It's not the first time it's been tried."

"It's the first time it's been tried by this method," Vidar said angrily. "And if the raiders are from within the Empires, where are they getting their ships from?"

Rallya glanced at Rafe, curious to see if he had the answer to that too, but he was still frowning at something unseen, as he had been since dropping into his seat and making his report.

"Take your pick," she told Vidar. "There are decommissioned fleets in every outermost zone, left to rot in orbit when their owners were absorbed by the Empires and found they couldn't compete with the Guild." She weighed *Hadra*'s web-reck and log in her hand thoughtfully. "Time somebody compared what we've seen of the raiders with what we know about those fleets. And what we know about the Outsiders with whom the owners of those fleets have contact. Only fools would use ships that could be traced back to them and whoever is behind this, they're no fools, to have got away with it for so long. Even though they won't have any success without . . ."

She censored the end of the sentence and turned to their silent companion. "I forgot to ask, Rafe. Had they been inside the secure space?" Even if he did not know the significance of everything inside, he would have checked.

"No. They left the R-K-D," Rafe answered abstractedly.

Vidar looked at him in surprise. "How do you know about

that?'' he asked. ''It's restricted information. ''Threes and above only.''

''Is it?'' Rafe looked equally surprised. ''I don't know how I know. I must have learned it before I was wiped . . .''

''Over a Webmaster's pillow,'' Rallya suggested, heading off Vidar's curiosity. ''Make yourself useful and play this.'' She tossed *Hadra*'s log to Rafe. ''Among the many things we don't know is how the crew died. There may be clues in there.''

As Rafe fitted the log into the rest-room's reader, Rallya thought with satisfaction that his awareness of R-K-D was confirmation that he had been a Commander before he was identity-wiped, in spite of the discrepancy with his apparent age. The drug was one of the Guild's most closely guarded secrets, its formula known only to a handful of the most senior members of the Webmaster's Directorate. Had it not been the only effective way to heal a damaged web, even its existence would not be known outside that group.

Rafe triggered the play-back of the log and the reader's screen flickered with nonsense and error messages. Looking puzzled, Rafe stopped the process and took the log out of the slot to examine it physically.

''No visible damage,'' he observed.

''Let me see it.'' Vidar made his own examination. ''Looks fine.'' He elbowed Rafe out of the way and fed the log into the reader again, as if his intervention would make it work. It did not.

''Verify the web-reck,'' Rallya suggested, passing that to Vidar. They could not interpret the data on it, except using *Bhattya*'s web's central monitor, and they required Joshim's authorization to do that, but they could check that the data was readable and consistent.

''Unreadable,'' he reported tersely almost at once. ''Both of them.'' He reread the labels on both recks, as if he suspected that Rafe had brought back the wrong ones. ''They've wiped them.''

''Easier to take them away,'' Rafe said thoughtfully. ''And they're not wiped, just scrambled.''

''As good as wiped,'' Vidar said stubbornly.

''Be interesting to find out if any of the other recks aboard are in the same state,'' Rallya commented.

''You think they were affected by whatever killed the crew?'' Vidar asked.

"Could be." Two mysteries aboard the same ship had to share a single solution. Rallya studied Rafe, who had withdrawn back into his silent preoccupation. "Care to share what you haven't told us yet?" she challenged him.

"I would, if I knew what it was," he said bitterly. "My memory isn't what it used to be."

"You remembered about R-K-D," Rallya reminded him, "and this is more important."

Rafe smiled sardonically. "Importance doesn't seem to have dictated what they left me. Knowing about R-K-D obviously wasn't personally significant to me. Knowing the connection between that tarnished hull, and the damage to those web-contacts, and the way those recks have been scrambled..." He shrugged expressively. "If I remember, I'll tell you. But I doubt that I'm going to remember."

"Some sleep might help," Vidar suggested. "You've worked right through your sleep period. Turn in. Joshim won't expect you to join him in the web for what's left of your shift, and Rallya and I can cover your next duty periods without you."

"It might help." Rafe sounded unconvinced. "If you've finished with me here, I'll get something to eat first."

When they had both gone, Rafe to eat and sleep, Vidar to set up some tests on the sample of hull metal that he had brought back from *Hadra*, Rallya put the log back in the reader and played it through slowly, looking for anything decipherable amid the nonsense. Not that she expected to find anything helpful: the placing of the bodies Rafe and Vidar had found—in cabins and workshops as well as in the web and the web-room—indicated that, when the raiders had attacked the ship, there had been no warning, no time to record the attack in the log.

The web-reck might be more useful, if Joshim could dredge anything from it, but that would have to wait until he came out of the web. And Rallya was not hopeful that either Joshim or Vidar would find a solution to the mystery, or even an intelligible clue. Perhaps the autopsies would help, but they would not take place until *Bhattya* reached Aramas, and Rallya would not be the first to learn the results.

Rafe's belief that he knew—had once known—something relevant to *Hadra*'s fate was interesting. Rallya had not given much thought to the way that identity-wipe worked; she had not realized that Rafe was aware of the gaps in his memory. Of course, they could not erase memories completely, not without

destroying the skills and knowledge that they sought to preserve. All they could do was make the memories inaccessible,
like unseen rooms behind locked doors. Finding a door revealed
the existence of a room, and the paths to the door were clues to
what lay beyond. It raised the possibility that Rafe could be
brought to remember what he had forgotten, both about the
connection between *Hadra*'s multiple mysteries and about the
truth of his past.

Rallya locked the log away in a storage drawer and rubbed
absently at her hip. Rafe would continue to worry away at the
missing memory without prompting, but a few new pointers
might help, if she could come up with any. And she could not
discount the possibility that he would never remember, or that
what he remembered would be of no use. Although he would
not be so distracted by it if he was not sure of its importance,
and she was beginning to value Rafe's judgment. Her instincts
and what she had seen of him said that he must have been a
damned good Commander in his time, almost as good as she
was . . .

Predictably, the gathering in the web-room was talking its
way around the same questions. It had not been possible to
keep secret the raiders' purpose, not when Peretya and Nikur
had seen the head wounds, and to suppress the idea that the
guilt lay within the Empires would have wasted the slight
chance that somebody in the web-room would put the pieces of
the puzzle together. The initial mood of fury had simmered
down into determination, Rallya was pleased to find; they
would think more clearly that way.

"You were told to go to bed," she reminded Rafe mildly,
breaking into his conversation with Jualla.

"Yes, ma'am."

It was said to pacify her, not as a statement of intent, but
Rallya let it go; Joshim would chivvy Rafe into compliance
when he came out of the web. She moved on to the cook-unit
and filled a plate with fish stew. Rasil's effort, by the delicate
smell of it; raised on a water world, he knew more things to do
with fish—and even mock-fish—than anybody else aboard,
including Joshim, who shared the same sort of upbringing but
disclaimed all knowledge of food preparation.

"Do you think we'll find more of the missing ships in this
system, ma'am?" Jualla asked.

"It's probable that they're here," Rallya answered. "I don't believe in the kind of coincidence that would bring us out of jump exactly on top of the only one. Whether we'll find them is another matter. We're on a tight schedule; we've only just enough time to drop the drones and jump on to Aramas to meet the convoy. We won't be making a search and, if we do come across another by chance, we won't have time to board."

She noted that Rafe was frowning intently at something she had said. It could not be their lack of time that had caught his attention; he already knew about that. The coincidence that had brought them out of the jump almost exactly on top of *Hadra* . . . The raiders were unlikely to move the ships that they captured any great distance from their point of entry to the system, she realized.

"Bring the gravity stress chart for this system up on a screen," she ordered Jualla. "Focus on the area where we found *Hadra*."

The chart was a patchwork of minor anomalies. Jualla highlighted the point where *Hadra* was still drifting. Rallya shoveled stew into her mouth as she studied it. There was a pattern to those anomalies, almost centered on *Hadra* . . .

"Trans-space breakthrough point," Rafe said crisply, identifying it from his survey training a second before Rallya did. "*Hadra* came here through trans-space."

It fitted: the damage to a hull never designed for exposure to trans-space, the input overload in the web as the sensors went wild and the safety circuits failed, the sudden death of the crew. Humans could not survive in trans-space, the dimension or dimensions that underlaid jump-space; experiments many years ago had demonstrated that. Rallya had never heard of any species who could.

"Who are they?" she asked Rafe, seeing that the frown on his face was deeper than ever, as if trans-space was not the answer he sought, only another pointer to it.

"I don't know." He shook his head to emphasize his frustration.

"If the raiders are making trans-space jumps, our drones aren't set to pick it up," Jualla pointed out. "Ought we to adjust them?"

"Good thinking," Rallya told her. "Although the gods know how we'll interpret the results when we get them. There are only a handful of people in the Survey directorate who know enough about trans-space to calculate a jump through it. Unless Rafe . . ."

He shook his head again. "If I could only remember..." he muttered.

"Remember what?" Jualla asked.

"I know of a species who use trans-space," Rafe explained. "I can't remember who, or where."

"How do you know about them?" Jualla asked impatiently. "Was it something you read, or something you heard? If you can remember even that much..."

Rallya saw the tension in Rafe's back as he realized the dilemma into which a combination of tiredness and preoccupation had brought him. Jualla would badger him ceaselessly until he remembered, or convinced her to give up. Rallya was curious to see how he would extricate himself.

"It isn't that easy," Rafe told Jualla ruefully. "I'm an Oath-breaker. I was identity-wiped ten years ago. Anything that happened before that..." He spread his upturned palms in a gesture of hopelessness.

The admission took Rallya by surprise, but only for a moment, not long enough to make her miss Elanis's hiss of dismay. Emperors, if she had needed proof of Rafe's tactical skill, this was it. Even if he did not know that the rumor had already reached Aramas zone, he must know that it would eventually. Prevarication now would harm him when the truth did come out, whereas his frank, unsolicited, admission would take the sting out of many of the criticisms that *Bhattya*'s web-room might make. Witness the looks of shock, not outrage, on the faces of his audience.

"Why?" Jualla was the first to find her voice, albeit one an octave higher than normal.

"I presume, for being unwilling to swear allegiance to the Old Emperor." Rafe looked at her without flinching. "I can only guess, of course."

"Of course," Jualla echoed uneasily. "And you really can't remember about..." She gestured at the gravity stress chart.

"I can't remember how I learnt about them," Rafe corrected her, moving the discussion further away from the realm of ethics into the realm of facts. "I might be able to remember what I learned, but it's difficult. I can't guarantee it."

"You're not going to let it go like that, are you?" Elanis demanded. "He's an Oath-breaker. He's admitted it. Don't you care?"

Rallya looked at the aristo with interest. He had been

dismayed when Rafe revealed the truth, but now he was trying
to make matters worse. Why?

"Rafe has never tried to hide his past," she pointed out. "It
was the first thing he told the Three when we began courting
him. Whatever he did or refused to do ten years ago, he paid
for it according to the Guild's law. Are you saying that the law
is wrong?"

"I'm saying that no decent webber wants to share a web-
room with him," Elanis said defiantly.

Rallya swept an interrogative look around the web-room.
"Anybody agree with that?" she asked them.

"As you said, he's paid for what he did," Jualla said uncer-
tainly. "We don't have the right to punish him further. Even if
we disagree with the law, we have to accept its results while it
is the law..."

From Jualla, that was generous, Rallya thought with satisfaction. It must be uncomfortable for her, torn between a belief in
the Unification of the Empires that made Oath-breaking uniquely
difficult to forgive, her envy of Rafe for getting the promotion
she had hoped for, and her legalistic passion for fairness. It was
the last of the three that was speaking and, if Rallya judged
right, it would continue to determine Jualla's reaction, making
her a strong supporter of Rafe where she might have been an
opponent if he had handled things differently. There were other
members of the web-room who might side with Elanis, but
Jualla was a key convert.

"Is there anybody who agrees with Elanis's definition of
decent?" Rallya asked.

"I'd like to know why Rafe didn't tell us earlier," Irinya
said.

"He's ashamed of it," Elanis sneered. "Who wouldn't be?"

"You, probably," Rallya retorted. "Except I doubt that
you'd ever be in Rafe's position. You'd rather swear a false
Oath."

"I resent that!"

"Go ahead, resent it," Rallya said cheerfully. "Threaten me
the way you threatened Joshim when he entered a formal
warning in your record, if you like." She grinned ferally. "I'm
not surprised nobody agrees with your definition of decent."
Turning to Irinya, she asked, "Did you tell your web-mates
every detail of your history as soon as you joined *Bhattya*?"

"No ma'am, but..."

"Do you agree with Jualla about the law and Rafe?"

"Yes, ma'am, but . . ."

"Stop browbeating her," Rafe interrupted sharply. "Irinya, part of the reason that I didn't tell you sooner was that my past didn't affect my work until now. But there was another reason too. I was scared of how you'd react. I'd been looking for a berth for over half a year before I joined *Bhattya*. I know how people can react when they find out." He smiled sadly. "I'll admit, I was hoping I wouldn't have to tell you. I didn't, on my last ship. It was never necessary. And, I suppose, I am ashamed of being an Oath-breaker, even if I don't remember why . . ."

"I suppose we can't really blame you for any of that," Irinya conceded.

"Most people would," Rafe remarked.

"You can't intend to go on sharing a web-room with him," Elanis protested.

"If you can't stand it, *you* leave," Jualla told the aristo curtly.

"There may be people who aren't here who agree with Elanis," Rafe reminded her quietly. "They have a right to be heard." He was playing his hand perfectly.

"I'll ask them," Jualla promised, nodding judiciously. "If they want to talk to you about it . . ."

"Of course," Rafe agreed readily. "But please, after I've had some sleep."

"I should think so," Rallya put in. "It's over an hour since I ordered you to bed." If Rafe wanted to make a timely withdrawal after that display of cunning, he deserved her support. She could hardly have done better herself.

She left the web-room herself shortly after Rafe, knowing that Jualla and the others present needed no further persuasion, in spite of Elanis's intriguing efforts to turn the tide. If those directing him wanted to keep Rafe under observation, he would hardly be doing his best to separate the two of them. He could not be intending to follow Rafe to yet another ship; that would arouse too many suspicions. Nor could there be another watcher ready to take over Elanis's role. If there were, the risk of using Elanis again would not have been taken. Besides, the conspirators would not want Rafe's significance known to any except a select few. Not that Elanis could be described as select, she thought with grim amusement.

So, if Elanis wanted Rafe expelled from *Bhattya*—and it must have been the aristo who planted the rumor in the convoy at Jalset's World, Rallya decided in passing—it was because something was intended to happen to Rafe, but not aboard *Bhattya*. Another murder attempt, made less risky because Rafe had no sympathetic web-mates to press home an investigation, or less risky still because Rafe had been driven out of the Guild completely? But if Elanis was a party to that plan, he must also have known about *Avannya*'s fate in advance, and it was his controllers who were responsible.

She was back to the question that she had asked herself fifteen days ago: if they wanted Rafe silenced, why wait ten years? Unless something had changed recently, and Elanis had reported something that made Rafe a greater danger to them. The return of memory, or the first signs of it? And if so, how had Elanis known about it?''

Rallya swore silently. She should have realized before. To be an effective observer, Elanis must have concealed snoops to help him. Where? Rafe's cabin was a certainty, Joshim's too, both audiovisual snoops and tracers on their consoles. The web-room and the rest-room would be monitored too. In fact, Elanis had had the opportunities he needed to scatter them throughout the ship, and any spy with the background support that Elanis had would have come equipped with the comp access needed to override any locks that he encountered.

Rallya shrugged indifferently, acknowledging that she could not make a search without alerting Elanis to her suspicions. So, let him watch and listen. He could not monitor her thoughts and she was not naive enough to trust any of this to a console. Besides, he probably spent all his time watching Rafe and Joshim together and blowing steam out of his ears.

Gods, she wanted to know why Rafe had been kept alive so long. It was so crazy, it had to be the key to everything else. If he had once been valuable alive, why were they now trying to kill him?

There was disagreement over him, she realized triumphantly. A party who wanted him dead, who had probably wanted him dead from the beginning, and a party who wanted him alive. If power had shifted between the two groups, or if one group was acting without the other's knowledge . . . She smiled contentedly. In a situation like that, there were ample opportunities for them to make mistakes that she could exploit.

What would they do next? There was no legal way for them to separate Rafe from *Bhattya* without the consent of her Three. The only options open to them were to kill him while he was off-ship or to destroy *Bhattya* herself. In their place, which would she choose?

Simple murder would invite a storm of questions so soon after Sajan's death when there were people who were aware of the link between them, but nobody would think twice about the loss of a patrolship in an active zone. An attack on *Bhattya* was the only safe alternative, in spite of the number of people who would have to be involved—they would have to send at least two ships to be sure of success, and it would be an insult if they sent less than three. They could not hope to use another EMP-mine; a patrolship did not follow a predictable course the way that a surveyship did. Or . . . Rallya caught her breath. They would try sabotage. A hidden explosive, or a modification to the drive, or something more subtle, a trap in the comp to send their navigation fatally wrong.

She could not bar Elanis from the maintenance areas without making him suspicious, anymore than she could bar the station techs from the ship at Aramas. And without knowing how widely Elanis had sown his snoops, she could not deliver a warning to Vidar and Joshim. But the snoops could only report locally without being detected, she realized; anything else would register in *Bhattya*'s comm sensors. And it would be no surprise when Elanis left the ship on Aramas; after all, no decent webber would share a web-room with an Oath-breaker. Once he had gone, *Bhattya* could be scoured of every snoop, tracer, and trap.

Rallya frowned uneasily. It was a calculated risk, balancing her forty years of familiarity with *Bhattya*'s comp and Vidar's intimate knowledge of every system aboard against the resources of the saboteurs. If they found nothing . . . They would find it, she promised herself, if they had to rebuild the ship around them in the process. She smiled wolfishly. There would be no retreating afterwards, and no more waiting for her enemies to act. Somewhere in Rafe's memory was what she needed to know to take the war to them. She promised herself she would find that too.

Conversation at the office
of Councillor Danriya Lady Carher

"The failure of the primary plan is unimportant. The agent reports that the second line of attack was activated before he initiated the first, and will be effective within ten days of his departure."

"Can't he be more precise than that?"

"The trigger selected makes the timing imprecise, but the results are certain."

309/5043:
ARAMAS ZONE, OLD EMPIRE

A tap on the door interrupted the long laughing kiss into which Rafe had snared Joshim as they were dressing. Reluctantly, Rafe rolled aside to let Joshim get up, then sat up and reached for his shirt as Joshim opened the door.

"Commander's compliments, sir, and would you join her and the Captain in the sun-side observation gallery," Fadir said.

"Now?" Joshim asked in surprise.

"She said immediately," Fadir confirmed apologetically.

"But she didn't say why," Joshim remarked resignedly.

"No, sir, but I did hear some good news that the dock supervisor told her, just before she sent me with the messages for you and the Captain," Fadir volunteered. "Elanis shipped out late last night, as a passenger on the fast courier to Keltam."

"You've got big ears," Joshim teased. "You're lucky Rallya hasn't trimmed them for you."

"Yes, sir," Fadir said seriously.

"She's plotting something," Joshim said when the apprentice had gone. "Though the gods know what. She doesn't usually drag me and Vidar off-ship to sanction her schemes. She doesn't usually bother to get our sanction," he added drily.

"Whatever it is, she's been plotting it since we found *Hadra*," Rafe remarked. "She's been acting like a woman with a stack of emperors in a game of drag, just waiting for the pot to reach a respectable size before she plays them."

"And not one of them was in the box that the other players drew from," Joshim agreed.

Rafe laughed and tossed Joshim's shirt across the room. "You'd better get dressed, or you may not leave here in time to see her slip them onto the table."

Joshim obeyed. "Will you take the training sessions if I'm not back in time?" he asked, adding with a wicked grin, "Churi will be pleased."

Rafe groaned. "Only Churi could think that being an Oathbreaker was exciting," he complained, thankful that the rest of the web-room had reacted more levelly to his admission. It was a relief not to have to hide his past from them any longer. He had not known when he confessed how they would react; there had not been time to consider the consequences, only to act on his instinct that it was the right thing to do. He was still warmly surprised by the scale of the acceptance he had received, by their willingness to judge him on what he was rather than on what he had been.

He frowned, thinking that he should not expect the same tolerance outside *Bhattya*'s web-room.

"I'm surprised Elanis didn't spread the news about me around Aramas station before he left," he remarked. "It's not like him to miss a chance to make trouble. Especially since he was more or less forced to leave *Bhattya* because of me. It would have been an obvious way to get even."

"Maybe he tried," Joshim suggested. "Our news about the raiders has pushed everything else into the background."

Rafe passed Joshim his tunic. "Maybe," he conceded. It was true that Aramas station was humming with speculation and counter-speculation. Everybody had a theory about who was behind the raids or about who was making them and, in the absence of any more facts than the few *Bhattya* had discovered, everybody's theory was equally viable and equally enthusiastically proposed. Everybody's theory except Rafe's, because Rafe did not have a theory. He *knew*. He just could not remember what he knew.

"Stop it," Joshim said firmly. "You'll just make yourself sick again."

Rafe flopped back to lie on the bed, scowling. "I swear you read my mind," he accused.

"No, just your body." Joshim sat down next to Rafe to put his boots on. "It's not your fault you can't remember. And whatever it is, somebody else will know it. The whole Guild—in both Empires—will be looking for the answer. You don't need to feel guilty because you haven't got it."

"It's not guilt. It's frustration."

"You're as bad as Rallya." Joshim wound one of Rafe's short curls around his finger and tugged playfully. "She thinks the universe ought to revolve around *her*."

"She told me it did." Rafe pulled Joshim down for a quick kiss, then reluctantly let him go. "You'd better not keep her waiting, or I'll get the blame."

"Mmm. And I know how scared of her you are."

Rafe tied his hair up on top of his head and watched Churi slip a headband around his.

"Ready?" he asked.

"Yes, sir." Churi hesitated then asked, "Can I try some internal monitoring this time?"

"The schedule says signal practice."

"I know, but the Webmaster said I could try monitoring as well."

Rafe gestured toward the doorway to the web. "Come and talk me through the display on the central monitor," he instructed.

The youngster described the basics competently enough, and identified the essential monitoring functions without too much prompting.

"If there's time at the end, you can try five minutes passive monitoring," Rafe conceded, adjusting the limits of the web to give Churi a manageable size for his first attempt. "I'll have a priority override on you and I'll probably need to use it. It isn't as easy in practice as it seems in theory. And remember: if I do override you, don't panic, just disengage normally. Understood?"

"Yes, sir."

Rafe logged his name and Churi's, and their purpose in the web. "In you go then," he told the youngster.

He watched Churi attach his quiescent web-contacts and sink below the surface of the shub, then moved around the circle to the next position. The web-contacts waiting for him were warm, active; as he attached them, he could sense the shadowy web beyond, quiet and empty. Most of *Bhattya*'s sensors were inoperative in dock; her drive was providing power for life support alone. The web was like a sleeper, waiting to be woken.

Breathing slowly and steadily, Rafe slipped into the shub. There was the inevitable twinge of otherness as he started breathing shub instead of air. When it had passed, he let go of his body and entered the web, exchanging the kiss of the circulating liquid against his skin and the familiar citric tang on his lips for a deep-felt awareness of himself at the heart of the silent ship.

He swept a trial signal through the empty circuits, measuring the echoes and checking the limits that he had set, then tested his override to be sure it was working. With that in place, the worst that could happen if Churi mishandled the monitoring was a mild web-burn for them both. Satisfied with his precautions, he activated Churi's contacts.

The youngster did not allow his eagerness to try something new to destroy his concentration on the routine of signal practice, Rafe noted with approval. Or else Churi realized that, if his signaling did not meet Rafe's standards, he would not be allowed to try monitoring. And there would be no arguing with Rafe's decision when it was made; even if he dared to try, Churi did not have the necessary inventiveness with signals. Not yet, Rafe corrected himself, not for another year or so.

As Churi worked on, Rafe mentally reviewed the possibilities of *Bhattya*'s next task, seeking to identify the one for which Rallya was maneuvering into position. There was no real purpose to the attempt; it was just an enjoyable challenge, to be able to predict her thinking. It would be even more fun to show her that he could; he could imagine what her reaction to being predictable would be.

It was easy enough to guess that she would not willingly accept escort duty again with the convoy gathering for Tarin's Outpost. And Noromi would not object too strenuously to her absence, Rafe added cynically. Now that *Meremir*'s Commander had learned how to organize a convoy effectively, he was eager to repeat his success without sharing the credit.

The obvious choice was a return to the system where they

had found *Hadra*, to retrieve the drones that had been left there
and to search for the other lost ships. The covert competition
for that duty would be intense, with its opportunities to learn
more about the raiders and its high probability of an encounter
with them. But Rallya had insisted on replacing *Bhattya*'s
missing drones as soon as they docked at Aramas, suggesting
that she did not intend to collect the ones they had left behind.
Nor did Rafe believe that she would look so permanently smug
if she was planning anything obvious.

The only other task in the Zone which called for a patrolship
was the routine patrol of the border with Zfheer space, and that
was a ceremonial duty, necessary only because the diplomats
had not yet agreed upon the final details of the treaty that
would bring the near-human Zfheer into the Old Empire.
Rallya would rather agree to convoy duty than undertake a
patrol whose highlights would be the rare meetings with their
peaceable Zfheer counterparts, Rafe decided with amusement.
Unless she knew something about the Zfheer that he had
missed in his research . . .

An irregular pulse out of place on the edge of the web caught
his attention and held it. It was not Churi's doing, he realized
immediately. Was it the echo that Khisa had reported in the monitor
circuits, the one they had not traced in spite of an exhaustive
search? Whatever it was, it was growing stronger, too quickly to
take any risks with it. Safer to examine it from outside the web.

[Immediate. Disengage.] He broke into Churi's practice with
the order.

[Acknowledged. Disengaging,] Churi replied promptly. Rafe
sensed him begin to obey, then halt abruptly.

[Disengage,] Rafe repeated.

[Inability.] Worry made Churi's signal less than perfect.

Rafe triggered the web-alarm by reflex, simultaneously sent
[Stand by for monitoring] to Churi.

[Standing by.] Still worried, but under control.

Rafe made a rapid survey of Churi's linkage with the web,
found nothing to account for his difficulty in breaking it. The
intrusive ghost was still getting stronger, interfering with the
signal circuits, threatening to cut them off from each other
before there was time to make a more thorough examination.
He had to get the youngster out now.

[Disengage. Will operate override,] he sent to Churi.

[Acknowledged. Disengaging.]

Rafe triggered the override as Churi tried again, using it to forcibly eject the youngster from the web. For an instant, it worked. He felt Churi disappear, felt him emerge into the dimly lit shub around him, felt him become aware that—incredibly—Rafe was still with him, felt the flare of panic as he dropped them both back into the ghost-ridden web, setting up a wild oscillation that drove them sickeningly back and forth across the boundary between body control and web control.

Rafe tried to damp down the feedback, but the ghost was amplifying it, blocking his attempts to contain the situation. He swung uncontrollably between the unstable web and the horrible awareness of sharing a body with Churi, not sure which of their bodies he felt struggling for breath in the shub, not even sure that it was the same body each time he occupied it. There was nothing but overwhelming fear coming from Churi, the emotion combining with the ghost to cloud Rafe's control and destroying any chance of coordinating their efforts to survive.

Close to panic himself, Rafe fought desperately to isolate himself, from Churi, from the web, from the insane combination they had become. He could feel his nerves being seared by the overload channeled through them, not yet true pain but the promise of it. He prayed that he was feeling the flow through Churi's nerves as well. His nerves would never survive that apparent volume of current . . .

He realized that Churi's terror was fading with his consciousness. The result of over-breathing in the shub, or the effect of the overload? If both of them passed out, both of them would die. One of them had to maintain a core of body control. Unable to check the overload or to pull free, Rafe gave up the losing battle, concentrated only on regulating their breathing, keeping it down to a level that the shub could support. It had only been seconds since he triggered the alarm; it would only be seconds before help came. Churi was no longer fighting him, consciously or unconsciously, but Rafe refused to think that he might be breathing for a dead body. He had no choice; breathing for himself, he had to breathe for both of them, until they were torn apart.

Now they were being pulled out of the shub, laid on their backs on the floor. Rafe had a confusing vision of Jualla and Lilimya bending over him, one superimposed on the other, their separate voices coming from the same pair of lips. The web-contacts were wrenched away from Churi's neck and wrists an instant before his own were torn off. He sank into the haven of one controllable body, seeing Jualla's frantic face through a blessedly single pair of eyes. Then his brain reregistered the damage his nerves had suffered. He screamed and thankfully gave in to unconsciousness.

*   *   *

"Attention, *Bhattya*'s Three. Attention, *Bhattya*'s Three. You have a Class One web-alarm. Repeat, you have a Class One web-alarm."

Joshim was moving before the repeat, leaving Vidar or Rallya to silence the broadcast. Class One was serious injury or death! He pushed through the packed corridor toward the docks, the webbers there making way as they saw his insignia and made the connection with the continuing broadcast. Gods, if they had still been in the observation gallery, instead of on their way back . . .

"Attention, all Webmasters. Attention, all Webmasters. *Bhattya* urgently requires assistance. Repeat, *Bhattya* urgently requires assistance."

"We're *Bhattya*! We'll handle it!" Rallya yelled from behind him as somebody else started to run.

Joshim ignored them all, concentrated on the end of the corridor ahead and the curve of the docking ring beyond. He swerved left as he got there, heading around the ring towards *Bhattya*'s open hatch. Hitting the ramp at a run, he bounced off the safety rail into the riser and triggered the speed override so that his stomach reached the top a second after he did.

The web-room was a blur of anxious faces, the web monitor a blaze of chaos that yielded no useful information.

"I'll get it," Rallya again, diving for the rest-room and R-K-D as Joshim entered the riser to the web without breaking stride.

As he emerged to the top, his first glance confirmed that the casualties were Rafe and Churi. He had calculated that it would be so, prayed that it was not. He dropped to his knees beside Lilimya, who was stubbornly breathing air into Churi's lungs as Peri and Caruya set up the respirator.

"What happened?" he demanded. "Anybody."

"Full wave compound feedback," Jualla said, looking up from Rafe. "And—we think—transference. Rafe's breathing for himself," she added, the simplicity of the statement underlining the harsh fact that it was the only good news she had to report.

"How long since you got them out?"

"Five minutes. Six since the alarm sounded."

Joshim had not even noticed the banshee wail of the web-alarm filling the ship.

"Turn it off, somebody," he called. "Lilimya, you're tired. Let Caruya take over."

If Rafe was breathing, he was in better condition than Churi. That made the junior Joshim's first priority.

"Churi was breathing when he came out of the shub," Lilimya reported, relinquishing her task. "He only stopped when we disconnected his web-contacts."

Joshim grimaced. "Was he breathing in time with Rafe?" he asked.

"Yes." Lilimya looked down at her hands in her lap, biting her lip. "That's why we suspect transference. And we haven't been able to start a pulse. Or get a brain trace." She gestured at the electrodes lying on the floor beside them, and the flat traces of the physio-monitor that they had already hooked up to the youngster.

Joshim took Churi's flaccid wrist, looked at the burned contact, the blue nails. Hypoxia, or the shock of third degree web-burn, either would have been enough to kill him. If there was no brain trace and they had not started a pulse already...

"Here." Rallya thrust a vial of R-K-D into his hand. "How bad?"

"Bad," Joshim said baldly, rising to his feet. "Get Churi onto the respirator. Lilimya, keep trying for a pulse." They had to go through the motions.

"Rafe?" Rallya asked anxiously.

"Breathing."

Gods, if Rallya had told him last night what she had told him this morning, none of this need have happened, Joshim thought angrily. He turned away, unable to trust himself not to fling that accusation at her, knowing that it was not her but Elanis and the vile shadows behind him that he ought to accuse.

Rafe's breathing was shallow with shock, his pulse erratic, his skin waxy pale under the congealing shub. But his brain trace was regular under the spikes of residual discharge and he had never stopped breathing, Joshim reminded himself hopefully.

"Has he been conscious?" he asked Jualla.

"For a moment, when we pulled him out. Long enough to

feel the web-burn,'' Jualla answered. ''I put ten units of Daraphine into him.''

''Good.''

The web-alarm fell silent and when Joshim looked up briefly, Vidar was moving away from the central monitor. ''Pass me an empty injector,'' he told Jualla, breaking the seal on the vial that Rallya had given him. ''Then get something to dry him off with, and a blanket to wrap him in.'' He took the injector and used it to give Rafe twenty units of R-K-D.

''How is he?'' Rallya repeated, taking the place that Jualla vacated.

''Alive,'' Joshim said shortly. ''Gods know how.'' He gestured angrily at the livid burns on Rafe's wrists and neck, evidence of the unseen damage to the nerves. ''Or for how long.''

Rallya frowned calculatingly. ''Can you move him?''

''Not far.''

''Your cabin?''

''That's what I planned.'' Joshim watched Rafe's brain trace as he spoke, looking for the first effects of the R-K-D.

''He's as tough as they come,'' Rallya promised. ''He's going to make it.''

''A pity Churi isn't so tough,'' Joshim said bitterly.

''Gods and Emperors, do you think I don't know it's my fault!'' Rallya hissed. ''Do you think I don't care?''

Joshim shook his head. ''I know you do,'' he muttered. ''And you couldn't have predicted this. Only filth like Elanis would think of this.'' He shook his head again, fixing firmly on the present. ''How is Churi?''

''On the respirator. Otherwise the same. Vidar's with him.'' Rallya leaned forward, ostensibly to watch the traces with him. ''Now listen,'' she whispered. ''Rafe is going to die—officially— shortly after you get him to your cabin. And you're going to stay in there grieving while we take his body into deep space for committal. Clear?''

Joshim nodded comprehension. Rallya's idea made sense, he thought angrily. The only way to keep Rafe safe—if he survived— was to convince his enemies that he was dead.

''I'll need more R-K-D than we have aboard,'' he warned.

''You'll have it. Anything else?''

''You could try praying, if you ever knew how.''

''I'm praying already,'' Rallya promised vehemently. ''For Rafe's life. And for vengeance.''

Death certificate dated 309/5043, Aramas zone, Old Empire

I, JOSHIM (OE-P5971-17529), Webmaster of *Bhattya*, hereby certify that RAFE (NE-P9000-42775) and CHURI (OE-P81113-07375) died this day as a result of injuries sustained in the web, namely (i) systemic nervous overload and (ii) transference shock.

Report by Palace Security Chief Braniya to the Emperor Julur

... His body has been retained by the ship *Bhattya* for committal in space. It will be possible to retrieve the body from space later, if you wish, but not to intervene at this stage ...

... I have already made arrangements to question Carher's agent. The explanations for his absence during this incident and the incident last year are plausible, but ...

... It remains a possibility that the death was an accident, although my preliminary investigations show that the ship *Bhattya* has an excellent safety record and her Webmaster is well regarded by his peers ... If it proves to have been an accident, all those guilty of negligence will be identified ...

... I will continue to investigate personally.

323/ 5043: ARAMAS ZONE, OLD EMPIRE

Rafe moved restlessly and muttered something unintelligible. Rallya paused in her jump calculations and watched him closely, until she was sure that he was not waking. Surely, it could not be much longer until he did wake, she thought in frustration. He had progressed so quickly to this point, just below the threshold of consciousness. She could not believe that he would hover there indefinitely.

Nor did Joshim's apparent patience fool her. He was as desperate as she was to know the true extent of Rafe's injuries. To know whether there was somebody they would recognize as Rafe within the body they were tending, or whether there was deep-seated brain damage that would never heal. However much of a miracle it was that Rafe had survived the overload at all, it would not be enough unless he made a full recovery.

There *were* hopeful signs, she reminded herself. Rafe's web continued to regenerate at a speed that only his near-human blood could explain. He moved and muttered and all his autonomic reflexes operated. He took food if it was placed in his mouth with a spoon, was no longer dependent on a network of tubes. Best of all, Rallya thought, Joshim now consented to leave his side, to eat in the web-room or to work a shift in the web. That must mean that the Webmaster was more optimistic than he claimed. Or that he had admitted to himself that there was nothing more he could do for Rafe . . .

At least Joshim's reappearance had steadied *Bhattya*'s web-room. The death of two web-mates in the web had shaken them so badly that it had been easy to persuade Maisa that they were only fit for the Zfheer border patrol. Learning the truth about Rafe and the reasons for Churi's death had jolted them out of their depression into a high pitch of anger and expectancy, but that had shifted into apprehension as the days dragged on and Rafe stayed stubbornly unconscious. Even the ritual farewell when they committed Churi's body to space had only been an antidote to their confusion for a few hours. Like Rallya, they wanted to be doing something positive, instead of waiting passively at the bedside of the only card they had left to play, not yet knowing whether he was an emperor or a fool.

Rallya still found it hard to believe that Elanis had out-thought her, that she had missed something as blindingly obvious as a trap in the web. Of course, they had found no snoops when they searched the ship; Elanis had removed them all before he left. Of course, they had found no explosives, no sign that the drive had been tampered with, no subtle changes in the comp to send their jumps astray, no evidence of anything except a tragic accident. Elanis—or his backers—had been thorough in covering their tracks.

They had provided an explanation for the accident, a heat-damaged monitor circuit which had failed catastrophically during the overload. The station web-techs had taken it away for examination, but they would find nothing unexpected, Rallya told herself sourly. To flood a web so rapidly, to bind its occupants so tightly, the circuit must have been modified by an expert. Somebody who knew their way around a monitor circuit, and how to turn one into a death-trap, and how to destroy the evidence afterwards. Somebody who had to be a webber or an ex-webber, Rallya added grimly. It was yet another piece of circumstantial evidence. They were submerged in circumstantial evidence, she thought savagely. What they needed was proof.

"Wake up, damn you," she urged Rafe angrily.

"Yours to command, ma'am." The voice was scratchy with disuse.

She swallowed her surprise immediately. "How long have you been awake?" she demanded.

"You can't please some people." He opened gray eyes and blinked at the light. "Not long." His voice was getting stronger. "How long have I been out?"

"Fourteen days."

"Gods." He moved his arms and legs experimentally.

"Everything works," Rallya assured him. "You've been thrashing around on that bed enough for us to be sure of that."

"My web?" Rafe craned his head to look anxiously at the monitor screen beside the bed.

"No permanent damage." Rallya confirmed what he could see for himself, a little envious of his self-control. He was hardly wasting a word as he set about getting the information he lacked. He might have planned the sequence of questions in his coma, she thought approvingly. Or while he was lying there, pretending still to be unconscious, she amended suspiciously.

"Churi?" It was the obvious next question.

"He died in the web." He would not thank her for withholding the truth, or for trying to soften it. He had been conscious throughout the overload; he would have felt Churi dying.

"Damn." He closed his eyes again. "The committal?"

"Five days ago."

"Damn," he repeated softly. "He'll hate being out there alone."

Rallya said nothing, knowing that she had not been intended

to hear his grief. There was no comfort she could offer him; even if there was, he would not accept it from her. His image of a lonely Churi drifting in dark space was one he would have to cope with unaided. All Rallya could do was to make it harder for him, by telling him the reason for Churi's death, and Joshim had extracted a promise from her not to do so until he was present.

"We've left Aramas," Rafe said after a short silence, unfastening the bindings on his wrists to release the monitor contacts as he spoke.

"Leave those," Rallya suggested, avoiding his unspoken question. "Save Joshim the trouble of putting them back."

Rafe carried on.

"Conscious, you're going to be a lousy patient," she predicted, reaching for her messager and using it to beep Vidar. Joshim was in the web; the Captain would have to relieve him.

"Conscious, I'm not going to be any kind of patient." Rafe pushed himself up the bed into a sitting position. "I can read those screens as well as anybody."

"Then fourteen days ago, you would have thought you were looking at a corpse," Rallya said flatly.

"Want me?" Vidar asked, coming through the door. Then he halted and smiled broadly, the first true smile that Rallya had seen aboard *Bhattya* since the web-alarm sounded. "Should you be sitting up?" he asked Rafe.

"No," Rallya answered.

"Yes," Rafe contradicted her.

Vidar laughed. "I'll fetch reinforcements," he suggested mischievously. "They're obviously needed."

"Do that," Rallya told him. "I'll try tying him down until Joshim gets here."

"You haven't told me where we're going," Rafe said when Vidar had gone.

His eyes said clearly that there was no hope of him acting the invalid for her. Even Joshim was going to have difficulty getting him to cooperate, Rallya judged. Not because he did not feel weak—there was a faint frown on his forehead that suggested pain behind it, and his hands were trembling slightly as they rested on the comforter—but because it was his way of dealing with Churi's death. If Joshim was not firm, Rafe would be out of bed and trying to work days before he was fit. Rallya decided that she would back Joshim to win that argument, but not by much.

"You can have all the answers you want when Joshim gives me the go-ahead," she promised honestly.

Rafe glared at her. "Does that include the ones you don't want to give me?" he asked.

"What makes you think there are any of those?" Rallya demanded, startled.

"The way that you're sidling around everything I ask, unless I can work out the answer for myself. The way you're waiting for Joshim's go-ahead, when you wouldn't bother if it didn't suit you." He ticked his reasons off on the fingers of one hand. "The fact that I'm here, and not in the infirmary at Aramas. The fact that you're playing nurse at my bedside, with a face like an explosion waiting to happen when you think nobody's watching you. Is that enough?"

That was the last time Rallya let anything show on her face, even if she was sure she was unobserved, she resolved. Damn him, how long *had* he been awake before she noticed?

"There's something unnatural about anybody who comes out of a fourteen-day coma and notices so much so quickly," she said tartly. "And you needn't think that you've won yourself any answers. I did promise Joshim I'd keep those until he was here and I wouldn't put it past him to throw me out if I don't. So sit still, shut up and concentrate on convincing Joshim you're well enough to be told. And that's an order."

"Yes, ma'am."

"You're the only person I know who can pack quite so much disrespect into that word," Rallya accused him.

"I try, ma'am." He closed his eyes, conceding a temporary defeat or conserving his strength. Rallya could not tell which. She realized with a jolt that she had pulled rank on him for the last time. Gods, he was unbiddable as a First; how much worse could he be when he knew that he had been a Commander?

"Who said you could sit up?"

Joshim did not wait in the doorway for an answer but crossed to the bedside, the relief on his face giving the lie to the tone of his voice. As he gripped Rafe's shoulders, Rallya had the distinct feeling that her absence would be appreciated, at least temporarily.

"I suppose they're swinging from the light fittings out there," she said. "Somebody should gō and supervise the riot."

The two people clutching each other on the bed gave no sign that they had heard her. And Joshim had warned *her* against overtaxing Rafe.

* * *

Half an hour ought to be sufficient time for them to disentangle themselves, Rallya thought as she backed through the cabin door with a handful of mugs and a bowl of stew balanced on top of them. And if it was not, they could save the rest for later; they would enjoy it more when Rafe was stronger. If he still felt like it when he had heard what she had to say.

"How long did it take you to reach that compromise?" she asked them, finding Rafe still sitting up but reattached to the monitor.

"He pulled rank," Rafe answered.

"When all else failed," Joshim admitted, taking the bowl of stew and handing it to Rafe. Just half an hour had eased the tension from the Webmaster's face, although it would take far longer to erase the lines that fourteen days of worry had carved there.

"Is he fit enough for some answers?" Rallya asked, setting the mugs down within reach of the bed.

"He's fit enough," Joshim said, less cheerfully. He slipped a protective arm around Rafe's shoulders. Unnecessarily protective, Rallya decided. Rafe was too tough to break under the weight of knowing that he was indirectly responsible for Churi's death. He might bend slightly, but it would be invisible and short-lasting. Nobody reached the rank of Commander without learning to live with the consequences of their actions, direct or indirect.

Rafe listened in silence as Rallya talked, his face showing little reaction to her words. Once he nodded sharply, urging her past the explanation of Sajan's death that she offered, making the connections for himself. Once he frowned, as if testing the name Yuellin Lord Buhklir against his memory and finding no match. But throughout, Rallya could sense his anger uncoiling to fill the room, could see Joshim reacting to the tension in his shoulders. The quality of the anger made her ache with sympathy, left her braced for an explosion when she finished speaking.

"Yes."

The word was exhaled more than spoken, and with it passed the possibility of a violent reaction. Rallya let her own breath go, less obviously than Joshim.

"Joshim, we talked about restoring my memory before." Rafe was already back in control of himself, his anger not blinding him to the essential next step. "How soon can we try that Aruranist technique?"

Rallya glared at Joshim. He had mentioned nothing to her about Aruranist techniques when she had been worrying aloud about restoring Rafe's memory. She had known it must be feasible; if his nervous tissue could recover so quickly from the random trauma of a massive overload, surely ten years was long enough for it to recover from the systematic damage of identity-wipe. And if the underlying nervous tissue had already healed, all they needed to do to release the trapped memories was to find the right key. She had spent a large part of the last fourteen days fruitlessly trying to identify that key.

"When did you two discuss this?" she asked, the implications dawning on her. If it had been before she revealed to Joshim her suspicions about Rafe, then they must have believed that they were discussing real Oath-breaking. It was a shock to realize that Joshim might have considered it.

"Don't ask us that, ma'am, and we won't ask you exactly when you worked out who I was," Rafe said coolly. "Joshim, how soon?"

"Not for several days," Joshim said firmly. "You nearly died in that web. You're still a lot weaker than you want to believe and you know better than anybody how much remembering takes out of you."

Rafe looked rebellious and Joshim tapped him sharply on the point of his nose, to Rallya's secret delight. "I want the answers as much as either of you," he stated. "The answers, and the people they lead to. When you're strong enough, we'll try it. But not before."

"Good enough," Rallya conceded, eight years' experience giving her the edge over Rafe in realizing when Joshim was immovable. "Wouldn't he feel better if he was horizontal?" she added innocently. "One way or another."

Rafe looked as if he wanted to throw his bowl of cold stew at her, was prevented only by Joshim taking it out of his hands.

"I think I preferred you when I was unconscious, ma'am," he said as Joshim lifted him bodily and laid him flat on his back.

"I'm sure you did," Rallya paused in the doorway. "Since you're now an honorary Commander, there's no need to call me ma'am any more."

"I'm sure there isn't," Rafe mimicked. "But I enjoy it, ma'am."

From the classic Aruranist text "Guidance for Seekers"

...Through the core of every life runs a vital thread of experience, or a succession of interwoven threads, around which that life was formed. If you would remember a life, seek its center. Find such a thread, follow its course, explore its linkages...

...Be guided by one who undertakes to journey with you, following at a distance, an anchor to the present. This one will remain in control where you will surely not...

333/ 5043:
ARAMAS ZONE, OLD EMPIRE

"When you're ready, move the fingers on your left hand."

Joshim's voice was filtered by the layers of relaxation that lay between Rafe and him. Rafe moved his fingers, detached from his own action by that same depth of relaxation, and dimly sensed the change in the air that he was breathing as Joshim fed the hallucinogen through his drug-mask.

"Remember, when you want the antidote, the signal word is Roshanir," Joshim reminded him.

"Roshanir," Rafe repeated obediently, still drifting through a haze of muted reality, waiting for the drug to bring the change that Joshim had promised. He had no intention of signaling for the antidote; they had too little of the arthane to waste any. There was enough for three doses, and Joshim judged that this first dose was unlikely to bring results, would only make Rafe familiar with its effects and the ways of controlling them. They would have been better prepared if Rafe had not turned down Joshim's idea the first time, but . . . If only won nothing except wasted time, Rafe reproved himself. He should be concentrating on the clues that he had to the memories which he was seeking.

Clues. Names. Yuellin Lord Buhklir. Sajan. *Janasayan*. The last of the three would be the best starting point, Joshim had suggested. Rafe's previous name might be only a label for other people to use, with less significance for him that it had for them; it was true that the name still woke no answer in him, for all the logic that said it had to be his. And by her own admission, Sajan had not been important to Yuellin. Although he had been important to her in the end, and to his web-mates aboard *Avannya*, and to Churi . . . Rafe turned away resolutely from that chain of thought. *Janasayan*: that was what he should be focusing on, the ship that he had commanded.

He had been a Commander, should still be a Commander: that felt satisfyingly true, a piece of a puzzle slotting into place, even though the pieces around it were still missing. And a ship's Commander too, not one of the primping politicians in External Liaison or the power-seekers in Central Support. That was the major flaw in the Guild's organization: the best webbers were allowed to cling to their ships and the real power fell into other hands. Rafe could almost hear somebody else—a nameless voice—saying that, and his own faintly guilty denial.

A ship's Commander, then. *Janasayan*'s Commander. Rafe cast around for a reaction to that fact, an echo to lead him on. The function of the hallucinogen was to release his mind from its familiar channels, to free him to follow those echoes through his dormant memories. And it had begun to take effect, he realized. There was a subtle change in the quality of the sounds and sensations reaching him, Joshim's voice, the texture of the bed beneath him. Curious, he opened his eyes and blinked at the world, the sphere around him that expanded with each indrawn breath and contracted with each exhalation. Joshim was still talking but the words had ceased to make sense, like a reck played alternately too fast and too slow. Rafe grinned reassuringly and Joshim smiled back, splitting his face into two halves that stretched in opposite directions across the cabin as Rafe watched, fascinated.

"You're well away."

Rafe knew that the words had to be Joshim's, but they bounced in a great circle around the universe before they reached him like rain.

"Cheap drunk," he responded, for the sake of watching his own words bounce back.

"Don't forget why," Joshim cautioned him.

"I remember why. *Janasayan*. My ship. One-third my ship." Rafe closed his eyes against the sight of the molten walls sliding into a puddle on the floor. "One-third my ship. One-third Hafessya's ship. One-third Baruchya's ship." He opened his eyes again smugly. "I do remember. Why are the walls melting?"

"Close your eyes again," Joshim advised him. "Let me worry about the walls. You tell me about Hafessya and Baruchya."

"Hafessya and Ruchya," Rafe corrected him. "Ruchya's Captain. Hafessya's Webmaster." It was easy to remember now; he could not understand why it had been so hard before. "She's a bully too." The walls were not really melting; it was the curtain of fluid falling in front of them that made them look as if they were. "Somebody should turn the tap off."

"They will." Joshim reached out with a hand inflated like a brown balloon and closed Rafe's eyes. "You concentrate on remembering. Where did you meet Hafessya?"

"Jenadir Station, when she and Ruchya were waiting there for a new ship. We got *Janāsayan* straight from the construction dock, the first Amsiya class patrolship in either Empire. I spent days just going round her, stroking the bulkheads when I thought nobody was looking. Except Hafessya was looking." Rafe blushed at the memory and felt his skin sing all the way out to his extremeties. "She used to threaten to tell the web-room about it when she couldn't control me any other way." He opened his eyes and watched his flesh ripple like waves on water, resonating with the lingering blush. "How does it do that?"

"Trust me. Don't worry about it," Joshim told him. "Carry on telling me about *Janasayan*. When was she commissioned?"

"Fifty-twenty-eight. Just in time for the F'sair troubles." There was no need to open his eyes to see; the room had seeped in through his eyelids and was painted on the inside in colors he had never seen before. "Can't we talk later?" he asked Joshim. "I want to watch the colors." He had never realized there were so many perfect colors.

"We'll talk now," Joshim insisted. "Do you remember why it's important?"

Rafe shook his head willfully and the colors broke up into dancing streaks of light. He laughed and his laughter broke into shards of glass that showered them both. He pulled Joshim towards him protectively. "Be careful. You'll cut yourself."

"I'll be careful," Joshim promised. "Tell me about the F'sair."

"Nice people, apart from a defective sense of property. Don't believe in other people's property. Steal anything that isn't bolted down. Stole me once."

"They stole you?"

"Apologized for it." Rafe giggled. "Very formal apology. Didn't give me back though." He could see the canine war-leader ritually offering food and drink, the interior of the warship, the ranked warriors drawn up to do him honor. And to stop him escaping. As if he could have escaped, the only human on the F'sair warship, not even knowing where they were headed. Scared, but that was something the F'sair must not guess. Take the food and drink. Compliment her on her ship, her warriors. Wait. Keep waiting . . . He shied away from the end of that wait, sensing the monster at the end of the tunnel. "Ugly, but nice people. Always did what they'd contracted to do." Joshim was dissolving in his arms. He grasped him tighter, felt him slipping between his fingers. "Don't go," he urged.

"I won't. Tell me, if the F'sair didn't give you back, where did they take you?"

"Don't know. Don't remember." As long as he did not move, he was safe.

"Don't remember, or don't want to remember?" Joshim prompted.

"Don't know. Don't want to know."

Rafe opened his eyes, looking for something outside himself to drive away the fear. He had shrunk in the darkness into a tiny body on a mountainous surface that would not keep still but bucked beneath him like an angry sea. Far above him, sounds were dropping out of an open cavern rimmed with white slabs of stone. He twisted away to avoid being crushed, clinging desperately to the sea that was trying to throw him off.

"Close your eyes and hold my hands. Come on. It's too soon to give in. Remember my name? Tell me."

Joshim. Rafe formed the word in light and felt it smear like warm oil across his skin, saw the cavern twist into an open mouth and a face behind it.

"Tell me out loud."

"Joshim."

"Good. Now tell me your name."

Rafe. Closest name, never rejected. All the others were escaping like water through sand. He clutched at the one that remained, anchored himself to it. "Rafe."

"Do you remember what we're doing?"

"Remembering." Rafe focused on that, on sorting Joshim's voice from the cacophony pressing in on him. "Out of control."

"Not quite. Ready to go on?"

"Ready," Rafe agreed. "Hold me still though. Don't let me move or I'll fall."

"I'll hold you. Shall we talk about your family? Your father?"

"Don't know who he was. Mother never said. Not even what he was, only near-human and anybody could have told that from looking at me. She needed a father for a child. Didn't matter who, only when. Wanted me born before my uncle's first child. And I was, by three days. She had me cut out of her, to make sure I'd be first. My uncle was furious, not to have thought of it himself. Tried to get it declared illegal. Couldn't. Had to accept me as his heir. Officially. Never really accepted me."

His uncle's face wavered in the air around them, with the angry scowl that was permanently reserved for Rafe. Rafe made a rude gesture in return and the old man vanished.

"He never believed I didn't want the title. Buhklir, I mean. All I wanted was to be a webber. Grew up on Guild ships. Never wanted to be anything else. Mother was a diplomat. Dragged me around in her baggage. Didn't trust her brother to keep me safe while she was gone. Wasn't much safer with her. She died on Hurth when the negotiations went wrong. I would have died too but they didn't kill children and they reopened the negotiations before I got old enough to be killed."

Bright blue sun, too bright to go out in full daylight. Dark underground warrens and shadowy Hurthfolk. Watching her being led away and waiting until she never came back. Spending a lifetime learning from the priests who guarded him how to play *anash* and *kerisduan*, all the games of waiting. The floor of the room was an *anash* grid scattered with bright grey game-pieces that moved of their own volition, breaking the rules as if there were none.

"What happened then?"

The voice cut across the babble of the dancing game-pieces.

They quivered and grew faces, all the same face, all Joshim's face, wheeling silently around the grid like coins. Rafe reached out for one and it burst like a bubble, spattering acid across his icy hand.

"Tell me what happened next. After Hurth."

"After Hurth? When I wasn't dead? Embarrassing as hell for my uncle. He'd had me declared dead, my cousin named heir. Had to get it all annulled. Never forgave me for not being dead." Rafe reached tentatively for the enormous face hanging over him, flinched as he touched it, relaxed as it did not shatter. "I'm babbling, aren't I?" he asked plaintively.

"You're doing fine. What was your cousin called?"

Rafe tried to form the name and was empty. "Can't!" he said in sudden panic.

"Don't worry. Tell me your uncle's name instead."

"Madranis Lord Buhklir." His panic subsided when he found that there were still memories open to him. "Scheming Lord Buhklir. Wanted me dead, but I did what he never expected. Didn't dare have me assassinated then. Couldn't even withhold permission for me to join the Guild. Had to smile and say yes. Thought he'd choke on it." Rafe laughed gleefully, tasting the sweet notes on his tongue.

"What did you do?"

Rafe groped for the answer and found outrageous darkness where it ought to be. Angry, he pushed at the wall, struggling to find a crack, a chink that he could slip through. After remembering so much, this failure was unfair, unbearable, unacceptable. He would remember. He would. He tore at the wall with his hands. If there was no chink, he would make one. He refused to accept that there was no way through.

"Don't force it. There's plenty of time. If you can't put it in words, can you make yourself a picture?" His hands were being held in a vice from which he could not break free. "A place, or a face?"

A picture, yes. If the words were all locked away from him, the visions were not, and a single face held the answer, all of the answers. He called light to his hands, wove it, stubbornly fought its tendency to unravel and fly out of his grasp, slowly built the face that was the key. There, he challenged the darkness triumphantly. You can steal the words but not the pictures. And I will have the name. All of the names.

As he stared at it, the face blurred, divided into two, into four, mirrored in every surface. It was a crowd: watching him, smiling at him, speaking to him, shouting at him, reaching for him, laughing with him, saying hello, saying goodbye, loving with him, crying with him, coming towards him, going away, giving to him, taking from him . . . And all cruelly nameless, mocking him.

He shouted in fury and the sound shattered the mirrors, dispersed the crowd, left only the single, known, unchanging face. Joshim. In bitter frustration, he recognized that the face he had so laboriously built had been Joshim; it had not come from behind the dark wall. He cursed vehemently, taking no pleasure in the complex of sounds but repeating it aimlessly to fill the uninvited silence in his head.

"That's enough for today."

Joshim drifted in and out of reach; Rafe made no effort to fight the motion.

"I'm cold," he announced. Joshim's motion was tuned to his shivering.

"Breathe in deeply. And out. And in . . ."

Rafe obeyed, wanting to be free of his helplessness, to be back in control, back in a reality where everyone had names.

"I really am cold," he complained, as the light in the room sharpened and the harmonics in Joshim's voice died away.

"That's normal." Joshim pulled the comforter over him. "What else do you feel?"

"Flat. All the edges have gone."

"That's normal too." Joshim smiled briefly. "How many fingers?"

"Three. Two. Four," Rafe answered dutifully. "And a thumb."

"Good enough." Joshim adjusted the valve on the canister attached to the drug-mask. Rafe watched him work, then closed his heavy eyelids for a second, just to rest them. "What is that stuff?" he asked suspiciously.

"The antidote."

"I didn't ask . . ."

"You weren't in any fit state to ask. Go to sleep. That's what you need most."

"What if I forget . . ."

"You won't." Joshim removed the drug-mask, dropped a soft kiss on Rafe's lips. "You did better than I expected."

"The faces were all yours," Rafe confessed.

"It happens like that, sometimes, the first time. It won't last."

From the rules of *anash,*
as played by
the priests of Hurth

... It is permitted to move your game-pieces when your opponent is not watching. But if your opponent correctly challenges such a move, the pieces moved are forfeit...

336/ 5043:
ARAMAS ZONE, OLD EMPIRE

"So, Commander Yuellin. The only halfway helpful thing we've learned from your excursions into Aruranism is that you were stun-gassed during a dirtside liberty on Gharan, and woke up on a F'sair warship, going you can't remember where," Rallya summarized. "Joshim, what are the chances that he's going to remember anything useful in the near future?"

"Not good," Joshim answered. "Somebody went to a lot of trouble to erase one group of memories more thoroughly than the rest. Now that the arthane has provided a context, they'll come back gradually but..."

"Not quickly enough that we can afford to wait for them," Rallya growled. At least the arthane trances had not been a complete failure. It would have been astonishing if the key memories had not received the most attention from the psych-surgeons, but the relationship between the gaps in Yuellin's memory and their context might still be enough to reveal the truth to anybody with the brains to look for it.

"Who was your heir?" she asked Rafe. "This cousin that you can't remember?"

Sprawled comfortably across a seat in the corner of the rest-room—as if he owned it, Rallya thought irritably—Rafe shook his head. "Buhklir goes down through the oldest child of each generation. I inherited from my uncle, and my niece—Madranya—will inherit from me. She's probably inherited already, if I've been declared dead," he added. "She would have come of age four years ago."

Rallya frowned. "And before she came of age?"

Rafe shook his head again. "No motive there. True, my cousin would have been Madranya's regent, but she was already regent for me. She'd nothing to gain by my disappearance, and a lot to lose. She'd have been my regent until I retired, not just until Madranya reached twenty."

"She?" Joshim queried.

"She?" Rafe echoed, puzzled, then nodded. "A female cousin," he agreed, smiling.

"The marvels of Aruranism," Rallya muttered.

Even if the damned cousin was not responsible—and she had to accept Rafe's assessment of that situation since, thankfully, she had no experience of aristo in-fighting—Rafe's abduction had to be linked with the tangle of his Buhklir heritage; that was the only thing that marked Yuellin apart from any other Commander. He had had no immediate ambitions beyond the hull of his ship—or none that he could remember—and no known enemies in the Guild. The answer had to be New Empire politics or aristo bloodlines.

"How old were you when you inherited?" she asked. "And since when did aristos let the family heir join the Guild?"

"My uncle died when I was seventeen. A year into my apprenticeship. My regent was . . ." Rafe stopped abruptly.

"The same gap or a new one?" Joshim asked sympathetically.

"The same." Rafe shrugged. "Also responsible for allowing me to join the Guild, ma'am."

"So now we know that the anonymous person who's wandered through your life at irregular intervals since you were fifteen is a benevolent relative," Rallya said tartly. "Another aristo, of course. Or wouldn't that have been a necessary qualification to be your regent?"

Rafe frowned. "Normally, yes. But not a relative . . ."

"A lover?" Joshim suggested.

Rafe nodded decisively. "Yes. And that might explain the faces..."

"Probably," Joshim agreed infuriatingly. "It's a common effect. I should have realized earlier."

Rallya ground her teeth silently. If she had been present during the arthane trances, or if Joshim had agreed to tape them, she would not have to contend with this conspiracy of censorship. Yes, Rafe was entitled to his privacy, but who knew what details he and Joshim had missed, and what vital directions Joshim had failed to explore?

"A male lover?" she inquired. "From Sajan's comments, and your current preferences..."

"*You*'ve never asked me my preferences," Rafe said casually. "But male, yes."

Vidar chuckled. "Any connection between this lover and your cousin?"

"Apart from their common anonymity?" Rafe asked. "There must be, but I don't know what."

"Who was Madranya's father?" Fire enough questions and something might escape from his subconscious, Rallya thought.

"Jalmair Lord Rarthen. Sorry."

Rallya had the distinct sense that she was following a line of questioning that Rafe had already exhausted privately, or with Joshim.

"It was only a thought," she said drily. "Based on the baroque intricacies of most aristo relationships. Tell me, have you deduced *anything* about this mystery lover of yours that I ought to know about?"

"Nothing worthwhile," Rafe said unrepentantly. "I'll let you know if I have a flash of inspiration."

"Is this getting us anywhere?" Vidar asked. "If Rafe doesn't have all the answers..."

"...and the ones he does have aren't admissible as evidence in any legal court..." Rallya interrupted sourly.

"...we'll have to collect some admissible evidence," Rafe finished. "Central, Commander?" he asked, arching an eyebrow at her.

"Central," she confirmed, glaring back at him. "And the records of Yuellin Lord Buhklir."

She was not yet sure that she liked having somebody only half a step—if that—behind her thinking. And two Commanders was one too many on any ship; once this was all over, Rafe would have to find his own. If they came out on top of the situation, that should not be too difficult, she thought wryly. And if they did not come out on top, a ship to command would be the least of his worries.

"The medical data in those records will put Rafe's identity beyond any legal doubt," Joshim was telling Vidar.

"And since being kidnapped on Gharan is not a legitimate precursor to identity-wipe, we'll have enough evidence to set an official investigation in motion," Rafe added.

"By the time Central Support set up that investigation—always assuming *they*'re not in this muck up to their armpits—the scum that we're looking for will have covered their tracks beyond finding. Or made a run for it," Rallya said testily.

"What do you want to do?" Rafe challenged. "Hunt each one down personally?"

"You're willing to settle for a lot less than I am," Rallya said angrily.

"I'll settle for the very most I can get, ma'am," Rafe said coldly. "But I won't gamble everything on an impossible drive for revenge. Or delude myself that we don't need help. I'll admit that Central Support is probably rotten at the core; I couldn't have been framed as an Oath-breaker without their help. But there are a lot of honest webbers who'll give us a hearing, and back us if we give them enough proof."

"Why do I have this insane urge to duck whenever I'm in the same room as these two?" Vidar asked Joshim in a loud whisper.

"That's not insanity. That's self-preservation," Joshim answered.

"You could always turn the fire-jets on us," Rafe suggested wickedly.

Rallya snorted. "Try it," she threatened. "You'll need to do more than duck." She swivelled her seat around and keyed a command into the rest-room console. Rafe was right, but she was not going to thank him for pointing out what she already knew. And she was not going to like it. "Here. I've done the calculations for a jump to Central . . ."

"Directly there?" Vidar queried.

"You and Jualla claim this ship can punch a jump through anywhere," Rallya reminded him. "This is your chance to prove it. Rafe, with ten years in survey behind you, you're better qualified than anybody else to check these results." A jump from the Zfheer border to Central was at the limits of

Bhattya's performance, even with all the unofficial modifications she had undergone at the hands of Vidar and his predecessors.

"Arrival point in the Disputed Zone?" Rafe asked, crossing the room to look over her shoulder.

"I wasn't planning to dock at Central uninvited and set off every alarm on the station," Rallya said tartly. "But nobody's going to pay much attention to another shuttle sneaking in from the Disputed Zone for some unofficial liberty."

Rafe grunted agreement. "I'll be in the web for the jump . . ."

"No, you won't," Joshim interrupted. "You *may* have put in some web-time before then, but you won't be fit to work a full shift. And certainly not to work during a jump that critical. And don't look at me like that, or I'll tell Rallya what Hafessya saw."

"You ought to play *anash*," Rafe said sourly. "The most important rule is only to cheat when you can get away with it."

"*Anash* sounds more like Rallya's game," Vidar said provocatively.

Rafe shook his head. "*Kerisduan* maybe. That's quick and nasty, won by going for the jugular. But it's too late for you to learn to play *anash* well, ma'am. You have to learn when it's the most important thing there is. And when you've got a lot of time to spare."

Rallya snorted; everybody with a new strategy game made the same claims, and every game she had ever learned could be reduced to a new set of rules and an old set of tactics. "How long did it take you to learn?" she asked.

"Two years, and I had nothing else to do," Rafe said with an odd smile. "A single game can last a lifetime, if it's played properly. The aim is to postpone the end, or to force your opponent to make the last move. *Anash* players are judged by the number of their unfinished games, and the length of time they've been running. I've only got two in progress. One on Hurth, from thirty-five years ago, and another . . ."

". . . with your lover," Rallya guessed. "It's been at least ten years since you made your last move in that one. Think he's still waiting for you?"

"Maybe." Rafe yawned. "I'll write you up a copy of the rules after I've checked that jump. I've got to have something to do, if I'm not allowed in the web."

Report by
Palace Security Chief Braniya
to the Emperor Julur

... In the light of the unsatisfactory interview with Carher's agent (transcript attached), I intend to question Carher herself. She is currently attending a Guild Council meeting at Guild Central. With your permission, I will leave for Central immediately...

339/5043:
CENTRAL ZONE

Joshim sensed Rafe disengage cleanly from the shuttle's web, noting with personal and professional pleasure that there was little sign in his web control of the injuries he had suffered. He still lacked stamina, and his range and extension had not yet returned to normal, but in another ten days he would be ready to web a full shift. Or to con the shuttle, instead of riding the journey out on filtered standby, a decision he had protested as strongly as Joshim's decision to keep him out of the web during the jump from Aramas.

"Ready?" Rafe asked, already waiting by the hatch as Joshim removed his web-contacts.

"Half a minute." Joshim fixed his infocorder to his belt, checked that he had the wad of credits that they would need to pass the dock supervisor. "Ready," he confirmed.

The section of dock beyond the hatch was almost deserted, only occupied by a pair of webbers passing supplies up through the hatch of the neighbouring shuttle. They stiffened when they saw Joshim's Webmaster's badge, then relaxed as Rafe gave them a high-sign. One of them signaled cheerfully back, then jerked her head at the dock exit and waggled a warning hand.

"How much?" Rafe asked softly.

"Thirty creds," she answered.

"Robbers. Who is it?"

"Shikur, still trying to make his fortune early," the woman said sourly. "Claims the price is higher today because there's some aristo from the Old Emperor's Palace on station and Security is out in force. Not that you'd notice it, anywhere except in Shikur's greedy imagination." She gave Joshim an inquisitive look. "Never knew Webmasters had to come in through the back door like the rest of us."

"We do if we want a quiet sight of the vacancy lists before Personnel hear we're looking," Joshim said easily. "Webmaster and Commander. Old Empire. Heard of anything?"

"Sorry. I'm New Empire. Luck to you though."

"You've done this before," Joshim accused Rafe as they walked on around the curve of the dock.

"Once or twice," Rafe admitted. "I was assigned to the *zone* for half a year when I was a junior." He grinned. "Twenty-eight years ago, but the routine is the same. The only thing that's changed is the price. And I've never met Shikur." He chewed his lip briefly. "Hope our friend was right about Security."

Joshim nodded silent agreement. The jump from Aramas to a point in the Disputed Zone just outside Central's border had gone without problems, thanks to the skill of *Bhattya*'s web-room, but the longer the ship waited out there, the higher the chances that their presence would be noticed and questioned. Any increase in Security activity on the station would make it harder for Rafe and Joshim to move around quickly and, if they were asked for an account of themselves, their story would only withstand cursory questioning.

The greatest risk was that Rafe would be recognized under either of his names. There was not much that could be done to disguise his diminutive stature or coloring, but they had to take the chance, since nobody else could gain access to Yuellin's records.

"I hear we've a VIP visitor," Rafe remarked as Shikur made out the docking certificate that they had bought for thirty credits.

"Uh-huh. Came in on the Old Emperor's Number One

yacht," Shikur told them. "To deliver a message for the Council, or something." He added an identity-code to the certificate which would certainly not tally with his own. "How long do you want this for?"

"Half a day," Rafe suggested. "Although, if we managed to buy some web-time while we're here . . . ?" His wink made it clear he was talking about web-time for two, without monitoring.

Shikur sniggered. "Call Jimsan, in Station Control. He might be able to arrange something."

"Mention your name?"

"Uh-huh."

"That's your reputation ruined," Rafe said playfully as they walked up the radial outside the dock. "Did you know you blushed when Shikur gave you that certificate?"

Joshim laughed and tucked his hand comfortably in the back of Rafe's belt. "I plead extreme provocation." The clowning helped to relieve his nerves, and Security were likely to be less suspicious of a couple obviously enjoying themselves than they were of two solemn faces. He hoped.

The radial disgorged them onto a hub walkway and they looked around for signs directing them to the library. Joshim had not been here before, and Central was built on a larger scale and to an older pattern than the stations near the borders of the Old Empire that he was used to. It took him a moment to adjust to the layout.

"Thirty degrees left." Rafe spotted the sign first and led the way around the curved walkway. It was midmorning, station time, and the walkways were busy with a mixture of station crew, webbers from the ships and shuttles in the docks, and occasional dirtsiders come to negotiate for one of the Guild's services. And, no doubt, to make a few private arrangements with their counterparts from the opposing Empire, if the opportunity arose; Central being the only place in the Twin Empires where such peaceful contacts were possible.

The library was two-thirds of the way along a radial, and three levels up. Joshim fixed in his mind its position relative to the dock where they had left the shuttle. Out to the ring, thirty degrees right and down: that was the fastest route back.

Inside the library, an uninterested clerk gestured them toward the rows of soundproof privacy booths. Rafe chose the nearest one to the entrance that was not already in use, locked the door behind them and then visibly relaxed.

"I feel like I've got my name—both of them—printed on my forehead out there," he complained softly. "How in hell do you look so calm?"

"Webmaster's secret," Joshim said. "We practice in front of mirrors." He spun the booth's seat around. "Sit."

Rafe sat, activated the console. "Before we go after my record, I want to check something else," he explained as he requested the station news.

"The Old Emperor's yacht?" Joshim asked, seeing what Rafe was scanning.

"Just curious."

Joshim read over Rafe's shoulder. The yacht *Havedir*, assigned for the Emperor Julur's use. One passenger, Braniya Lady Rujur, personal aide to the Emperor, and her entourage. Arrived two days ago, duration and purpose of visit unspecified.

"Personal aide?" he queried.

"Means she's somebody important," Rafe explained. "The ones without explicit titles are the dangerous ones . . ." He froze; another memory had returned, or almost returned. Joshim waited but Rafe finally shook his head in frustration. "Don't say it," he said ruefully. "I'm getting a lot of practice at patience."

He cleared the news off the screen and keyed in the access sequence for Active Records, New Empire, followed by an identity-code. The screen spat Unknown Record at them and Rafe swore mildly.

"You'll have to try the Historical Records," he told Joshim, vacating the seat. "I'm obviously dead, for the third time in my life."

Historical Records required a Webmaster's general access rights. Joshim entered his identity-code and inserted his hand in the bio-probe for confirmation. When his name was displayed on the screen as a signal that his access rights had been noted, he entered the sequence for Historical Records, New Empire.

"Identity-code?" he asked.

"NE-P8271-31586."

Joshim keyed it in as Rafe supplied it. The screen said Specify Access Privileges. Joshim answered None and the screen said Access Denied.

"Bio-locked, as we guessed," Rafe said thoughtfully. "Be interesting to find out who has access besides me, if we can crack those locks."

"And if they haven't removed your access," Joshim said

pessimistically, re-entering the enquiry sequence. To the question about access privileges, he replied Bio. Rafe submitted to the bio-probe and they were looking at the record of Yuellin Lord Buhklir.

"012/5032. Gharan, Yerjin Zone. Accidental death," Joshim read the last chronological entry aloud.

"Some way that didn't leave any identifiable tissue," Rafe predicted. "Go on to the personal details. Next of kin."

Joshim obeyed. "Just a comm destination code," he said in disbelief. "You were expecting your lover's name?"

"My previous lover," Rafe said deliberately. "Though that would have been too easy." He reached around Joshim to scan rapidly through the rest of the record. "Nothing else we should follow up here. Let's copy it and go."

As they left the library, Joshim glanced back along the radial towards the hub.

"Damn. Provosts," he alerted Rafe quietly. "Identity spot-checks, by the look of it."

Rafe looked back. "Act normally. Maybe they'll pick somebody else to hassle. Especially since you're wearing a Webmaster's badge."

They walked on towards the outer ring, hyperconscious of the team of provosts behind them. There was no reason for them to warrant special attention, Joshim told himself repeatedly, wishing there were more people in the corridor to give the provosts a choice.

"Damn it," Rafe said vehemently. "You'd think they could keep the faffing risers working, wouldn't you?" He gestured angrily at the Out-of-use sign on the riser gate. "We'll have to go the long way round, via the hub."

"Identities?"

The challenge came as soon as they drew level with the provosts. Predictable, Joshim thought savagely, trying to remember which gods he had neglected recently and offering a blanket prayer as an insurance policy.

"OE-P5971-17529 Joshim," he answered. "Webmaster, *Bhattya*." They would have the extra information on their portable console soon enough, and it might help to remind them of his rank.

"Verify, sir." The provost-sergeant squinted at the readout of the bio-probe. "I hadn't heard *Bhattya* was in the Zone."

"Just arrived," Joshim explained. "We're on station to pick

up the latest gossip. And to check the vacancy lists.'' He was talking too much, he realized; he should just let the woman get on with her job.

"NE-P9000-42775 Rafell," Rafe said when he was asked. "First, *Bhattya*."

"Yes?" The sergeant looked at Rafe suspiciously; Joshim's heart sank as he realized what was wrong. "Verify," the woman continued. Rafe obeyed and she looked bemused. "Chadir, will you take a look at this. Ever seen anything like it?"

The second provost looked at the data on the console. "Says he's dead."

"Dead?" Rafe protested. "Do I look dead? What kind of joke is this?"

"No joke." The woman showed him the screen. "Deceased on 309/5043." She grinned. "It's going to make the top-sergeant's day, having to sort this one out. Chadir, call in and tell them we're on our way home."

"Emperors," Joshim protested. "You're not going to haul us in over a stupid mistake?"

"We're not hauling you in," the sergeant said, offended. "We're just going to help you sort out the problem in your First's records."

"I can do that from *Bhattya*," Joshim growled. "And we're due on patrol too damned soon for this nonsense."

"Can't have dead people wandering about Central unescorted," the woman said gleefully. "Even if you don't look very dead, short-stuff," she told Rafe, "appearances can be deceptive."

Did they teach you that in provost-school, Joshim wondered sourly. It was probably all they taught, that and the art of finding any excuse to cut short a patrol.

He sought Rafe's eyes, found agreement there. The corridor was not the place to jump the provosts, not with their escape route blocked off at one end. They would have a better chance in the hub, with the crowd to lose themselves in and a choice of exits.

"Let's get on with it," he told the sergeant resignedly.

"This is a waste of time," Rafe remarked as the provosts escorted them along the radial. "Once the Commander finds out why we're late back, she'll kill me anyway."

Joshim grunted an acknowledgment, thinking ahead. The provost's office would not be far from the hub; he and Rafe would have to act almost as soon as they reached the walkways. They might get some covert support from the webbers in the crowd; evading the provosts was a time-honored sport for liberty parties. Since the provosts were not expecting trouble, they would have the advantage of surprise, and there was nothing to link them quickly with their shuttle, whose arrival had gone undocumented on anything except the flimsy in Joshim's pocket. They could get away with it yet . . .

"Isn't that the Old Emperor's high-class go-fetch? In ten lengths of gold lace?" Chadir asked as they stepped onto the walkway.

"Where?"

As the sergeant turned her head to look, Rafe and Joshim dived into the crowd. In opposite directions, but the important thing was to get away, Joshim told himself as he dipped in and out of the bystanders; they would meet up at the shuttle.

The provosts took a second to react, long enough for Joshim to put several convenient bodies between him and them.

"I'll get the dead one," the sergeant yelled to Chadir as Joshim swerved around a pack of goggling dirtsiders. "You call in for help!"

That left Joshim free of immediate pursuit. He rounded an angle in the walkway and plowed through a bunch of laughing juniors.

"Maintenance hatch back here," one of them hissed, pushing him in the right direction. By the time Chadir passed the group, Joshim was tucked safely in the access space, hoping that Rafe had had the same kind of luck. From here, he could take the ladder down to the level of their shuttle and circle back round to meet Rafe.

"They got your friend," his rescuer whispered, halting him as he started down the ladder. "Damned Security jumped him . . . Wait a moment. There's some kind of argument going on. Between Security and the provosts and some aristo, the one who came in on the Old Emperor's fast yacht. Now the provosts are moving on. The aristo's got her arm round your friend. He doesn't look too healthy—Security must have hit him hard. Now Security are leaving too, but they don't look pleased about it. Your friend's being carried away by those two thugs that the aristo calls her entourage. Looks like he's out cold. The aristo's going with them, towards the VIP dock. Now they're all out of sight."

"Thanks," Joshim said through the acid taste in his mouth. "Which is the fastest way to the VIP dock?"

"Are you crazy? With the provosts and Security looking all over for you?" his rescuer objected. "Let the search die down first."

"No time," Joshim protested. "I . . ."

"Hold it, provosts," another junior interrupted.

Joshim dropped down below floor level as the juniors moved to shield the hatch. Gods, why had Braniya intervened, and what did she want with Rafe? He remembered the touch of memory that Rafe had felt in the library, the way he had thought it necessary to find out about the aristo. Did it mean that she was involved in his past, that her presence at Central was no coincidence?

"All clear," the signal came at last.

"The VIP dock," Joshim repeated urgently.

"Down one, right forty-five." As Joshim moved out of hearing, the voice added, "He's crazy."

"He" probably was, Joshim reflected grimly as he descended. The Security presence around Braniya's ship would be heavy; not even the Old Emperor's aide could snatch a webber from the Guild's custody with impunity. Worse, Joshim had very little time in which to act; soon his connection with the unregistered shuttle would be recognized and he would be cut off from it and from *Bhattya*. But he could not abandon Rafe without trying.

The access ways took Joshim out along a radial as far as the VIP dock and then stopped dead at the dock's safety bulkhead. By crouching down beside a maintenance hatch half a length from the end, and peering through the air-grille, he had an angled view of the dock entrance and the two sets of guards standing there, a full team from Guild Security and an equal number wearing the livery of an aristo. From the tension in their stances, they were as wary of each other as they were of anybody approaching, but Joshim had no illusions that they would not act in concert for as long as it took to capture him, if they were given the chance.

He retreated down the radial. It was worse than he had expected. There was no way through that entrance to the VIP dock, and no visible access to the dock's maintenance space. It would take time to backtrack, to search for a way in, time that Security would spend tracing him back to their shuttle. Even if he did reach the dock, there would be further guards there and inside *Havedir*, and if the guards outside the ship were only armed with sleepguns as the Guild demanded, the guards within would be lethally armed. Joshim clenched his fists in angry impotence, seeing no way that he could rescue Rafe.

"Let us through. We wish to speak to Lady Rujur."

"I'll ask if she wishes to speak to you."

The curt exchange carried from the entrance to the dock. Joshim crept back towards its source and crouched motionless by the air-grille to watch and listen. Two webbers were waiting by the dock entrance, denied access by Braniya's guards. The sleeve of one of them bore a Councillor's insignia, and he guessed that the other was equally highly placed. They must have come to demand Rafe's return, he decided uneasily. Without knowing why Braniya had snatched Rafe, or who his enemies on the Council were, it was impossible to know where he would be safest.

"The Lady Rujur will be here shortly."

"We wish to talk to her aboard her ship."

"The Lady Rujur will be here shortly," the guard repeated stolidly.

"Very well." That was the second of the two Councillors, the woman. Her companion looked annoyed at the capitulation but did not argue publicly.

Would the benefits of waiting to hear this conversation outweigh the risks of being trapped aboard the station? Joshim fretted. Yes. They had to. He must learn what he could about Braniya's intentions and the Council's; if nothing else, he must return to *Bhattya* knowing in whose custody Rafe was.

The sealed hatch behind the guards opened and a woman came though. Dressed in ten lengths of gold lace, one of the provosts had said, and the description fitted Braniya exactly, but the lace was the only softness about her. Commandingly tall, with glossy black hair cut unusually short for an aristo, she had a presence that fitted Rafe's description well: the ones without explicit titles are the dangerous ones . . .

"Councillor Lady Carher, Councillor Ferin. You wish to talk to me about the unfortunate incident earlier?" Her voice was pitched low and level.

"We do," Ferin agreed grimly. "More precisely, we wish you to return the webber whom you removed from the custody of our Security police."

Braniya laughed. "I should be glad to do so, had I custody of any such webber. But I only have custody of a young lad who thought it would be amusing to impersonate a webber.

When your provosts discovered the deception, he panicked, with the unfortunate results of which you are aware."

"There were two webbers involved," Ferin retorted. "One of whom was positively identified."

"And was my ward also positively identified? I believe that the identity he claimed was that of a webber who died in a recent, tragic accident. A careless decision, I thought." She smiled coldly.

"Lady Rujur, there are many things about this affair which are not easily explained," Ferin said stubbornly. "We request that you make your ward available to answer questions."

"I regret that will not be possible at this time," Braniya parried smoothly. "He is still recovering from the injuries caused by your Security police. Injuries which will undoubtedly distress the Emperor Julur, who has a certain fondness for the youngster. You will recall, Councillor Lady Carher, that we have discussed the lad in that context recently."

"We have," Carher admitted stiffly. She was scared, Joshim recognized. Why?

"And you would recognize the lad if you saw him, would you not?" Braniya continued. "I'm surprised you didn't recognize the description given by your Security police. He is, after all, very distinctive. Not the sort of person about whom one easily makes a mistake." The aristo seemed amused by the idea. "Would it satisfy you both if Councillor Lady Carher verified that my ward is who I say he is and not some abducted member of your Guild?"

"Councillor Ferin should also verify that your ward meets the description of the webber we seek," Carher said quickly.

"Of course, Councillor Lady Carher." Braniya smiled widely. "Since I'm accused of the abduction of a webber, I can understand your desire for safety in numbers." She was taking pleasure in baiting Carher, her words seeming to have a hidden, uncomfortable meaning for the Councillor.

"On reflection, I see no need for either of us to verify your ward's identity," Carher said hastily. "The description I heard could be nobody else." Ferin glared at her but she ignored him.

Carher was scared that, if she went aboard Braniya's ship, she would not be allowed to leave, Joshim realized. And she knew who it was that Braniya had rescued from Security. Which could only mean that she was one of those responsible for what had happened to Rafe.

"My ward does have a reputation for causing trouble, does he not?" Braniya was murmuring. "Now that this matter is resolved to universal satisfaction, you'll allow me to return to his bedside? We shall wish to leave soon. The Emperor will wish his protégé to recuperate in the Imperial Palace." She gave Carher another of her freezing smiles. "We will have to continue our discussions at a later time, Councillor Lady Carher. But be certain, I shall find time to fit them in."

And that was a threat, not a promise. *A careless decision, I thought. The Emperor Julur . . . has a certain fondness for the youngster . . .* Notice was being served that Carher would not escape retaliation for the attempts on Rafe's life. As Braniya disappeared through the hatch to the dock, Joshim did not find it reassuring that Rafe was in her hands.

*   *   *

Rallya plucked at the pins that held her shub-coated plaits close to her head as she sat at the edge of her web-position to hear Joshim out. The intervention of the provosts had been pure bad luck, but it seemed that in every direction that they turned in this tangle, there was a new hand meddling. Braniya, aide to the Old Emperor . . . Rallya slowly licked the shub from her lips. That was raising the stakes in this game higher than she had anticipated.

"I want ears open for any whisper of this on the full comms band," she told Jualla, who was waiting anxiously for orders. "And I want to know the movements of every ship within sensor range."

So. The obvious precautions had all been taken. *Bhattya* was on full alert, her sensors wide open, her web full, her comp programmed with a sequence of escape jumps in case they had to flee. All that remained to be done was to extricate Rafe from Braniya's clutches. All, Rallya snorted silently. The little scut caused havoc in no proportion to his size.

"Are we going to get him back, ma'am?" Jualla lingered to ask.

Rallya pressed her lips together. "One way or another," she promised. "Although I hadn't planned to take on the Old Emperor as well as the Guild Council. At least, not at the same time." *And when Jualla repeats that, the web-room will think that everything is under control,* she thought wryly.

"You think the Old Emperor *himself* is involved?" Joshim asked in disbelief when Jualla had gone. "If he's broken his Oath..." He trailed off, unwilling to follow that thought to its unsettling conclusion.

"Braniya is his Palace Security Chief," Rallya said bluntly, "or so the rumor goes. When she moves, it's because he's pulling the strings. Gods, Joshim," she exploded, "why can't your pretty boy be satisfied with the kind of enemies that the rest of us make?" She gestured angrily that she did not expect an answer. "At least now we've put names to both sets of his enemies. If there are only two," she added drily. "He seems to have a talent for collecting them."

Joshim smiled tightly. "And they for collecting him." He moved restlessly to the center of the web, watched the activity displayed on the monitor there. "We've got no choice now," he said abruptly. "We've got to petition the Council for a hearing, before they allow Braniya to take Rafe away."

Rallya sighed. "We can't do that," she said gently. "Rafe is only safe with Braniya as long as she believes that his significance is still a secret. No matter how important his life is to the Old Emperor, Braniya would kill him rather han let him give evidence about Julur's Oath-breaking. And *Havedir* is an immune ship," she added, forestalling Joshim's next protest. "If we tried to take him back by force, we'd be fighting every other ship in the zone. And if by some miracle we won against odds like that, we'd have forfeited any chance of getting a hearing afterwards."

"What *are* we going to do then?" Joshim demanded. "Slink back to Aramas and pretend nothing has happened? Let Braniya take Rafe to the Old Emperor, who doesn't give a two-credit kiss for Rafe as a person, only as a pawn? Who may decide to give him another identity-wipe and another identity outside the Guild? Who may decide to kill him after all because he isn't worth the trouble or the risk any more?" He stopped shouting as abruptly as he had started and turned his back on Rallya. "I should have tried to get him out when I had the chance," he said bitterly.

Rallya stood up, ignoring the twinge in her hip, seized his shoulders and shook him fiercely. "You never had a chance," she said vehemently. "If you had, you'd have taken it, and Rafe will know that too. So stop wallowing in guilt and answer this. What use is a pawn to Julur? Any pawn?"

Joshim turned back to face her, his attention caught. "Ultimately everything Julur does is aimed at Ayvar," he said slowly.

"The New Emperor," Rallya confirmed. "If Julur has a use for Rafe, Ayvar will want to know what's going on."

Joshim's face clouded. "What good can he do?" he asked. "He can't dictate to the Guild. If he could dictate to Julur, we'd have one Empire, not two. And Rafe will still die as soon as Julur realizes that he's a threat."

"Possibly," Rallya conceded brutally. "There isn't any certainty in this, Joshim, but it's the only chance we've got. Rafe's life is the least important thing at stake now," she added ruthlessly. "Julur's broken his Oath. At least one member of the Council has broken hers. If we don't act against them now, we can say goodbye to the Guild that we know. And we can't win against opposition like that without support from an Emperor as well as from within the Guild. And we have to have something ready to fill the vacuum that will be left when we've won. Which means we need Ayvar." She laughed without humor. "Not that I think he's any better than the other one. He may even be worse. But he's the only Emperor I've got left to play."

"You're talking about giving both Empires to Ayvar? About changing everything?" Joshim breathed.

His doubts helped to ease Rallya's own. "If necessary," she said more confidently. "If there's no other choice. Most people live their entire lives without caring how many Empires there are, or who claims to own them. It only makes a difference to dámned aristos like Rafe who get themselves involved with matters above their heads. And it's long past time the Guild stopped shoring up a ridiculous war whose sole purpose is to stop two immortal fools from getting bored."

Joshim inhaled deeply, then let his breath go in a rush. "The worst thing is, Rafe would agree with you about this," he said grimly. "Well, if we're going to change the shape of history, we'd better get started. I'll take over from Vidar in the web. You go and tell the web-room what's going on."

Rallya nodded, then took his wrists affectionately.

"Don't," Joshim said, refusing the comfort she wanted to offer.

*   *   *

Rafe splashed cold water on his face, dribbled it over his head, temporarily driving back the unmistakable after-pain of a sleepbeam. A stateroom was the last place he had expected to wake; neither the provosts nor Security habitually provided such accommodation for their guests. Which left a very large question to be answered: whose guest was he?

Or rather, whose prisoner. When he tried the door of the stateroom, it was locked. There was an intercomm on the wall that might yield the answers, but he ignored it in favor of a rapid examination of the rest of his surroundings. Standard model luxury stateroom, the storage units empty except for a selection of clothes that were suspiciously close to his size and had the look of new fabric. An inactive console, hidden behind a decorative panel of real wood. A range of personal items in the san, all new. Nothing that suggested how he had arrived here, or why.

He remembered being trapped between Security and the provost sergeant, catching the edge of a sleepbeam as he moved to avoid it. After that, his memory was less clear. A condition he should be accustomed to by now, he jibed at himself. There was a vague impression of being supported by somebody, then the deadening sensation of another sleepbeam. Then nothing until this stateroom.

He contemplated the intercomm. Notify his captors that he was conscious, or wait for them to come to check? Or did they have the stateroom under observation, and already know that he was awake? It might be informative to wait, to confirm that he was being watched. He lay back on the spacious bed.

Wherever he was, he was not aboard a ship in transit; the almost subliminal vibration of a ship's drive was absent. Still at Central then. Or had they kept him unconscious long enough to take him elsewhere, he thought in an instant's panic. No. If they wanted to keep him unconscious so long, they would have used drugs, not a sleepbeam. His headache had the heavy overtones that only a sleepbeam left behind.

"They could have provided me with some painkillers," he said experimentally.

Had Joshim escaped? If he had not had the same bad luck as Rafe, there was an excellent chance that he had, Rafe decided with relief. Which meant that *Bhattya* had the evidence of Yuellin's record. My old record, he corrected himself, although Yuellin's memories still did not seen an integral part of him.

That would come, Joshim had promised; it was the gaps that caused the illusion of distance.

The stateroom door opened with a whisper. Rafe opened his eyes and looked at the woman who stood there. Ten lengths of gold lace, one of the provosts had said, and Braniya Lady Rujur was still wearing it. He remembered the moment in the library when a memory had almost returned and was only slightly surprised.

"Did you bring the painkillers?" he asked impudently.

She inclined her head courteously. "I did." She placed two tablets on a convenient surface. "Should I introduce myself?"

"It would eliminate the possibility that I've guessed incorrectly," Rafe told her, sitting up and reaching for the tablets.

"Guessed?"

"I don't recall that we've ever met." Rafe examined the tablets. They looked like the painkillers they were said to be and he dissolved them in his mouth gratefully.

"Braniya Lady Rujur, your host," Braniya confirmed. "And you are Rafell, a member of the Guild of Webbers. Or you were until your recent death. And you're correct. We have never met."

"I shall have to take your word for that, Lady Rujur, since I have trouble with my memory from time to time." Rafe bowed politely. "Including the period covering my arrival here, and the reasons for it." Had Braniya discovered his identity before she intervened, or afterwards?

"You're here because it suits me to have you here. And since you are officially dead, the Guild cannot reclaim you," Braniya added with cold humor. "Which is to your advantage as well as mine, since there are certain interests within the Guild who would wish to turn an official fact into reality."

Rafe grinned back. "I had noticed," he said plainly. "It can be dangerous to be associated with me."

Braniya took a seat, her lace rustling around her. Armor-cloth, not lace, Rafe realized. And there was the faint glow of a field-shield around her head. A powerful woman with her own enemies. Rafe shivered without moving. Braniya knew too much about him for hers to be a recent interest. Was she the one who wanted him alive, but identity-wiped? He would have to guard every word, in case she realized how much he had remembered. Aide to the Old Emperor... A ferreter in corners, an enforcer of secret policies? Gods, was he part of one such secret policy?

"We could amuse ourselves indefinitely, fencing with each other for information," Braniya said when she was comfortable, her hands clasped incongruously on her lap like a highbred child. "However, for reasons which need not interest you, I have a desire to learn certain specific facts from you and no others. In return for your answers, I offer equally specific answers to certain of your questions."

"And if I don't take your bargain?"

"Then you will never receive your answers, but I will receive mine, eventually."

"Whether I wish to give them or not," Rafe deduced. "Tell me, Lady Rujur, do you conduct your own interrogations?"

"I have said, there are things about you I have no wish to learn. But you will be interrogated, yes." She frowned momentarily. "Or perhaps not. The decision is not mine."

"Whose decision is it?"

"Answers for answers, Rafell."

"What happens if I inadvertently tell you something you'd rather not know?" Rafe asked mischievously.

"At the worst, I would have to submit to a partial memory-wipe," Braniya said calmly.

"I don't recommend it," Rafe advised. "It's an unpleasant state in which to live."

Braniya smiled wintrily. "It is nevertheless a state of living. My predecessor made the mistake of trying to learn too much about you; it lead to his death. I shall not repeat his error."

Or at least, not when there is a chance of it being discovered, Rafe thought cynically. Braniya did not seem to be somebody who would accept willingly a restriction on her curiosity. And it would be instructive to learn how she knew about her predecessor's mistake.

"Were you the one to report his transgression?" he asked provocatively.

"Your profile says that you're clever," Braniya conceded. "Clever enough to accept my bargain?"

"Or fool enough," Rafe agreed, lying back on the bed with his hands under his head. "Your questions, Lady Rujur?"

"Clever and cocky," she said measuringly. "Why are you at Central?"

"Because there have been two attempts on my life. To my

knowledge," Rafe added thoughtfully. "I may have missed others. Or they missed me."

"Two attempts only," Braniya said confidently. "The attempt to destroy *Avannya*, and the malfunction in *Bhattya*'s web."

"Which you believed had succeeded," Rafe said casually.

"Which I was investigating." That was all that Braniya would admit. "Whose idea was it to report you dead?"

"Not mine. At the time, I *was* very nearly dead."

"*Bhattya*'s Commander," Braniya decided. "She's got a good reputation, in her limited field." She would not say that if she had ever met Rallya, Rafe thought with bleak amusement. It was a slight comfort to think that Braniya was underestimating one of her enemies. "Why did you come to Central?" Braniya continued.

"Something Sajan said before she died." Rafe saw the briefest frown on Braniya's face. She did not know about Sajan, but she was not going to admit it. "I reminded her of somebody she knew in the New Empire. An aristo called . . ."

"Not the name," Braniya said sharply.

Rafe considered giving it to her anyway, out of spite. But the woman had information he wanted, and might withhold it if he provoked her too far.

"An aristo from the New Empire," he continued. "I came to Central to see if I could read this aristo's records. Which I couldn't," he added flatly. "The rest you know."

"Your companion?" Braniya waited a few moments, then accepted that Rafe was not going to answer. "Your Webmaster lover, no doubt. You'll be pleased to hear that he escaped. A shuttle left the station shortly after you both escaped from the provosts, and joined a ship just over the border of the Disputed Zone. The ship—which I assume to have been *Bhattya*—jumped within an hour of the shuttle's return, without making any attempt to contact Central about a missing crew-member. You wouldn't care to speculate about their plans?"

Rafe shook his head. "I couldn't begin to guess what Rallya will do," he said truthfully. Rallya had the evidence that Rafe and Yuellin were the same person, and that Yuellin could not have been lawfully identity-wiped. Was she going to gather support from within the Guild, thinking that Rafe was being held by Central Support, and thus losing his trail when Braniya took him . . . ?

"Where do you intend taking me?" he asked.

"To the Imperial Palace." By which she meant the Old Imperial Palace; like most aristos in the Old Empire, she only admitted the existence of one Palace.

"For the Emperor, or am I not quite that important?" Rafe asked with a pretense of arrogance. The idea unaccountably started his stomach churning.

"For the Emperor," she said imperturbably. "As you've discovered already, you'll travel in comfort. The Emperor has ordered that you come to no harm."

"Was that before or after the efforts to kill me?"

"There will be steps taken against those responsible," Braniya promised. "Elanis Lord Khalem is already enjoying my hospitality." She smiled again, with her mouth alone. "Not as much as you are, I assure you. And he will enjoy it even less, now that his guilt in this is proven."

Nobody had told Elanis that the Old Emperor was involved, Rafe guessed; the arrogant aristo would never have had the nerve to go against Julur's wishes. But he would get no sympathy from Rafe; for Churi's death, he deserved whatever punishment Braniya planned.

"I may give Danriya Lady Carher her freedom a while longer," Braniya said thoughtfully, unclasping her hands. "She will make a suitable diversion to occupy your Commander." She nodded with satisfaction. "Yes. Carher will fight for control of the Guild, for the power she hopes will save her. And while the guild tears itself apart, who will be looking for a long-dead Oath-breaker?"

Rafe withheld his reaction, knowing too well that what she planned was possible and the repercussions would be disastrous. A prolonged power struggle within the Guild would destroy the impartiality on which its strength was based, giving the Emperors a chance to gather up the fragments. He was chilled by the thought of the Guild split between the Emperors, carrying the war out of the Disputed Zone into regions where people lived. Gods, would Rallya see the risk? Even if she did, and abandoned the battle before it began, Carher had nothing to lose.

"Have I answered all your questions?" Braniya inquired.

"What does the Emperor plan to do with me?" Rafe asked. "Or is that something else he won't let you know?"

"I can't say," Braniya said haughtily. "He has a certain regard for your physical health, but I expect you to undergo a new identity-wipe. And perhaps cosmetic surgery to alter your appearance before you're placed in a new environment. That will be my recommendation.''

"Recommend another twenty cents in height, would you?" Rafe asked cheerfully. "I'm getting a pain in my neck looking up at you."

When she had gone, Rafe closed his eyes and for a moment gave in to despair behind them. By the time Rallya had wrested control of the Guild from Carher—and he had to believe that she would do so because the alternative was too bleak to consider—his memory would have been ripped from him again. And his face, and his web, he realized bitterly. And this time there would be no mistakes made in the identity-wipe, no loopholes left through which memory could return. Under interrogation he would reveal all that he had remembered— nobody could hold out against the truthseeking drugs—and they would finally and irrevocably steal him from himself.

If he waited for them to do it, he thought angrily. How would Julur react if Braniya delivered a self-killed corpse? Although, he realized as he thought about it further, there was nothing in the stateroom with which killing himself would be easy or certain. He recoiled from the grotesque self-mutilations that were his only choices if he wished to commit suicide. And from the idea of giving in when there was still time left to fight.

What did Julur want him for? Gods, it made no sense, that the Old Emperor had broken his Oath to the Guild for Rafe's sake. If the truth were ever discovered, the Guild could withdraw its Oath to Julur and their services from his Empire. The chaos that would follow could topple Julur, which was the real reason that the Emperors kept their Oaths. Even if the danger of division within the Guild made it likely now that Julur would escape the full consequences of his action, ten years ago when he had Rafe kidnapped he would have had no such reassurance.

Somewhere in the missing memories between the F'sair warship and waking as Rafell the Oath-breaker, a memory of Julur must be lurking. Of Julur, of Braniya's predecessor, of interrogation, of the process of identity-wipe . . . No wonder he shrank from remembering that part, Rafe thought ruefully.

Braniya had aroused no memories, or nothing specific, only the odd certainty that she reminded him of somebody. He was probably thinking of her dead predecessor, he decided sourly.

Would meeting Julur trigger anything fresh? A memory that gave the reason behind this inexplicable tangle? Joshim had said that meeting somebody who figured in the missing memories could cause them to return.

There was something that could be deduced from Julur's interest in him, he thought darkly, and that was that the New Emperor must have a corresponding interest. Yuellin had been an aristo in the New Empire and the head of a family; surely he must have met the New Emperor at some point in his life. As a child, he had been presented for the Emperor's acknowledgement as the Buhklir heir. He strained to remember, but it was too long ago or too unmemorable to the infant he had been; all he could recall was being dressed with great precision by his nurse, and the stern back of his uncle preceding him up an endless aisle. When he tried to remember another occasion he had been at court, he failed.

Was that the pattern of the residual identity-wipe? he thought excitedly. Did it cover the periods when he had visited the New Imperial Palace? If Yuellin's lover had been at court, Julur would have taken extra trouble to erase those memories, to expunge everything to do with the Emperor Ayvar.

His excitement faded as he realized that knowing the pattern of the missing memories was no help in recovering them. There were a thousand explanations he could invent for the pattern, and Joshim had warned him that true memories were easily concealed by an overactive imagination. Rafe wished miserably that Joshim was with him, to comfort him, to drive away the fear that Braniya had sown so effectively. Still, if he could not have that comfort, he could have the satisfaction of applying Joshim's Aruranist techniques to consolidate the memories he had and to chip away at the barriers remained. *Havedir* could not reach the Old Imperial Palace in less than ten days, not when Julur's paranoiac security stopped ships from jumping into his defensive sphere. By the time Julur tried to steal his identity again, Rafe swore he would have reclaimed it fully. And when he knew what had happened to him in the old Emperor's hands last time, he would be better prepared to change things this time. As long as he knew who he was, he still had a chance.

Security alert dated 346/5043,
for the attention of Yulenda,
Head of Security, New Imperial Palace

Facial pattern HA-72541 matched on entry at Main shuttleport. Subject identifies self as Guild Webmaster Joshim, accompanied by Guild Commander Rallya. Webber status verified by bio-probe. Routine surveillance continues.

347/ 5043:
IMPERIAL ZONE, NEW EMPIRE

"We're being followed," Joshim said without warning. "Tall, dark-haired woman, yellow-brown skin, deep brown tunic. At the top of the steps now."

Rallya squinted in the bright sunshine, looking along the trackcar platform for the woman that he described and cursing the milling crowd of tourists blocking her view. Everything on New Imperial was hidden behind a crowd of tourists, or else—like the New Emperor—swaddled in layers of equally impenetrable bureaucracy. But at least the bureaucracy could be bypassed, or would be when Rallya had her way. The only good thing that could be said for the tourists was that they allowed her and Joshim to move anonymously around the city. And if Joshim was right, they were not even doing that effectively.

"She's out of sight now," Joshim said. "She'll pick us up again down the street."

"Are you sure she's following us?" Rallya asked sceptically.

"Certain," Joshim insisted. "She was outside the hotel

when we left. She didn't get onto that trackcar until she was sure we were taking it. She waited until we got off before she did. And she watches everyone around her all the time. With the notable exception of us. Every time she looks at us, her eyes skid past as if we were greased.''

Rallya grunted less doubtfully. Even distracted with worry about Rafe, Joshim could be trusted to notice a detail like that, and to interpret it correctly. But, if they were being followed, who had arranged it? Nobody should have been able to guess where *Bhattya* had gone after Central. Nobody should have been able to locate them so quickly on New Imperial, unless they had been spotted at the shuttleport when they arrived. And if that was the case, the place was more thoroughly riddled with Julur's agents than Rallya had expected. They were right to be avoiding the official channels for contacting Ayvar, the channels that would have carried their request to every interested ear in the Palace. Safer—and quicker—to find somebody to help cut through the bureaucracy and get them a secret audience with the New Emperor. Yuellin's lover or his cousin, once either had been identified. If one of them could be trusted—and if the presence of the woman following them had not changed everything.

What instructions had Julur's agents been given about *Bhattya*, and when? Braniya must have sent a warning to watch for *Bhattya* before she left Central; the woman deserved credit for covering all the options, Rallya admitted grudgingly. The important question was whether she had issued instructions only to watch and report, or orders to prevent them from making contact with Ayvar.

''Is she alone?'' she asked Joshim as they took the steps down to street level themselves.

''I've not seen anyone else.''

''Hmm.'' If Joshim said she was alone, she *was* alone. Which suggested that she only held a watching brief; that Braniya had not guessed their intention when she issued her orders. So, they were in no immediate danger. And if they could dislodge the spy or distract her, maybe they could still accomplish what they came to do.

When they reached the street, the woman was examining the fruit in a street vendor's booth a few paces away. As they passed, she glanced up to watch them in the mirror behind the display of fruit. A few moments to let them get a safe distance ahead and she would be in place behind them again, Rallya judged. Did she know she had been spotted? If she was wearing an audio-enhancer, she must know, but in the crowd of tourists an audio-enhancer would be a liability. Even if she did know and had called for help, it would not arrive in time to forestall what Rallya planned.

"Let's get something to drink," she said, leading Joshim into the nearby eating-house which occupied the ground floor of one of the massive creamstone buildings that formed the heart of the city. Inside, she chose a booth screened by the greenery that New Imperial's citizens miserably failed to keep in its proper place, out of doors: let the woman read their lips through that!

Joshim gave their order to the table attendant and sat back, glancing significantly at the choice of exits. The woman entered and took a booth that would allow her to see when they left but not close enough to draw their attention. She did not know she had been spotted, Rallya decided with satisfaction, or was not sure of it.

The drinks arrived, refreshing in the morning heat. Rallya waited for the attendant to withdraw, then said, "We leave here one at a time in different directions. She'll have to choose one of us to follow. Whoever it is takes her on a fool's errand." She scowled, reckoning that as Commander, she would be the one condemned to a wasted day. But Joshim knew more of Yuellin's history, would be more competent than she was to do the research that needed to be done. And with Rafe's life at stake, she could rely on him to be wary about whom he approached for help. "The other goes on with our original plan. We meet up again this evening at the hotel." And be careful; no need to add that.

"If one of us goes missing?" Joshim asked bluntly.

"Scrap the plan and go for the direct approach," Rallya told him. "Make as much noise about it as possible. We'll have lost the advantage of secrecy anyway." If one of them went missing, it would be because the watcher's role had changed; neither of them was a match for a professional assassin. She was glad that she had left Vidar behind with *Bhattya* rather than bring him along to be yet another target. She snorted angrily. If she was starting to congratulate herself on obvious decisions like that, it was past time that they were moving.

*   *   *

"And here is the Great Throne Room," the guide announced, gesturing dramatically through an enormous pair of double-height doors. "Here, the Emperor meets his subjects in cere-monies going back to the dawn of the Empire. Masked, upon his Great Throne . . ."

Joshim tuned out the commentary as he followed the rest of the tour party through the doors, a few paces behind his faithful shadow. He wondered sourly if she was enjoying herself on the fool's errand that Rallya had called for, and also, angrily, why she had chosen to follow *him*. It was hard enough to know that there was little he could do to help Rafe; it was unbearable to be prevented form doing even that little.

Rallya would have reached the Imperial Archives by now, might even have discovered the names they needed to know, be on her way to ask for help from one of them. Rafe's cousin, probably. She would be the easiest to find; New Imperial was the Buhklir homeworld and the Buhklir estate was on the edge of the city. If Rallya had listened when she was told that Rafe had been confident that his cousin could be trusted, they could have gone straight there without wasting any time. Or one of them could, he reminded himself bitterly.

He glared round the cavernous room, remembering the role that he was playing. Walls clad in fine mosaics and studded with precious stones, a floor tiled with clouded crystal, and at the far end of the room, a simple wooden throne raised on a dais and another pair of double-height doors. Beside the dais, a pair of impassive guards stood, dressed in a ceremonial black and silver livery and armed with far from ceremonial flash-swords. Two more guards stood in front of the doors behind the dais, the four of them the only sign of security Joshim had seen during the tour. Were they there to reinforce the dignity of the throne, or were they guarding something else? The doors, of course. The New Emper-or would not enter his Throne Room through the public halls; the doors behind the throne must lead to the inner palace.

Joshim crossed the floor to the foot of the dais. A pair of children were standing there, daring each other to climb the steps to the throne, apparently ignored by the guards. That would change as soon as one of them plucked up courage, Joshim thought. He grinned as he watched the girl push the boy—her brother, by the look of them—onto the first step. The nearest guard moved, as if to warn them away, then looked at Joshim and, to his intense interest, hesitated as if doubting his approval.

Why should his presence and apparent indulgence influence her?

"Come way from there!" the children's escort called and they went back to him guiltily. Joshim gave the guards another experimental grin and was rewarded by a visible stiffening of their backs. They thought that they recognized him, he realized excitedly. Who did they think he was? And more importantly, where did they think he was allowed to go?

The guide was shepherding his charges out of the Throne Room, promising them the delights of the Crown Jewels. Joshim's shadow would leave without a glance behind her, too cautious to betray herself by overt interest and quite reasonably convinced that there was no way he could escape her inside the palace. But if he could get through those double doors... Although, what would he do if he could? Well, there was a way of finding out. And the gods knew he had been praying for a chance to do something; they would not offer it again if he refused it now.

He lingered until he was the last in the room, then walked casually around the dais, jerked his head at the doors and raised his eyebrows in what he hoped was an obvious gesture, not wanting to speak because his voice might betray him. The guards at the door saluted smartly. One of them spoke a word into the voice-lock, pressed his palm onto the contact pad; his companion pulled the door open. Joshim nodded his thanks and walked through. The door closed silently behind him.

To his relief, the wide corridor immediately in front of him was empty. On either side of him, stairways led up; above him, the lowered ceiling suggested a viewing gallery looking out over the Throne Room. He paused to think. How far would his luck take him? Just entering the palace should bring him quickly to the attention of a higher level of authority than he and Rallya could have reached through the normal channels. Should he settle for that, or should he try to reach the New Emperor? He laughed at his own presumption. He could hardly wander unchallenged around the palace until he found the man; his impersonation might have fooled the guards, but it would not survive a sterner test.

The corridor led to an octagonal courtyard, a sunny water-garden surrounded on all sides by shaded walkways. There were three more corridors beyond the walkways, and nothing to tempt him up any of them. There was also a seat where he could sit and watch the fountain; it was as good a place as any to be found. He did not want his intentions to be mistaken, and he certainly did not want to give the New Emperor's security staff any reason to think he was dangerous; it was too important that he get a hearing. If he waited here until they came for him—and they would, once his absence from the tour party had been discovered and the guards in the Throne Room had been questioned—he might intrigue them enough for them to listen.

It was thirty minutes before anybody came, just one woman with curly grey hair, short, plump, Joshim's age or a little younger. Dressed in black and silver that echoed the livery of the guards in the Throne Room, she wore a flash-sword at her belt, but she was not a guard. Joshim studied her with interest, wondering who had taken his bait.

"You like the garden," she said with a hint of amusement. Her voice had the soft accent that he associated with Rafe and he flinched momentarily. She did not miss it.

"Something wrong?" she asked.

"Your voice reminds me of somebody," he told her.

"And you bear a close resemblance to somebody else." She sat down beside him.

"So I've discovered, although I don't know who."

"Don't you?" She patently did not believe him. "That didn't stop you taking advantage of it."

"I have a need to be here," Joshim said mildly. "A need to talk to the Emperor."

"Have you?" the woman said dangerously. "Have you indeed, Webmaster Joshim?"

They had worked quickly to discover his identity. "May I know your name?" he asked.

"Yulenda." She watched him closely for a reaction, as if he might recognize it. "If you have a need to talk to the Emperor," she continued, "why are you sitting here?"

"Would I have found him if I'd looked?"

Yulenda laughed, genuinely amused. "No. And you won't find him by asking to see him either. Not until I've heard what you've got to say."

Joshim searched her face. Not an honest face, because it hid a great deal, but a face he trusted instinctively.

"It's about the Old Emperor and the Guild and somebody called Yuellin Buhklir," he said, making his decision.

"Is it?" She stood up abruptly. "Then it's nothing we should discuss out here. Come to my office to talk."

"The name means something to you," Joshim realized, alarmed by the strength of her reaction.

"Among other things, he was my cousin. And a very good friend."

"It's an interesting story," Yulenda said thoughtfully. "Do you have any proof that your Rafe is the same person as Lin?"

"I've Rafe's record and Yuellin's in my infocorder." Joshim set it on the desk in front of him. "If the bio-locks are compared with each other, and with his medical records if they still exist..."

"I'll have it done now." Yulenda clipped the infocorder to her belt. "You have a personal interest in this, don't you?" she added shrewdly.

Joshim nodded. He had not tried to keep his feelings out of his story, was not surprised that she had detected them. "If the bio-locks match, what will you do?"

"I'm going to take your story to my superior. He'll make that decision." She paused to study Joshim's face and smiled, the first time she had done so. "If you're telling the truth—and I'd like to believe you are—your face is one hell of a coincidence. And if you're not telling the truth, it was done by one hell of a good surgeon. It isn't a perfect match, but it's damn close."

"Who *do* I look like? Somebody Yuellin knew?"

He had the answer before she spoke. Yuellin's lover. Rafe had not seen Joshim's face in the arthane trance; he had seen the face he had been struggling to see. If they had only realized that then, Joshim thought bitterly, it would have unlocked the rest of his memory and they would not have needed to make that catastrophic visit to Central...

"You look like my superior," Yuellin was saying. "He may want to talk to you and Commander Rallya himself, so I'll have her collected and brought here, when you tell me where to find her."

"The Archives," Joshim said automatically. "Trying to find out who you are. And Yuellin's lover." How much of Rafe's love for him had been an echo of his love for the stranger who shared his face? Gods, as if that mattered now, when there was no guarantee that he was even alive...Let us get him back safely, Joshim prayed, before we start dividing him between us.

"You'd better warn whoever approaches Rallya to be careful," he remembered to warn Yulenda. "She's ready for trouble. One of Julur's agents was following us this morning. That's why we split up.''

"Tall woman, with you when you entered the palace?'' When Joshim nodded, Yulenda frowned. "She's mine. When we've time, I'd like to know how you spotted her. It shouldn't happen, at least not when she's trailing amateurs. But Rallya's right to be careful. Braniya and her successor are very thorough. Too much interest in Lin's history will bring somebody around to ask why.''

*   *   *

Rallya dismissed the Court Record (300-325/5008) from her screen and called up the next in the sequence, cursing under her breath at the procession of old and worthless news. Aristos getting born and dying, making alliances and breaking them, winning court appointments and losing them . . . Everything, in fact, except the one item she was searching for, the appointment of a regent for the underage heir to Buhklir.

Getting the date of Yuellin's succession had been simple; his obituary gave it, and the name of his cousin, and the names of the aristos who had attended his memorial rites. But there was no indication that one of the aristos had meant more to him than the others, that any of them had attended out of more than duty, in spite of the glowing words of the death-notice. *Held in deep affection at court* and *sorely missed* . . . Rallya snorted derisively; after she was dead, they would tell similar lies about her.

She had just started to scan the next Court Record when there was a quiet tap on the door of her carrel. As she turned to look, the door opened and a stranger stepped inside without waiting to be invited.

"Excuse me, Commander. I must ask you to come with me,'' he said politely.

"Not without knowing who you are,'' Rallya said flatly. "And why.'' There was no getting past him to the door, and her ears told her that he had at least one companion outside; they did not intend to lose her again. She wondered anxiously what had happened to Joshim and, in passing, how they had found her.

"Emperor's Security police, ma'am. That's all I can tell you here.''

Which Emperor? she asked herself sourly, as if she did not know. "Prove it," she challenged him.

"My identification, ma'am."

Rallya took the proffered card, handed it back after a close inspection. "Picture looks like you," she conceded. "And the card looks impressive. It could be the real thing." She was willing to bet that it was close enough to convince anybody who came in response to a call for help. And though it seemed that they wanted to take her away without attracting attention, if she refused to move they might find it worthwhile taking her out unconscious or dead. In neither of those states would she have any chance to escape. So let him think that she believed him, that she would go with him meekly.

"Just let me finish up here . . ." she suggested.

"No need for that, ma'am. One of my colleagues will tidy up after we're gone."

To make sure that there was no record of the material she had been consulting, no doubt, in case there were questions asked after her disappearance. Rallya stood up slowly, deliberately favoring her hip. If they had not been fully briefed, they might believe that she was lame, an advantage that she could use later.

"I'll have to search you, ma'am. Orders," he said apologetically.

Rallya smiled wintrily. "I understand." She cooperated in silence during the search, turning around clumsily when asked.

"This way, ma'am," he said when he was satisfied that she was unarmed.

He had two companions outside. One of them slipped into the carrel that Rallya had just vacated, the other took up position behind her. Her original captor walked beside her, slowing his pace to accommodate her limp. It was a short walk to the entrance down the dimly lit exhibition hall with its displays of ancient documents. As they stepped outside, the intensity of the light made them all blink. Rallya took her chance before her captors recovered, swerved away from them down the broad gentle steps to the plaza below, pushing through the crowds of tourists, seeking shelter in their numbers.

"Police! Stop her!"

The shot that Rallya expected did not come. Held off by fear of hitting someone else in the crowd? One of the tourists made a halfhearted grab for her; she kicked him on the knee and left him clutching that instead. The next one might not be so easy to dissuade . . . She grabbed the nearest person that was smaller than her and too slow to get out of her way, wrapped an arm around his throat and jabbed two fingers into his back, praying he was scared enough to take them for a weapon.

"Back away, or I kill him!" she shouted harshly.

The crowd moved back reluctantly, clearing a wide circle around her and her hostage.

"Stay where I can see you!" she ordered her one-time captors. Not that they cared about the boy's life, but they had a role to play and the presence of the crowd would make them obey. She hoped.

"It's a bluff! She hasn't got a gun!" the one who had searched her shouted.

"You missed the knife in my boot!" Rallya yelled back. If there had been such a knife, only a contortionist could have removed it on the run, but the crowd was so scared they would believe anything and Julur's agents had not had clear sight of her since she broke away from them.

"You can't get away!" he threatened, a bolt-beamer now in plain sight.

"Am I trying to?" Rallya said scornfully. "I'm going to wait here until the *real* police come to see what's happening. I assume somebody's had the sense to call them."

The boy in her arms was trembling; belatedly she realized that she was throttling him and she relaxed her hold just enough to let him breathe. No point in saving herself to face a murder charge.

The hum of an aircar cut through the angry murmuring of the crowd. Reinforcements for the enemy or support for her? By the look on the faces of Julur's people, by their sudden inclination to slip away out of sight, it was nobody that they welcomed.

"Emperor's Security police! Nobody move!"

The announcement broadcast across the plaza was enough to sway the crowd. Julur's agents found their way blocked, the beamers wrenched from their hands, everyone a hero now that no real risk was involved. Rallya let her captive go, judging the crowd might take it upon themselves to force her if she did not. He ran for the dubious shelter of his friends' arms, as if she might change her mind if he lingered too long in her vicinity.

"Commander Rallya?" The woman who stepped out of the

aircar was the woman Julur had spotted that morning. "You're wanted at the palace. Your colleague is waiting for you there."

Rallya rubbed at her hip, which was taking its revenge for the unexpected exercise, and watched Julur's agents being hustled into the aircar. How in hell had Joshim got himself into the palace?

"If I ask you for proof, you'll only show me another of those fancy identity cards," she told the woman tartly. "Well, I suppose you can't all be on the same damned side."

The resemblance was impossible, Rallya decided, watching Joshim and Lord Dhur study each other. Face, height, build— all so close, they could be twins. What were the odds against such a coincidence? Not just of their appearance, but of their role in Rafe's life? She shivered; she was too old to start believing that it was not a coincidence. Far too damn old.

"It's disturbing," Dhur said into the uneasy silence. "I almost didn't believe Yulenda. Having lived with this face so long, to see it on somebody else . . ."

Their voices were not the same, Rallya heard with relief; that one difference made the similarities less intense.

"You have something else in common," she reminded them, calling their attention to the reason they were there.

"Somebody very precious to both of us," Dhur agreed.

"And currently very precious to the Old Emperor," Rallya said sharply. "If the little scut is still alive."

"He is," Dhur said, with an irritating and totally unfounded confidence. "If Julur found a reason to keep him alive for ten years, he won't kill him wantonly now." He gestured around the room to which they had been brought. "Please, sit down. You weren't hurt at the Archives earlier, Commander Rallya? You seem to be limping quite badly."

Now she knew who had honed the edge on Rafe's tongue, Rallya thought as she seated herself with icy precision opposite Dhur, disciplining herself not to favor her hip.

"Nothing was damaged at the Archives earlier. Except the secrecy I'd hoped for," she admitted grudgingly.

"I think not even that," Yulenda put in. "I sent a team to clean out Rhalan's nest as soon as the bio-locks proved Lin was still alive; we netted Rhalan himself on the plaza. And a F'sair diplomatic courier was involved in an unfortunate accident at the shuttleport an hour ago; while he was receiving medical care, the contents of a certain unmarked message capsule were edited. It will be several days before Braniya realizes I've taken Rhalan out of circulation and asks herself why."

"That may be enough." Dhur pressed the points of his fingers together and looked at them consideringly. "If we move quickly, we can be in a position to stop Julur before he does anything irreversible to Lin."

"Rafe isn't important," Rallya told him bluntly. "If we can get him back safely, it will be a bonus, but..."

"On the contrary," Dhur interrupted her. "The *only* important thing is to retrieve him safely."

"I doubt the New Emperor would agree with that," Rallya snapped. "Or that you've the authority to make that decision for him."

"Let us consider your authority first, Commander Rallya," Dhur said softly, leaning back in his seat. "You're offering the support of the Guild of Webbers to strip power from the Old Emperor and hand it to the New. Tell me, is control of the Guild included in the bargain, or do you intend to keep that for yourself? And how much support do you have in the Guild, outside your own web-room full of Oath-breakers? What gives you the right to alter the balance of power in the Empires?"

"Should I let Julur get away with Oath-breaking?" Rallya countered. "Should I let him worm his way into control of the Guild, with all that would mean for the balance of power? No, Lord Dhur. Control of the Guild is not included in the bargain, neither for Julur nor for Ayvar nor for me. But I will have its support, once I expose Julur's Oath-breaking. And if the New Emperor doesn't think that's important enough to take action over, the Guild will be reconsidering its loyalty to him too."

"I believe you." Dhur sounded more amused than anything, to Rallya's added fury. "Now we've established that your authority is spiritual whereas mine is only temporal, shall we try to agree to a set of common goals? Given that I insist on Lin's safety, and you insist on the Guild's independence and renegotiation of the Emperors' Oaths."

"Which will include an end to the war in the Disputed Zone," Rallya said promptly.

"Agreed."

"You can't..."

Rallya stopped, belatedly recognizing the sound of total self-certainty. Dhur did have the right to negotiate with her; he was doing it on his own behalf. She looked at him, past the likeness to Joshim, past the infuriating patience with which he waited for her to realize exactly how much authority he *did* have. How had she expected an immortal to look? she asked herself angrily. Not like Joshim, and that had blinded her to the preternatural depth of this man, his almost physical aura of power. She laughed aloud, first ruefully at herself, then more forcefully at Rafe's hubris. The New Emperor's lover. It made truth of that ridiculous obituary—*held in deep affection at court*—and it made sense of Julur's interest in him.

Or partial sense. "I understand now why Julur might have wanted Rafe dead," she said, "but why take the risk of snatching him? And why keep him alive this long?"

"It wouldn't have been enough for Julur, just to kill him," Ayvar claimed. "He would have wanted to own him, to have the pleasure every day of knowing that he had stolen something from me and made it his. And the pleasure of knowing that I didn't know what Lin was suffering," he added bleakly.

"Why did you put Rafe in that position?" Joshim demanded. If he was impressed by his doppelganger's identity, it did not show, to Rallya's approval.

"I held out against him for three years," Ayvar said mildly. "He was sixteen when he first tried to seduce me." A smile at the memory. "He was fighting for survival and he needed a friend more powerful than his uncle. He decided it was going to be me. I took his side, but I didn't take him into my bed—I knew what the dangers for him would be if I did. He isn't the first lover that Julur has reached."

He released the pressure on his fingers, as if he had only just remembered what he was doing, and watched the color flood back into their tips.

"Three years later, he was on his half-year leave, between his apprenticeship and taking his Oath. There was no doubt that he would take the Oath, and I thought that it would only be for a short time, that it wouldn't last after he took his Oath. I was wrong," he said ruefully. "And I was wrong when I thought that the one person who would be safe from Julur was a webber," he added bitterly. "Even when he died in an aircar crash, I didn't guess. And I should have guessed—you *can* blame me for that," he told Joshim.

"I hardly took better care of him," Joshim muttered. "Do you really think Julur will keep him alive, even now?"

"Alive, yes," Ayvar said. "But he's still in danger. There are things Julur might do that couldn't be reversed . . ."

"Tell me, Commander Rallya, did you come here hoping that I had the answers, or do you have some suggestions of your own?"

"All I require from you," Rallya said stiffly, "is a guarantee that you won't interfere between the Guild and Julur. Which I assume I have, in view of your obsession with Rafe's safety."

"Obsession? Yes, it could fairly be called an obsession," Ayvar said, unruffled. "But you don't have a guarantee. Not unless you can guarantee Lin's safety in return."

"Nobody can do that," Rallya objected.

"Then I feel free to interfere. After all, there are other ways to obtain what *I* want. I could negotiate with Julur directly. Offer him my support against the Guild perhaps . . ."

"You won't do that," Rallya said shrewdly. "You can't afford to lose the Guild's services any more than Julur can."

"The Guild isn't irreplaceable," Ayvar commented.

"No, but could your Empire really survive the change?" Rallya challenged. "Do you think the F'sair would wait for you to build up an effective space force of your own? Are all your aristos so loyal that they wouldn't make private treaties with the Guild, treaties that encouraged them to secede from the Empire?"

"And you'd stand by and watch that happen?" Ayvar asked.

"If Julur gets control of the Guild, neither of you will have a choice," Joshim snapped. "Which is more important? Finding out who's going to have the last word—and I would have thought it was obvious, Rallya; he's had several thousand years more practice—or doing something to stop Julur?"

"You're right, Joshim." Ayvar made a gesture of apology to him. "I'm afraid I find it difficult to resist a new challenge." He repeated the gesture to Rallya. "You should be glad he isn't wearing your face, Commander. It's disconcerting to be told off by your own double."

"He's usually right," Rallya muttered. "That's what I like least about Webmasters." Not that she was convinced that a few thousand years made so much difference, but there would be time to settle the point later.

"Since you've no real intention of negotiating directly with Julur, even if he'd listen to you, which I doubt, what do you intend to do?" she asked directly.

"Support you in regaining control of the Guild, and then use you as a lever to make Julur negotiate." Ayvar's face clouded. "He won't bend to a threat to withdraw the Guild's services from his Empire; he can afford to wait out a few hundred years of chaos. And he knows there's a limit to what I will allow to happen to him. I won't take his Empire from him." He raised a hand to forestall Rallya's protest. "What would you do with an Empire without an Emperor? Rule it yourself? Give it to me? Neither of us could hold it together, and if one Empire falls, they both do.

"And what would you do with an Emperor without an Empire? He won't retire to a backwater world to watch the flowers grow, and he won't disappear gracefully off the edge of the map. And even if you could bring yourself to kill him, I couldn't allow it."

Rallya scowled. It *was* uniquely obscene, the idea of killing a person who might otherwise have lived forever, the thought of destroying an unbroken thread of existence. And that was the reason the Empires were saddled with a pair of immortal fools. There *was* nothing that could be done with them, other than make them gods or Emperors. And if it was not done for them, they would do it themselves, like oil inevitably rising to the top of water. Or scum separating out, in Julur's case.

"If we can't threaten to kill him, and we can't threaten to take his Empire away, just how *do* we persuade him to give Rafe back and renegotiate his Oath?" she demanded.

"I didn't say you couldn't threaten to kill him," Ayvar corrected her. "If the Guild were to besiege Old Imperial, I wouldn't be able to prevent you. I might protest convincingly from a safe distance, but that's all I could do. And fear for his life is the one thing that will make him release Lin."

"It would be a dangerous precedent to set," Rallya said slowly. "Let some of Julur's aristos—or your own—know that it can be done and they'll be hiring Outsider fleets to try it themselves. The Empires would be run by whichever aristos most recently scared you shitless."

"Not if the Guild guarantees our protection," Ayvar argued.

"I don't like it," Rallya said stubbornly. "And it isn't necessary. We can break Julur's hold on the Guild without it, and maybe even renegotiate the Oaths." She snorted. "For what that would be worth in his case."

"But we couldn't get Lin back safely," Ayvar said flatly. "I told you, Commander, that matter is not negotiable."

Could five thousand years warp a perspective that far, Rallya asked herself in disbelief. "What if the Guild decides that Rafe is expendable?" she questioned. "That we aren't willing to spend the lives it would cost to get him back." And it would cost lives, she thought grimly; Old Imperial was not a soft target.

"Whatever it costs, you won't leave him," Ayvar said confidently. "You won't found *your* Guild on a betrayal like that, Commander Rallya."

Damn you, Rallya thought furiously. I would like to pull the cocky little scut out of the trap he sprung on himself when he jumped into your bed. I would like to drag Julur out of his palace and send him on a one-way jump to the other edge of the galaxy. But I will not condemn the people of the Old Empire to a few hundred years of chaos. I will not throw away webbers and ships to salve your pride. And I will not have my options dictated by you.

"I'll need a fleet to dislodge Carher," she told Ayvar coldly. For now, let him think she had capitulated. "I want every ship you've been assigned for use in the Disputed Zone; you can change *their* orders without anyone questioning it. And I want Khirtin station too—that's your command center for Zone operations, isn't it? I want the ships assembled there in five days time. Flash a message to the Stationmaster to call them in. Tell them to reserve the first arrival slot for your yacht and another one four days from now, also to be notified to you. And I'll need a coded tight-beam to pass that information on."

She would have like to have *Bhattya* there earlier in the sequence, but it could not be done. The shuttle with Caruya and Peri aboard would not reach the ship for three more days. And Vidar would want to move out of the rings around New Imperial's neighboring gas giant; that was no place to start a fixed-window jump with only a Second and a Third to back him in the web.

"You'll have all of it," Ayvar assured her. "Yulenda, warn *Khetya* to expect us. Four passengers: Lord Dhur, yourself, and two anonymous guests."

"You're not coming," Rallya decreed, standing up to leave.

"Commander, you and I still have guarantees to discuss."

From the Guild of Webbers' Guide to Navigation

Imperial Zone, Old Empire: a Class One restricted zone. Prior authorization to enter must be obtained from the Imperial Palace; access is permitted via a single jump point (O-I-1). A defensive sphere is maintained around the system; any unauthorized ship penetrating this sphere is liable to attack without warning.

349/5043:
IMPERIAL ZONE, OLD EMPIRE

It was impossible to know, Rafe thought shakily, which one of them would speak first. Or, if the Old Emperor was first to break the silence, whose victory that would be. Blurred memories—which he was struggling to rebury, in spite of the days that he had spent aboard *Havedir* fighting futilely to unearth them—told him that, in some warped way, it would be Julur's victory if Rafe outlasted him, because Rafe dared not speak until he had control of his voice and the same blurred memories had deprived him of that control.

The waiting had ended without warning, ten days of isolation curtailed by the soporific that had flooded his stateroom. Rafe had regained consciousness strapped into this seat, free only to see, to hear, and to speak, in a room brightly lit around him and shadowed at the edges. Julur was in the shadows: visible, not recognizable, but it could only be Julur. Cat-and-mouse would not be Braniya's style, not once the hunt was over, but Julur took delight in it. Rafe fought off more unwelcome images, of a similar room or the same one, of a similar struggle for silence.

He had no way of knowing how long it had been between losing consciousness and regaining it, no way of knowing what they had done in that time. Had they sorted through his head, to discover how much he had remembered, and how much he had not? What else might they have done? There had been games that Julur had played the last time . . .

"Shall I call you Lin or Rafe?"

A triple shock. The ending of the silence, for all that he had known Julur would speak eventually. The voice, better remembered than the face, because it had been possible to close his eyes but not his ears . . . And the name, Lin, indisputably his, bringing with it a stream of fresh associations that he could not dam, ice-clear memories of the man who had bestowed it upon him. And because no reaction was more appropriate to the enormous irony of that shared face: Rafe laughed.

"The question did not warrant hysteria."

"I'd explain the joke," Rafe said, sobering abruptly, "but as I remember, you've no sense of humor."

"And yours, I remember, is odd in the extreme. And fails you eventually."

Julur came out of the shadows, his appearance no new shock because Rafe's newly intact memory had primed him. Blond, blue-eyed, slightly plump, even for his unusual height, and his face alarming in its apparent youth. A thousand years or more older than Ayvar, he looked as if he had been frozen as a gauche adolescent while Ayvar looked like a . . . a forty-six-year-old Webmaster.

Let nobody tell me the gods have no sense of humor, Rafe thought bitterly.

"You do remember me, I see," Julur remarked, watching Rafe intently. "And how much else?"

"All of it," Rafe said flatly. A denial would do him no good.

"That would be surprising, since you were hardly coherent for much of your time with me. I take it that you mean you remember your life as Lin."

"Which you took so much trouble to erase. Yes."

It gave Rafe perverse pleasure to think of that wasted effort. There was no other success he could claim against Julur, no information about himself that Julur had not drawn from him. He flinched from remembering how easily he had answered questions at the end, answered them before they were asked, volunteered information out of fear of the pain, out of terror of what the drugs did to him. The other choice had been to submit to the pain and the drugs, to pay a higher price for providing the same knowledge with the same scant dignity. His choice had not eventually mattered; Julur had used the drugs anyway, had vindictively inflicted the pain. And in a final, grotesque and unseen gesture to Ayvar—who surely could not know—he had destroyed Lin and given the Oath-breaker Rafe to the Guild.

"Was I supposed to be grateful that you left me alive?" he asked rashly.

"You are asking whether I intend to repeat my generosity, are you not? I do, but not perhaps in the same form." The Emperor stretched his damp lips to show his teeth. "It is unfortunate that the identity-wipe failed. The alternative is more drastic, forfeits more of the original and there are aspects of the original worth preserving. The intelligence, for example."

"Has anybody ever accused you of being subtle?"

"Humor, I believe, is an inevitable casualty of personality disintegration." Julur returned to the shadows and Rafe heard the whisper of his clothes as he sat down. "Before that, however, I shall discover why the identity-wipe failed. It would be a pity to destroy you so thoroughly when something less might serve."

Silence would be interpreted as capitulation; a defiant response as desperation. Neither was far from the truth, Rafe thought miserably, choosing silence. A tactical problem for you, Commander Rallya. You are the prisoner of a mad Emperor—a paranoid Emperor who wears armor-cloth for every hour of the day, who has not left his palace for over a thousand years, a palace infested with fanatically loyal guards trained from birth. You are unarmed and unable to move. Discuss methods of escape. He sighed wryly, reckoning that even Rallya would not get far with the problem.

What was she doing now? Probably gathering support against Carher. Lin had known Carher by reputation, an ambitious woman, elected to the Council half a year before he had his "accident." Her record as a patrolship Commander was solid, not outstanding; she had won her place on the Council largely by virtue of being unopposed by anyone better qualified. He

felt a flash of guilt over that. The councillor elected for the New
Empire in the same election had been equally undistinguished.
He—Lin—had been urged by his friends and by Ayvar to fight
that election; he had refused, not ready to give up the joy of
commanding *Janasayan* for the responsibilities of a councillor.

Not that it would have been long before Julur relieved him of
those responsibilities, he reminded himself angrily. And if he
had joined the Council, he would always have been open to
accusations of being influenced by Ayvar, of being the New
Emperor's passport to control of the Guild, as Carher had been
intended to be Julur's. At least Rallya would prevent that, and
the scouring she would undertake would be thorough enough to
leave Julur—and Ayvar, he acknowledged dryly—no possibility
of replacing their pawns for several years.

"What do you intend to do about Carher?" he asked boldly.
Better to concentrate on that than on his own predicament,
about which Rallya could do nothing, primarily because she did
not know about it. *Bhattya* probably thought he was dead, he
realized with a pang of grief for Joshim. When Ayvar learnt the
cause of the conflict within the Guild, he would know that
Julur was involved, but by then it would probably be too
late . . .

"There is no need for me to do anything. Lady Carher will
be dealt with by her opponents within the Guild."

"It's unlike you to neglect an opportunity to be vindictive."

"You seem to be feeling better." Julur was moving about;
Rafe could hear the rustle of armor-cloth, the chink of
metallic items being gathered together. "Lady Carher has a
certain utility in distracting interest from you. If she outlives her
usefulness, Braniya will arrange her execution."

He moved out of the shadow, began to arrange the items he
was carrying on the table to Rafe's left. Rafe refused to turn his
head to watch. "You should not use my interest in you to judge
my interest in mortals like Lady Carher. You have a certain
quality that makes you uniquely rewarding."

Or a certain relationship with the only person you care about,
Rafe thought bleakly. The only person who is real to you.
Gods, Ayvar could be strange at times, when he talked about
somebody a thousand years dead as if he had spoken to them
only yesterday, when he wore that haunted expression that told
of the events around him having been played out before by the
same characters wearing different faces . . . But at least he knew

that mortals were real. Real enough to take one as a lover, to bind him with a mixture of fierce possessiveness and brusque insouciance, so that he would hold Lin bruisingly tight all night as if he were the one person who would never leave him and then send him back to his ship at the end of his liberty with a joke about the queue to share his bed when Lin was gone. Sometimes, Rafe thought ruefully, it was a struggle not to be swallowed whole by the man and at others, it was impossible to get close to him...

"Do you remember the effect of this?" Julur inquired, showing Rafe an injector. "Gadrine. Not unduly unpleasant, but effective."

Not unduly unpleasant if you had no objection to losing control over your tongue, to spilling out the contents of your head for Julur to pick through. Rafe remembered Joshim's support during his arthane trances, the anchor to reality that he had provided. Julur would not be so concerned for Rafe's sanity, for the necessary distinctions between past and present.

"We're going to explore the failure of your identity-wipe," Julur continued. Rafe felt the injector enter his arm. "The stimuli that caused it, the speed with which it progressed." He smiled as he withdrew the needle. "If you are fortunate, the failure will not be inherent in the process, but will be due to something in your environment. If that is so, I may not resort to personality disintegration..."

Gods, Rafe thought frantically. Joshim. Of all the factors— his work in the web, Commander Rallya and *Bhattya*—Joshim must be the most significant, his likeness to Ayvar the essential trigger. And Julur did not know about him yet. When he did know, how much danger would Joshim be in? If Julur took pleasure from destroying somebody who had been Ayvar's lover, how much would he enjoy destroying somebody who wore Ayvar's face? It was painful enough that Rafe had unconsciously used Joshim as a substitute for Ayvar—and that was what he had done, he realized in a tide of raw guilt—but now he was going to expose him to the danger of Julur's hatred, and he knew he could not avoid it.

From the History of the Empire
by Dhelmen Lady Hjour,
taken from a copy made in 3087

...And the Emperor Ayvar came in haste to Khirtin, bringing with him such of his establishment as were loyal to him, and on Khirtin they abided for a year. But Khirtin is a poor world and so Boronya Lady Buhklir came to the Emperor Ayvar and offered him her homeworld of Buhklir to be his home for all time and he was gracious to accept, raising her family high in his affections...

...And a great assembly was held at Lhorphenir and the Empire was divided...

351/ 5043:
KHIRTIN ZONE, NEW EMPIRE

"So that's what's happening now," Joshim said wearily. "Every ship assigned to Ayvar for the Disputed Zone is coming here. The Stationmaster is going grey watching them come out of jump and praying they all get their calculations right."

"I don't blame her," Vidar said feelingly. "Five minutes after us, a courier arrived so close we could read the markings on its hull unmagnified."

"Stop complaining. At least *Bhattya*'s got a place in dock. The couriers and the supplyships are stuck in a holding pattern. The priority is getting the patrolships battle-ready."

"Uh-huh." Vidar stood up. "Back in a minute," he promised.

He was, with a mug of alcad he put into Joshim's hands. "Sounds like you need that."

"I've been talking my throat raw. Every Three that comes in wants to hear the story from the source."

"I'll take that on," Vidar offered. "After six days in those damned dust rings with nothing else to do, this ship is in better condition than when she left the construction dock."

"I expected as much." Joshim gave him a tired smile of gratitude. "We won't see much of Rallya before the fleet leaves here. When she isn't talking tactics with the other Commanders, she's arguing with Ayvar."

Refusing to accept his priorities; refusing to commit herself to anything beyond ridding the Guild of Carher, least of all an assault on Julur. Balancing possibilities and costs: the future of the Guild, the future of the Empires, the lives—all of them, not just Rafe's—that could be lost if the upheaval she started got out of her control. And Ayvar was insistent on Rafe's safety, at any price. Gods knew what was driving him: injured pride perhaps, a determination not to yield anything to Julur. Not even an immortal could love Rafe so fiercely that he was willing to sacrifice the peace of both Empires for him. Or maybe I won't allow anyone to love Rafe more than me, Joshim thought wryly.

"Is the Emperor here at Khirtin?" Vidar asked.

"That isn't public knowledge," Joshim warned. "Officially, Lord Dhur, the Emperor's representative is here. Confusing the hell out of anybody who's met me."

"How close is the resemblance?"

"It's frightening. Like looking in a mirror." Joshim blew on his alcad to cool it down.

"No wonder..."

"...Rafe fell for me. Yes."

"No wonder Rafe started remembering," Vidar contradicted him. "What's he like as a person?"

Joshim shrugged. "I'm not the person you should ask. I'm trying not to like him."

Vidar grunted. "How many ships will we have at Central?" he asked, changing the subject.

"Twenty patrolships, if they all get here in time. Five armed couriers. The supplyships are staying here." Joshim yawned. "That reminds me. We're leaving the apprentices behind too."

"They won't like that."

"Fleet Commander's orders. Says they'll only be underfoot."

Vidar laughed, knowing as well as Joshim that Rallya wanted the apprentices out of danger.

"She's expecting a fight then?" he queried.

"She's ready for one. Although Carher might run for it," Joshim said hopefully. "She must know that even if she wins Julur will still want her hide. It depends on how good she thinks her chances are of making peace with him."

"What opposition will we be facing?"

"Open a book on it," Joshim suggested, yawning again. "If it hasn't already been done."

"Not this time," Vidar said somberly. "You should . . ." He stopped, held up a hand to silence Joshim while he listened to his messenger. "There's a visitor for you," he reported. "Lord Dhur."

"Tell him to go away," Joshim said. "Tell him I'm asleep."

"You should be," Vidar agreed. He relayed the message, listened to the reply. "He's already on his way up," he reported.

Joshim swore.

"I'll keep him out," Vidar offered.

"No." Joshim found a strained smile. "Let's not all three of us get on the wrong side of him. Not until Rallya's got no use for him anyway."

There was a tap on the rest-room door, characteristically Fadir. "Come in," Joshim called.

"Lord Dhur, sir." The apprentice's eyes swivelled from Ayvar to Joshim and back again, looking for differences.

"Thank you, Fadir," Ayvar said, smiling slightly.

"Sir." Fadir backed out, still comparing.

"You have a fine ship, Captain Vidar," Ayvar said. "Don't let me keep you from your work."

"You'd better let the web-room know what's happening," Joshim said resignedly. "And break the news to Fadir and Rasil that they don't get to join in."

"You need some sleep," Vidar said pointedly. "I'll be back in an hour to make sure you get it."

"Thank you for seeing me," Ayvar said when Vidar had gone. "I won't keep you long. But we ought to talk about Lin—Rafe, if you prefer—while we can."

"Before we know he's alive?"

"Trust me," Ayvar said gravely. "I know Julur. He won't kill him."

It would be a relief to have his certainty, Joshim thought with longing. Not to live with the misery of not knowing. Not to lie awake in the dark cataloging the possibilities. Maybe he *was* right; the gods knew, there was nobody else qualified to understand the workings of an immortal's mind. Or maybe Rallya was right, and Ayvar was as far from sanity as Julur was, if in a different direction.

"What are you thinking?" Ayvar asked.

"You're right, or you're insane, and I can't tell which."

"And you've no talent for believing something because you want to believe," Ayvar said sympathetically.

"I'm an Aruranist," Joshim said, amused. "I've heard it said that that's wishful thinking."

"About reincarnation, I wouldn't know. But the rest . . . somebody gave you my face and put you into Lin's life so that he would remember me."

"Maybe." Joshim had had the same thought himself. "Maybe they put you into Rafe's life so that he would recognize me when he found me." He ran a hand over his chin, trying to remember when he had last depilated it. Four days ago, on New Imperial. He must look as disreputable as he felt. "He isn't an Empire to be divided up by treaty," he said angrily, knowing what Ayvar really wanted to discuss.

"That wasn't what I intended," Ayvar said. "I just don't want to make it any harder for him than it has to be. Julur won't kill him, but he won't be gentle to him either. He'll need time to recover, when we get him back. He'll be in no condition to make a decision between us."

"So you want to make it for him now." Joshim was still furious.

"Not that either." Ayvar sighed. "He makes his own decisions. He always has, and they're often not the decisions I'd have him make. Like staying in the Guild. I've asked him to leave before. I shall be asking him again. This time, perhaps he'll agree. He's always said that his Oath binds him, but if the Emperors' Oaths can be rewritten, his can be dissolved."

"He won't give up webbing," Joshim said confidently. "If you could web with him, you'd know that." He felt a tinge of jealous pleasure at the knowledge that Ayvar could never do so.

"He needs the power it gives him," Ayvar admitted, "but there are other ways he can have that."

Joshim shook his head, although there was truth in what the Emperor said. Power would always be a lure for Rafe, the power of the web or the power hanging in the air around Ayvar which would call him like a sailfly to a flame. But webbing was not only power. There was the magic inherent in sharing that power with others, in guiding a junior who was learning their first skills, or working in the web in perfect concert with a team. Nothing that Ayvar could offer would give Rafe that joy, or the trust and companionship of a full web-room.

"You don't know him as well as you think you do," he observed.

"I know that he'll be grateful to you. To everybody who helps to rescue him. And he's obsessive about paying his debts."

So he may be generous to me, out of gratitude? The Rafe I know... could be that stupid, Joshim realized painfully. What if it *was* my face that attracted him, if he thought he loved me because of his love for Ayvar... Gods, it was too tangled to see a way through. Especially at Ayvar's persuasive prompting.

"I'm not fighting over him," he said flatly. "He isn't mine to fight over, any more than he's yours. And neither of us can be sure what he'll feel, what he'll do. After ten years as Rafe, he isn't the Lin you knew, and once he's remembered Lin, he won't be Rafe either."

"That may be true," Ayvar conceded. He was silent for several seconds, then shrugged gracefully. "Go to bed, Joshim. And be glad you've got something useful to do. Having given your Commander a fleet and pointed her at Julur, there's nothing for me to do except wait. And Lin would tell you, that isn't my favorite role. It makes me bad tempered. Makes me want to settle the things that I can settle." He laughed briefly. "And the things that I can't."

It was an apology of a kind, or a peace offering. An appeal for sympathy. "You are worried," Joshim realized.

"The thought of Commander Rallya with a fleet at her back and an Emperor as her target would make any sane man worry. What if she decides she does want control of the Guild? And of both Empires? What would be the cost of stopping her?"

"No. Not Rallya," Joshim said positively. "You'd have to back her into a corner with no choices left before she'd accept any of it. And even then, she'd probably find a way to wriggle free.''

''I'll remember that.''

''Want to tell me what you're really worried about?'' Joshim suggested.

Ayvar looked at him quizzically. ''Lin always said that Webmasters could read minds.'' He linked his fingers together, stared at them. ''What will you do, if what we get back isn't Lin or Rafe but something that Julur has twisted or emptied?'' he asked abruptly. ''Something mindless or insane.''

Joshim shook his head in distress. ''I don't know. There would be ways of healing him . . .''

''I hope so, yes. Could you be part of that, Joshim, if you were needed? For as long as it took?''

Gods, that was a question. Joshim took a deep breath, let it out without speaking. Was that the measure of how much he cared for Rafe, that he hesitated to give up the web for him?

''I don't know,'' he said finally.

''That's an honest answer.'' Ayvar took Joshim's face in one hand and studied it as if he would find a different answer there. ''We could be twins. I wonder how deep it goes . . .''

There was a knock on the door. Ayvar released Joshim's face.

''Come in,'' Joshim called.

''General broadcast, just received,'' Fadir said excitedly. ''The Captain said you'd want to see it at once.''

''Thank you.'' Joshim took the flimsy that the apprentice was clutching, scanned it rapidly. ''Did he tell you what it meant?''

''He said we'd be fighting at Central, sir. If Commander Carher has declared *Bhattya* renegade, it means she's decided to oppose us.''

''She has no choice,'' Ayvar said harshly. ''If she runs, one of her supporters will execute her for Julur. But she thinks she'll have something to bargain with if she fights and wins.'' He laughed contemptuously. ''It won't be enough, but she won't find that out until it's too late. If Julur doesn't kill her, I will.''

''Couldn't we tell her that?'' Fadir asked.

''In my experience, Fadir, things are rarely that simple,'' Ayvar said kindly.

''The Commander will have thought about it,'' Joshim promised. ''But Carher wouldn't believe us, and it would do her no good if she did. The best she could hope for from us is identity-wipe, and I doubt the Commander would be that merciful." He sighed. "You'd better start packing, Fadir. The Commander may take us out early, before Carher gathers too much support."

"Do I have to stay behind, sir?"

"Yes," Joshim insisted.

"I shall be needing somebody to carry messages for me," Ayvar said. "Can I borrow Fadir from you?"

"Do you mind?" Joshim asked the apprentice.

"No, sir. I suppose it will be better than doing nothing," Fadir said dejectedly.

"Good." Ayvar smiled generously. "If you remember to call me Lord Dhur in public, you can call me Ayvar in private."

"Really?" Fadir swayed in shock. "Is he, sir?" He looked to Joshim for confirmation.

"He is," Joshim said.

"But only you and your Captain and Webmaster know that," Ayvar warned. "And Commander Rallya, of course."

Fadir nodded gravely, the effect spoiled by the fact that he was blinking so rapidly that his eyelashes were almost a blur. "I'll remember, sir," he promised.

"Good. I'll wait here for you while you pack," Ayvar offered.

Fadir paused on his way to the door. "Can I bring Rasil with me?" he asked. "Two of us will be more useful that one, don't you think?"

"You'd better bring Rasil then," Ayvar agreed.

"That was kind of you," Joshim said when the lad had gone.

"The three of us can be miserable together," Ayvar dismissed it. "Don't worry. I won't lay a finger on them. I only make my mistakes once, and anyway, they can't have half the charm that Lin had at that age. At any age." He lifted the pendant that hung around Joshim's neck to examine it closely. "Will the Commander respond to that broadcast?"

"She'll have to, or we'll be fighting ships at Central that think Carher is telling the truth." Joshim grimaced. "We probably will anyway."

Ayvar let the pendant fall. "What will she send?"

"I'm guessing," Joshim warned. "A broadcast accusing

Carher of Oath-breaking. Of murder. Of unlawful identity-wipe. Of conspiracy with Julur."

"She can't," Ayvar said tautly. "If she mentions Julur, he'll know I know about Lin."

"She has to mention Julur. None of the rest makes sense without it. You won't talk her out of it. She has as much responsibility for the people that might die because they don't know what's happening as she has for Rafe." Joshim closed his eyes in despair. "You think it will stampede Julur into hurting him."

"The gods know. Julur knows the value of what he's got. That's why he tried the identity-wipe first. He'll move slowly while he thinks he's got the time. And he won't believe that Rallya has the nerve to attack Old Imperial until it happens," Ayvar said hopefully. "If she does . . ." He put a hand on Joshim's shoulder and shook gently. "Get to bed, Webmaster. You're dead on your feet and I'm relying on you to keep Rallya pointed in the right direction."

General broadcast from Rallya, Commander *Bhattya*

To all ships and stations:
Be advised that serious charges of Oath-breaking will be laid against Councillor Carher at the first opportunity, to include: conspiracy with the Emperor Julur to subvert the Guild; unlawful identity-wipe of a Guild member; and conspiracy to murder Guild members. Evidence will be presented at Central to support these charges. It is requested that Councillor Carher be detained until that time.

Directive from the Emperor Julur
to Palace Security Chief Braniya

...I will move to the deep levels of the palace imme diately. The prisoner will be transferred with me...

352/5043:
IMPERIAL ZONE, OLD EMPIRE

"The Emperor is pleased that you keep yourself fit," Braniya announced herself from the entrance to Rafe's stateroom.

He paused in the daily sequence of exercises that he had set himself, to fill a little of the time while he waited. He did not have access to a console; nobody visited him except the pair of silent guards who delivered his meals. He had exhausted the possibilities for escape from the stateroom, not by trying them but by satisfying himself that there were none. All that was left for him to do was to be ready for the possibilities that there might be, in other places, at other times.

"And the Emperor must be pleased at all costs?" He was pleased that his voice was steady, without a trace of his apprehension about her visit, his fear that it meant another session with Julur.

"Most people find his pleasure rewarding."

"Faced with the prospect of a second identity-wipe—or worse—to please him, I can't share their enthusiasm." Rafe stood up and stalked through to the fresher to find a towel to dry his sweat. His legs were surprisingly steady too. "Was the state of my health the only reason for your visit?" he called back to her.

"No. You're being moved. Immediately."

"May I dress first?"

"Do. Everything else will follow you."

Rafe chose breeches and a shirt at random. "Where am I going?" he asked as he pulled them on.

"Down," Braniya said succinctly. "The Emperor has chosen to move to the deeper levels. You're to go with him."

"How deep is deep? This palace is rumored to go a long way down, and I'd hate to be trapped at the bottom by a surface strike."

"Don't alarm yourself unnecessarily," Braniya advised. "The life-support systems down there are good for a few hundred years, and the planet would have to be destroyed to seal all access to the deep levels." Her lips twitched. "Accommodation down there is not a privilege extended to many."

And you would dearly like to know why I am honored, Rafe thought with malicious amusement. It was interesting to know that Julur was worried about an attack on his palace. Fear of the Guild might be enough to make him scuttle for shelter, if he thought they knew what he had done. Rafe tucked that speculation away for later examination.

"Do I walk or will I be carried?" he asked Braniya lightly.

"It would be quicker if you walked, and there are other matters which require my attention." Her lips twitched again. "I am allowed to tell you that one of them is the execution of Lord Khalem."

"You could tell the Emperor that there are gifts I'd like better than Elanis's death."

"I understand that the news is the gift, not the death. Are you ready?"

"Does it make a difference?"

"The Emperor requires you to be treated with courtesy."

That was not the description Rafe would have used for the interrogation Julur had carried out; but then the Emperor was exempt from his own requirements. It had been a shock afterwards to wake in a luxury stateroom with his mind—he believed—still intact; there had been no similar treatment ten years ago. He distrusted it, as he distrusted this move, judging that it was meant to unbalance him.

There were six guards waiting for him outside, anonymous behind their visors. Rafe let Braniya set their pace, not bothering to conceal his interest in the route she chose, just as she did not bother to conceal her amusement at his interest. Not much profit in memorizing it, he reckoned, but he did anyway, in the faint hope that there was a pattern that would help him if he was ever free to chose his own route through the palace.

The riser to which Braniya led him was locked to her voice, its controls not labeled with the levels it served. The descent took ten minutes at high speed: a very long way down. Rafe's ears popped with the changing pressure and his nose itched with the faintly musty smell that greeted them when they stepped out, the smell of infrequent occupation.

The tunnels at the lower level were less ornamented than the upper corridors, their walls heavily reinforced and each junction marked by bulkheads waiting to be swung into position. It was possible to believe that Julur could live through a few hundred years down here. Rafe wondered if there was a similar bolt-hole beneath Ayvar's palace. It was more likely that Ayvar had his hiding place somewhere else, somewhere his enemies would not know to look; he did not have Julur's phobia of the universe beyond his palace.

"Gods." Rafe swore aloud at the sudden shooting pain in his arms and back, leaned against the tunnel wall with his eyes closed fighting it. Web-cramp, he thought hazily, twisting away from one of the guards who was trying to urge him on. "Wait," he pleaded.

"What is this, Rafell?" Braniya demanded.

"A minute," he insisted. "Just that." The pain was receding, to a level where he could stand straight again. He squinted at Braniya through watering eyes. "No trick," he promised.

"You're ill." It sounded like an accusation. As if she suspected him of arranging it deliberately.

"Web-cramp," Rafe said, moving away from the wall experimentally. "It's over now. For the moment." It would be back though. He had last worked on the day that Churi died, more than forty days ago, and he would not be back in the web for the foreseeable future, he thought bleakly.

"You can walk?" Braniya asked. "It isn't far now."

"Your concern is delightful."

"The Emperor requires you to be kept in good health," she said stiffly. "I will be reporting this episode."

Much good it would do Julur to know about it. The cure for web-cramp was webbing, or deactivating the offending web, both of which would require the cooperation of the Guild. And if Rafe was right, the cooperation of the Guild was in short supply for Julur at the moment. He smothered a cynical grin. He might still manage to frustrate the Old Emperor's plans. Admittedly, at the cost of considerable discomfort, but that was probably down on the agenda already; the web-cramp was just hurrying things along. The thought made him perversely cheerful.

"In here," Braniya ordered. "Wait outside," she told the guards.

"Impressive," Rafe said honestly, looking around him. "All for me?"

"Leisure accommodation, sleeping room, sanitary facilities. And a small gym. Please explore," Braniya invited graciously.

"Later. The wisest thing I can do now is lie down," he told her frankly.

Braniya followed him into the sleeping-room. "How serious is web-cramp?" she asked.

"In my current circumstances?" Rafe gave her one of his best smiles. "Probably fatal."

"That can be checked."

"Ask Julur. He knows everything I do."

When she had gone, he curled on his side on the bed. Web-cramp was a perpetual headache and creeping weariness and unpredictable spasms like the one in the corridor. If he were back on *Bhattya*, Joshim would give him a tablet to ease the headache and then, when his concentration could be trusted, he would put him in the web to stretch the cramp away. If he were back on *Bhattya*, Joshim would . . . as well wish to be an apprentice back on New Imperial, with the choice that had led him here still unmade.

Joshim would have problems of his own now, supporting Rallya when she made her bid to oust Carher. And afterwards, avoiding Julur's attention without knowing that he needed to do it. For survival's sake, he needed to know about his resemblance to Ayvar, but it hurt to know how much that knowledge would hurt him. Hurt to know what Joshim would think. Hurt to think that it was partially true, and that Joshim would talk himself out of being angry about it. Everybody had the right to be angry about a gods' trick like that.

Ayvar would be angry when he knew. Not about the gods' trick. About the wasted mourning he had done ten years ago—*I save it for the people who are worth it, Lin*—and about the fresh mourning he would have to do, knowing there was nothing he could do to rescue Rafe, nothing that would not cost more than Rafe was worth. He would protect Joshim, as well as he could, and maybe Julur would be wary enough of the Guild to leave the Webmaster alone. But there was no power in either Emperor that would make Julur hand Rafe back, not without letting chaos loose. The Old Emperor need not worry about an attack; Rallya would not do it, had too much sense to do it, however much she hated to back off. Some deal would be made to cover the cracks between Julur and the Guild, and everybody would hope fervently that Rafe was dead. Which he would be, if Julur was pressed for evidence; his body would be produced with apologies and Braniya would be handed the blame. Rafe hoped that Rallya and Ayvar would insist on proof; Ayvar at least would know the importance of that.

The hiss of a sliding door told him that somebody had entered the suite. Braniya, or somebody bringing the clothes that had been provided for him. He curled up tightly, ignoring the footsteps coming towards the sleeping-room.

"You are unwell."

Gods, that voice. Julur, come to see if he was to be deprived of his entertainment.

"I have web-cramp." Rafe uncurled slowly, balancing hatred for Julur against a desperate wish not to push him too far too soon. Braniya was there as well, a sleepbeam trained on him in case he indulged himself and tried for Julur's throat.

"You did not suffer this on a previous occasion."

"How would you know? How would I have known? I wasn't identifying every piece of pain."

"You will not die of it."

"Is that a request or an order?"

"It is not usually fatal."

"Not when there's a chance of webbing, no. Or when there's somebody around who knows how to deactivate a web. Going to ask the Guild how to do that?" Thank the gods that was a secret that not even the Threes knew.

"That will be the long-term solution," Julur said evenly. "But the Guild is currently preoccupied with internal politics. Such a request would not be welcome."

"If you don't come up with a short-term solution, you won't need the long-term solution," Rafe said spitefully. "You could give me access to *Havedir*'s web. If your yacht's webroom swallowed my abduction from Central they'll swallow that."

"You will not leave the palace."

"Then I suggest you enjoy watching it while you can."

"This web is a complication that endangers your health," Julur said, as if Rafe had not spoken. "Braniya, he is to be sedated for my investigation. And have the Webmaster of *Havedir* brought to me."

Braniya coughed. "*Havedir* are still refusing to accept our orders, sir. Until the situation within the Guild is clarified."

Julur muttered something that sounded like a curse. "Are you capable of commissioning a web?" he demanded of Rafe.

"How large a web?" Rafe asked, intrigued. Julur had a web within the palace?

"It was used for amusement only."

"It's not my specialty, but I should get by," Rafe said cautiously. "Providing it isn't too far from what I'm used to." Gods knew how old it would be; if Julur was anything like Ayvar in his memories, that amusement could have been fifty years ago or five hundred. "Where is it?"

"If medical examination proves the necessity, you will be taken to it. Braniya, you will arrange for the supply of the necessary tools and technicians."

"Expendable technicians?" Braniya queried.

"The prisoner's existence is to remain a secret," Julur agreed. "You," he added to Rafe, "will commission the web for your own use. You will be interrogated before you are permitted to use it, to verify that what you have done is acceptable.''

Rafe nodded, not understanding why he was being given this lifeline when his life was measured in tens of days anyway, but finding that he could not turn it down. Julur was mad. There was no understanding him except on his own terms, and he was the only one who knew what those were. But if he could not be understood, perhaps he could be manipulated a little. If he did not want Rafe to die of web-cramp, Rafe would not die of web-cramp. But it would take time to commission a web, time in which—perhaps—Julur would put off any other action.

Broadcast from
Commander Rallya

To all ships in Khirtin Fleet:
The fleet will depart at 03:00/353/5043 . . .

353/ 5043:
KHIRTIN ZONE, NEW EMPIRE
AND CENTRAL

[Fleet Group Three in position for jump,] Vidar reported,
relaying the message from the Group Commander. [Fleet Group
Six undocking complete.]

[Acknowledged.]

Rallya checked the information against the timetable for the
jump. Still on schedule and if the gods were kind—or at least
looking the other way—still with the advantage of surprise.
The charges against Carher had been broadcast from the other
side of the Disputed Zone; no message had been sent from
Khirtin without her approval; no ship that had approached the
station had been allowed to leave. There was no way that
Carher could know the scale or timing of what she faced.
Unless the pickets around Khirtin had missed the jump flare of
a spy's arrival, and Rallya would have somebody's ears for
web-bands if they had. If they *were* going to jump into a
shooting gallery around Central, she wanted to know about it in
advance.

Whatever they were going to jump into, she would have
liked to know about it in advance. But there had been no

response from Central to the charges she had made, neither from Carher nor from the rest of the Council. There would have been a denial if the Council was backing Carher; the silence meant that Carher was in control, but without their support. Which meant that she would only be able to rely on her coconspirators to defend her, and there was no knowing how many of those there were, or how quickly she could gather them at Central. Which meant there was no knowing what was waiting for Rallya's fleet when it came out of jump.

[Damage control Team One in place,] Vidar signaled. [All nonessential power drains being shut down.]

[Acknowledged.] That, too, was on schedule, *Bhattya*'s own preparations for the jump and afterwards. It was a familiar routine, familiar to her but to very few of the other members of the fleet's web-rooms. To them, real fleet battles were history, in the Homir wars and before that. All they were used to were the push-and-shove imitations in the Disputed Zone, or kiss-and-run encounters with Outside raiders, not full-scale shooting wars where both sides had everything to lose. It had made Rallya feel damned old to realize it and damned worried about how they would stand up to what was coming.

[Damage control Team Two in place. With passenger.] There was a flavor of amusement in Vidar's message.

[Query passenger,] Rallya sent sharply.

[Fadir. Found in his cabin.]

Rallya swore inwardly. Of all the times for Fadir to find out that he had some initiative . . . Only he would be stupid enough to give up a safe berth running errands for Ayvar in favor of being underfoot on a patrolship in battle. Or maybe not, she conceded; in his position, she might—just might—have pulled the same stunt. And he had done well to remain undiscovered for so long, until there was no time left to put him off. There might be some hope for him yet.

[Query Rasil,] she sent.

[Negative.]

At least they had one apprentice who knew how to obey orders. [Message to web-room for Fadir,] she told Vidar. [Sit down, shut up, and consider a future without ears. Copy to web and damage control teams.]

Since he was aboard, he might as well be useful. Tension was building up in the web; she could feel the undercurrents of fear. It would be worse where Jualla's team and Lilimya's

waited in the maintenance spaces with nothing to do until—
gods forbid—the ship took damage. It would do them all good
to know that Fadir had sneaked aboard, give them something to
laugh about. Battles were not only won by conserving every
erg of energy for fighting with, they were won by knowing
your web-room's strength, by knowing how to blunt the razor-
edge of waiting that cut away at concentration.

[Fleet Group Four in position for jump,] Vidar reported.

Two more groups still maneuvering into formation. Ten more
minutes until jump. Ten minutes in which to consider all the
mistakes she might have made, the possibility that Carher *did*
have the support of the Council, that she *was* waiting at Central
with the capability to destroy all of them as they came out of
jump. *If* she had enough warning, *if* she had enough ships, *if*
somebody miscalculated the jump from Khirtin and emerged in
somebody else's shadow...

[!] The signal from Joshim was just a flicker, a warning that
her jitters were leaking out into the web. Disgusted with
herself, Rallya returned an equally brief acknowledgement.
Pre-battle nerves were another familiar part of the routine, but
she had never forgotten herself so far as to let them show. Only
Joshim would have noticed, but that was no excuse. Nor was
being tired from five days of drumming sense into a collection
of Commanders' skulls. If a junior had made the same mistake,
she would have expected Joshim to dump them from the web.

[Fleet Group Five in position for jump.]

No trace of nerves in Vidar's web-presence, not even concern that his beloved ship systems were out of his control.
Comms control was a senior's job in battle, but *Bhattya* was
short of seniors and Rallya would not trust her link with the
fleet to anybody else. She wanted somebody she could rely on
to feed her the information she needed when the data inflows
were too great for a single person to handle. Somebody who
would know which messages to pass to her, which messages to
handle themselves. Somebody who would not crumble if things
went wrong.

Joshim's presence in the web was so light that it was
possible to forget he was there. Until he flicked you a warning
that your web control was slipping. Or decided that you were
fading and swapped you out to filtered standby to snatch some
sleep in the shub. He had better think carefully before he tried
that with *her*. She had designated him as her backup because he

had insisted she choose one. He was the best Webmaster she had worked with in years, and an adequate tactician for Outsider encounters. He was not a Commander. Especially not a Fleet Commander.

[Fleet Group Six in position for jump. All Commanders report ready and counting.]

[Acknowledged. Five minute warning.]

The alert confirmed what everybody knew, that jump and combat were imminent. Rallya felt the telltale shift in concentration throughout the web as minds and bodies tensed in anticipation. She sent a test signal down her direct channels, to the sensors team, the drive team, the weapons team, the shields team. Ritual more than routine, a final reassurance for her and for them that they were in contact, that she was in control of the ship, that *Bhattya* was part of her body as the fleet would never be, although they took her orders too.

[One minute warning.]

The drive team signaled readiness; the parameters for the jump were locked into the system ready to be activated. Rallya put the shields on triggered standby; they would be raised as soon as they came out of jump. She switched her primary input to the wide scanner, for an instant overview of Central when they emerged.

[Activating jump.]

She rode it with her inputs open, shedding the chaotic data that flowed in for the no-time they were in jump space. As the shields came up and the vanes moved out to restore the drive field, she drew the wide scan matrix into herself, looking for threats, immediate and deferred.

The fleet had come through in perfect formation, a slowly contracting sphere focused on Central. There were several ships in dock, others forming a ragged shell between the station and the fleet. Ten . . . eleven of them. Patrolships by their sleek lines and the heat patterns on their hulls. Patrolships with their shields up and their weapons primed but still taken by surprise by the fleet's arrival, their weapons targeted on the station, outnumbered two to one by the incoming ships.

[Fleet broadcast,] Rallya flashed to Vidar. [Status one.] Which was fire only when fired upon, by the code she had agreed with the other Commanders. [General broadcast: Invitation to surrender. To Central: Query situation.] To the sensor team, she sent [Identify all hostile ships.]

Some of Carher's ships were moving away from the station, sacrificing its shelter to give themselves more room in which to fight. Or run, if they could escape the station's mass-shadow. No Commander who deserved their berth would like such uneven odds. Their web-rooms would probably prefer to surrender if they were given the choice. Most of them would be cut off from the comm circuits, deaf to everything that their Threes did not want them to hear, but their sensors would show them what was going on. It would not take them long to work out what their chances were and nothing crippled a ship more effectively than discord in the web.

[Message from Central,] Vidar notified her. [Station secure. Long-range comms damaged. Unable to assist.]

Not with four armed patrolships looking down their throats, Rallya agreed grimly. Stations were never armed, could not be shielded, were too complex and fragile to invite being fired upon. And the ships in dock could not move without jeopardizing the station. Unless some of them were hostile, but there was no sign of activity among them. It looked as if she had interrupted an attempt to capture the station. As if none of Carher's ships had reached dock or they had been forced out by the station's resistance. Where was Carher? On one of the ships preparing for action, or still clinging to the shelter of the station? At least she did not have control of the station; that was the bloodiest of the scenarios that Rallya had planned for.

[General broadcast,] she told Vidar. [All ships to hold current position or be fired upon. Fleet broadcast: status two.] Select targets and prepare to fire on signal.

The sensors team were feeding her names for Carher's ships and for their Threes; the station must be broadcasting the data, doing as much as they could to help. Carher's name was tagged to *Keldir*, hugging the station within *Bhattya*'s field of fire. Rallya marked her down as the prime target for the weapons team. There were other names that she recognized, names that held no surprises. Most of the Old Empire aristos in the Guild had swarmed to Carher, like flies to a dung heap. She saw Meresya's name on one of the outbound ships, and Dhanar's. Thirty-five years ago they had both slipped through the Council's ineffective net. But not this time.

[Message from *Keldir*,] Vidar sent. [Withdraw, or we will fire on station. Also coded broadcast, same source.]

Instructions to her other ships, as Rallya was instructing

hers. [Fleet broadcast: code five,] Rallya responded. Fire on any ship that tries to jump. [No reply to *Keldir*.]

Carher was bluffing. Outnumbered and caught in Central's mass-shadow, she was hoping to negotiate a way out of the trap, trying for time to regroup and try again. As long as she believed she had a chance of winning, she would try to preserve Central and the secrets it held: the formula for R-K-D and the drugs that deactivated a web, the navigation libraries, all of the other keys to the power that she needed to survive. And she was gambling that Rallya would not risk crippling the Guild by endangering Central's records. Hellishly stupid to have kept them in one place, Rallya thought fleetingly; that would have to change. After she had seen Carher's bet.

[Lock on target,] she ordered the weapons team.

[Acknowledged.]

One of the outbound ships folded its vanes and dropped its shields in a single well-planned move. Then it was debris, hit by fire from two directions as it tried to jump.

[We have surrenders,] Vidar reported almost immediately. [Four. Now six.]

It had taken those web-rooms long enough, Rallya thought angrily. Gods knew if the webber who had just died had been the most fanatic or only the most stupid . . .

[Nonnegotiable conditions,] she sent. [Dropped shields, folded vanes, cold weapons. Skeleton team in each web, the rest of the web-room in suits on the hull. Group One Commander to take possession. One ship from each group to assist.] And gods help anybody who got in the line of fire if Carher made a break for it, friend or enemy. [Fleet broadcast: status two.] There were still four ships to deal with. [General broadcast: will open fire in five minutes.]

[Message from *Keldir*: will surrender at station.] There was a ripple of disbelief in Vidar's signal, an unnecessary flicker of warning from Joshim.

[Negative. Conditions for surrender have already been stated. Remaining ships will move away from station before surrender will be accepted.]

Nobody willing to double-cross Julur would fold so easily. Carher had something planned; every length she moved away from Central reduced the danger that the station would be caught in the cross fire when she tried it. Though gods knew what it was: *Keldir* was too deep inside a mass-shadow to try for a jump, too outnumbered to fight free. Surrender was the only sane option, but it still was not believable.

[Conditions accepted,] Vidar reported.

As Rallya watched suspiciously, *Keldir* lowered its shields and edged away from the station, tamely copied by the other three ships.

[Message to *Keldir*: we will approach you,] she told Vidar, angling *Bhattya*'s vanes to take them out of formation. The weapons team was still locked on target. The sensor team fed her a heat scan of the approaching ship: shields lowered, cannons cooling, no more activity from the drive than could be explained by the gradual movement. Nothing apparently out of place. Even the vanes were ...

Space rippled with the stress of a ship jumping inside a mass-shadow. Rallya grabbed for the drive controls, slammed *Bhattya* in *Keldir*'s wake. The web convulsed in a struggle to adjust; dimly she was aware of Joshim damping the shock waves to allow her to work. The cannons were still primed and aimed where their target had been. She bypassed the weapons team, praying that they had come out of the jump in the right orientation, that *Keldir* was the blurred image in the sensors that had survived. She fired. The blur scattered into a sparkle of fragments. As it did, somebody—Vidar?—took the ship back into jump space, back through the hole that was closing behind them, back to the fading echoes of their departure.

There was utter silence in the signal circuits as the web steadied, as if nobody quite believed what had happened, neither *Keldir*'s insanity, jumping inside a mass-shadow, nor Rallya's, riding the wake. Gods knew, nobody could expect to survive such insanity twice in a lifetime, Rallya thought, pulling herself together. Luckily, once had been enough. But it had been earned luck, she told herself exuberantly, the luck of having the right team in the web and the right kind of suspicious mind. Although if they drifted much longer in a battlefield, half-blind and congratulating themselves, they would deserve something else.

Not that there was a battle still going on. Not that there had been a battle at all, only a swift but conclusive skirmish, but the histories would call it a battle, and the web-rooms of her fleet would boast about having taken part in it. Let them, Rallya thought resignedly. Only two ships lost, and those both the enemy's: it was more to be proud of than a bloody fight with heavy casualties on both side. There was still clearing up to do, guilt to determine in the web-rooms of the ships that had surrendered, but it was a good beginning.

[Query comms,] she sent crisply to Joshim. First priority was a situation report, to confirm what she was getting from the sensors that were left. The growing activity in the web told her that Vidar was already busy collating a damage report that he would hold against her for years. [Casualty report,] also to Joshim. The damage control teams would have taken a battering in those two rapid jumps. [Well-done,] to the rest of the web.

[No casualties,] Joshim replied. [Message from Group One Commander. Situation stable. All hostile ships being boarded. Fleet moving to defensive formation.]

Situation stable? Huh. It would be a long time before the situation in the Guild was stable again. [Query Central.]

[From Central: sending tug to assist us to dock. Council waiting for you earliest opportunity.]

[Advise accept assistance,] Vidar added accusingly. [80 percent sensor loss, 60 percent vane loss, total shield loss. Other minor damage.]

[Accept,] she sent to Joshim. She could imagine what the Council—or what was left of it—wanted. Help to sort out the chaos their incompetence had brought down on their heads. Well, if that was so, they would take it on her terms or not at all. She had not risked the lives of every webber in *Bhattya*'s web-room to see the Council throw away what they had won.

[Take key,] she told Vidar, relinquishing control of the web. Carher had lost because she had not been given enough time to win; the Council were going to learn the same lesson. Hit them now with what was required of them, while were they still reeling from the shock of Carher's defection, and the Guild would come through this a hell's length stronger than it had ever been.

General broadcast
from Guild Council

To all ships and stations:
The coup instigated by ex-Councillor Carher has been decisively suppressed in a brief battle at Central... Commander Rallya of *Bhattya* and the Old Empire has been co-opted onto the Council...

354/5043:
IMPERIAL ZONE, OLD EMPIRE

"The work would go faster if you had help."

Rafe glanced across the floor at Braniya's feet, all that he could see of her from under the antique web's casing. "I don't need help." He pulled another circuit out of its mounting and inspected it carefully for visible signs of damage.

"You don't want to endanger anybody," Braniya corrected him.

"It would be a waste," Rafe agreed. "Especially since you won't find a tech who knows anything about this." Not even within the Guild, unless one of the historians had come across something similar in the records...

"Not even the little that you know?" Braniya asked. "Perhaps not, but would an extra pair of hands not be useful?"

"This," Rafe said, sliding out from under the casing and standing up to place the circuit in the test-rig that he had found

with the web, "was designed for a single person to maintain
and use. An extra pair of hands would just get in the way."

What else it had been designed for, he had been unable to
discover. Self-contained, even to its power-source, it had no
sensors, no control linkages, only a bank of comms circuits to
connect it to the world outside. There was a single couch
covered by a full-length hood, with web-contacts that would fit
his and provision for a nutrient feed. For amusement, Julur had
said; somebody had had a damned solitary vice.

"The Emperor is concerned that your web-cramp is occur-
ring more frequently and with greater severity."

"The Emperor is not the only one."

The test-rig displayed the symbol for test-in-progress, then
the symbol for test-complete-without-errors. They were the
same symbols that the Guild's test-rigs used, produced by
equipment of an age Rafe could not guess. The area where the
web was installed had been vacuum-sealed; when the guards
had unsealed it, it looked as if it had not been visited for
centuries. And the web itself—the principles of its construction
were familiar, if all the materials were not, but for it to have
survived so long without deteriorating . . . Unless the test-rig
was faulty—and he had to trust that it was not—every circuit
that Rafe had checked was functioning perfectly.

"It may be that the equipment will need to be maintained for
some time," Braniya said. "Any tech brought in to help you
could expect to live for some years."

Rafe raised his eyebrows. Braniya was telling him that
something had changed in the Guild, something that made it
unlikely that Julur would get any cooperation from them for
years. For the Guild's sake, that was good news. For himself?
If Julur wanted to keep him alive, he had to preserve his skill in
the web; otherwise web-cramp would kill him. The only way to
do that was another identity-wipe, which was preferable to the
personality disintegration he had been threatened with. Very
marginally.

"I don't need any help," he said stubbornly. He would not
jeopardize anybody else's life. And he would not share the
excitement of this web with anybody. Working on it stopped
him thinking for hours at a time about Joshim and Ayvar and
what Julur intended to do with him. And about his web-cramp,
except when the spasms took him.

"The Emperor wishes your work to be checked, to be certain that the web is safe to be used."

"Only a webber could tell him that." Rafe slid back under the casing to replace the circuit he had just tested, to extract the next one. "He'll have to rely on my judgment. He'll be questioning me under gadrine; he'll know I haven't done anything deliberate to hurt myself. For the rest, he'll have to assume I know what I'm doing. It's my life I'll be risking when I hook in. If I'm not ecstatic about him meddling with my sanity, I'm hardly going to endanger it by mistake."

"Your life belongs to the Emperor," she contradicted him icily.

"If you bring a tech down here, I shall stop work," Rafe told her equally coldly. "Maybe the tech could complete what I've started. Maybe you and enough guards could get me hooked into the web without doing permanent damage to my web-contacts. But you couldn't make me use it."

When he stood up again, her lips were pressed into a thin angry line. It must be difficult for her, he thought without sympathy, to have a prisoner whose terms of imprisonment were so contradictory, about whom she was forbidden to ask questions. Almost as difficult as it was to be that prisoner, not knowing when Julur's indulgence would end.

"If you want me in this web as soon as possible," he informed her, "you can stop distracting me. And you can tell Julur that it will be ready for use first thing tomorrow. I'd appreciate it if he'd schedule his question session then."

He shrank from the thought of more gadrine, but if it was the only way to get into this fascinating web . . . Not just because of the web-cramp, but because he itched to explore it from within. He would never know whose it had been or why it was here in the Old Imperial Palace. He would never share what he did learn with anybody else, but just once while he was still Rafe who had been Lin, he wanted to web again. He wanted a world where *he* was in control, he admitted to himself ruefully, somewhere where his every breath did not hang on the whim of an Emperor.

From Central Station News

. . . The Council will meet in private session in the Council Chamber at 04:00/355/5043 . . .

355/ 5043:
CENTRAL ZONE

Rallya flung the sheaf of flimsies that she had accumulated during the Council meeting onto the desk in the office she had been allocated. Carher's office, and noticeably larger than the other Councillors'. The flimsies made a satisfying scatter on the floor as they slid off the highly polished surface. If she could have been bothered, she would have dumped them in the waste disposal.

Gods and Emperors, it was easy to see how Carher had been able to get away with so much. Half the Council was incompetent and the other half was worse. No, that was unfair. There were one or two brains struggling to remember how to function, Ferin's for one, and the woman with one arm, Rhonya. The rest of them . . . If she had needed proof that democracy was no way to choose a governing body, the Council was it, but having been elected, they could at least have the decency not to try to unload their responsibilities on the first savior that came along. Yes, she was willing to take them by the hand and drag them in the right direction until she was sure they could carry on by themselves. No, she was not going to accept leadership of the Guild, not even until they could arrange for fresh elections."

"Excuse me, ma'am." Fadir hesitated in the doorway, one foot just inside the office as if he was testing the temperature before venturing in. "Message from the Stationmaster. *Khetya* is coming into dock and Lord Dhur would like to speak to you as soon as possible."

"Who. invited him here?" she demanded. "No, don't try to answer that, Fadir. You might wear your brain out thinking, and you wouldn't want to be the only one around here with a used brain. Message to the Stationmaster. I'll see Lord Dhur as soon as *Khetya* has docked. Let the idiot who calls himself my secretary know too."

"Yes, ma'am."

Lord Dhur obviously thought he did not need an invitation to Central, Rallya thought darkly as she dropped into the high-backed seat. That was one mistake he would not make again. If he thought the loan of his fleet—which he was not going to get back—entitled him to special treatment, he was wrong. And if he thought he could persuade her to besiege Julur, he was also wrong. Blood and hell, the man was stubborn. Joshim stood more chance of changing her mind and at least he knew better than to try.

"Lord Dhur, ma'am."

"Thank you, Fadir. Find out if the idiot in the outer office can produce some alcad, and bring it in yourself." She nodded to Ayvar, gestured at the empty chair. "If you were in such a hurry to be here, you should have stowed away with Fadir."

"Fadir didn't tell me what he planned." Ayvar took the seat he had been offered. "I came to find out what you plan."

"What I plan or what the Guild plans?"

"For current purposes, the two are the same."

"No, they aren't," Rallya objected sharply.

"The Guild Council is ready to accept any suggestion you make," Ayvar said smoothly. "No," he added, holding up a hand to silence Rallya, "I don't have a spy in the Council. I've seen the same situation in other places and times—in so many thousand years, there's little new. You're strong. You have strong ideas about the Guild. And you're willing to put them into action. It's inevitable they look to you for a lead."

Rallya snorted. "Well, they are not going to be led into

besieging Julur. Rafe's life isn't worth what it would cost. And he would agree with me, no matter what Julur does to him.''

''Is that your final word?''

''If I can win Rafe's freedom by negotiation, I will. But I will not throw away the peace of both Empires to do it.'' She studied him suspiciously. It occurred to her that there was another potential source of a fleet, the F'sair who had taken Julur's hire in the past, who might take Ayvar's hire in the future. Was he so intent on Rafe's freedom that he would go that far?

''I think, Lord Dhur,'' she said slowly, ''that you had better resign yourself to an indefinite stay at Central. I want you where I know what you're doing.''

Ayvar looked at her without expression. ''You aren't worried that holding me will provoke the same chaos as besieging Julur?''

''Not if you make no protest,'' she said calmly, ''and you won't, will you?''

''I'll give you two days to try negotiating,'' Ayvar conceded. ''But I warn you, Commander Rallya, I will hold you personally responsible if I lose Lin.''

Rallya stiffened at the threat in his voice. ''Julur might release him in exchange for you,'' she suggested provocatively. ''One webber—any webber—is worth more to me than an Emperor. No doubt the reverse is true for Julur.''

Ayvar shook his head. ''Even if you offered, he'd refuse. I've told you, nothing will make him give Lin up except fear for his own life.'' He stood up. ''Two days, Commander. And for Lin's sake, don't bring my name into it.''

Rallya called the Stationmaster when he had gone, to warn her not to let him leave on any ship. Then she sat glaring at her reflection in the glossy desktop. If Ayvar was convinced that what she had to bargain with would not gain Rafe's freedom, then it was not enough. Gods, was she going to be forced to abandon Rafe? She felt sick to her roots at the thought.

''Alcad, ma'am.'' Fadir halted in the doorway, looking in vain for Ayvar.

''Bring it here,'' she said irritably. ''He couldn't wait.'' She took one of the mugs off him. ''Make it yourself, did you?'' He nodded. ''Then you may as well drink the other one. And sit down while you do it. You make me uncomfortable standing up.''

"Yes, ma'am." He sat so close to the edge of the seat that the weight of the mug should have unbalanced him.

"Have you been aboard *Bhattya* today?"

"Yes, ma'am."

"Good. You can tell me how the repair work is going." She had not been back aboard since they docked. She needed something simple to worry about and damn it, it was still her ship. "Vidar still angry with me?"

"I think so, ma'am," Fadir said cautiously. "Although not as angry as he was yesterday."

"His temper is directly proportional to the amount of damage still to be repaired," she said drily. "If you ever make it to command rank, Fadir, remember that all Captains have an unnatural attachment to the fabric of their ship. If you ever want to annoy one, bring their ship into dock a virtual wreck. Even if it is in a good cause, they won't talk to you for days."

"Yes, ma'am." Fadir sounded justifiably uncertain whether that was the response expected of him.

"How's Joshim?" she asked.

"He's . . . working very hard. And not very happy," the apprentice said bravely. "I think he's worried about . . ."

"Rafe. We're all worried about Rafe," Rallya said heavily. So much for something simple to worry about.

From Central Station News

...The Guild has withdrawn its services in the Disputed Zone from both Emperors...

355/5043:
IMPERIAL ZONE, OLD EMPIRE

"These are where the attachment is made?" With distaste, Julur examined the bunch of web-contacts lying on the couch. "Barbaric. It should not have been allowed."

"It was my own choice," Rafe argued, probably unwisely. "Are you convinced yet that it's safe?"

He held his fingers rigidly straight, to prevent his nails from digging into his palms. After the latest interrogation under gadrine, there was nothing else he could do to convince Julur. Was it all a hoax? Had Julur never intended to allow him in the web? Had he held out the possibility for the pleasure of denying it?

"You may use it." Julur dropped the web-contacts. "I will observe." He crossed the room to the seat he had had carried in. "How long a period will you require for good health?"

"Initially, two or three hours," Rafe said cautiously. "I'm accustomed to webbing for eight hours a day. To prevent the web-cramping recurring, I should maintain that level of activity."

"It will be permitted." Julur sat down. He had dispensed

with his guards again, brought only Braniya with him. "You may begin."

Rafe stretched out on the couch, removed his web-bands. His web-contacts would need cleaning—vividly he remembered Joshim doing just that—he would not ask Braniya or Julur to do it for him. He strapped the signal-contacts onto his wrists; they were warm, already active. There was no monitor for him to check their placing, only experience to tell him that they felt right. He strapped the control-contact to his neck, hardly aware of his audience in his eagerness.

At the instant of engagement, there was a disconcerting impression of size from the web, larger than it should be within the confines of the casing. He fought that down; it was the strange configuration disorienting him. He wanted to stretch out to the edge of the available space, to give his nerves the freedom they had lacked for so long. He fought that down too. In a web as strange as this, he had to be cautious. At least while there were still things to learn about the web.

The strangest thing was being alone, the knowledge that there was no one on the end of his signal circuits. It made the web cold, less inviting than the Guild's webs. Or was that just his imagination? Whichever it was, he was not comfortable, did not feel safe, felt like a child tiptoeing through a deserted building.

Tentatively, he sent a signal, expecting it to vanish into nothing or to be reflected back to him. What came back was neither silence nor an echo. Intrigued, he repeated the experiment on a different set of circuits with the same result. The response was nothing he could understand, but it was not the signal he had sent.

Slowly, he extended along a single circuit, looking for the terminus. He found nothing, even stretched so far that he would have reached the edge of *Bhattya*'s web. He withdrew, sent the same probe down other circuits. All of them seemed endless, reinforcing his initial impression of size.

There were no external sensors, but were there status banks, information banks from which he could read a matrix? Nobody built a web as complex as this for amusement, whatever Julur claimed. It had to have another purpose. Station webs held information about arrival and departure schedules; he remembered hearing the suggestion that all the Guild's records should be held in the same way. There were no circuits in this web whose function he had not understood, no excess storage that he had noticed. The only anomaly was the large bank of comms circuits, approaching the complexity of a ship's comms circuits. Were they a link to storage elsewhere? Was he misinterpreting his signal circuits? Direct comms circuits would be openended, he thought excitedly. If he could just master the signal system . . .

Doggedly, he ran through every signaling system he knew, starting with the training signals that were the first that a junior learnt, working through the standard fives used upon the cargoships, the eights of a surveyship, the extended tens of a patrolship. When he ran out of options, he repeated himself, varying the patterns across the array of signal circuits in case the connections were made differently than they were in the webs he was used to. If nothing else, the exercise was driving the web-cramp away.

Just when he had given up hope, was repeating the sequence out of stubbornness, not conviction, he got an answer that he could interpret. Extended tens, but with the connections made in reverse order. He sent [Query status,] received [Acting.] An instant later he felt the unmistakable tingle in his input circuits that was a matrix forming. He opened to it.

It was a visual analog. It took him several seconds to build the picture in his mind. The first try made no sense, but when he inverted it along both axes, it was a text bank, written in almost recognizable symbols, symbols that could be the precursors of the alphabet he knew, symbols that could be as old as the web he was in. The web lost the fragile veneer of familiarity that the signaling exercise had given it.

Struggling to hold the image clearly, he tried to understand it. There were several lines of text, each with a corresponding signal glyph. The top line might be "web." The rest . . . possibly "complex" and "surface" and others he could not interpret. He sent [Query web] and the matrix reformed.

A mixed text and diagram bank, less difficult to visualize because the adjustments he needed to make were becoming familiar. "Power" and a figure were easy to recognize, but harder to interpret without knowing the scale; he assumed it referred to the web's internal power source. "Lock" and the symbol for "off" implied that something could be locked but was not. The diagram could be interpreted as meaning the web was fully functional, or it could mean something else entirely.

He sent [Magnify] with a pointer to the area of the diagram and watched it reform on a larger scale, spanning four of his input matrices. He thought he would go crazy, shifting them from their old relationship to the new upside-down back-to-front world, but he got them there in the end, concentrating so fiercely that he knew he would have a headache when he came out of the web.

Now he was seeing a schematic of the web's circuits, dotted and continuous lines. Assume one set was signal, one set was control. Which was which? Concentrations of both kinds led to a cluster of arrows pointing out of the web. The comms circuits? Did he have control over something outside the body of the web? Outside the casing that he knew about, he corrected himself. How far did this web extend? And most importantly, what could he do from it?

There were control circuits terminating within the casing, if his interpretation was correct. "Lock," he remembered from the previous matrix. Lock the hood? It was sturdy enough to be worth locking, if he had remembered to slide it over him. Could he manage the mixture of body and web control that would take, if he had a good enough reason for doing it? And would locking the hood also lock access to the circuits? Surely yes, if it was intended as protection for the person in the web.

[Query,] he sent, wondering what further information the web would supply about itself. One of the circuits on the schematic doubled in intensity and a description appeared; as it did, he felt an itch in his own—corresponding?—circuit. Gods, he thought, this was how juniors learned their way around a web. The teaching was done by a Webmaster, not the web itself, but if the web was designed only to hold one person . . . The description was incomprehensible. He sent [Acknowledge] and another circuit was identified for him, also leading off the edge of the diagram.

It could take days to learn his way around by this method. How long had he been in the web? He had lost track of elapsed time, but it must be close to two hours. When would Julur expect him to emerge? And would he be questioned about what he had done? If Julur learned that this web was not the limited thing he had believed, he would not allow Rafe to use it again. Was it worth taking the risk—if he could learn how to do it—to lock himself in and anger Julur in return for . . . Gods knew what possibilities. Yes, it was, when he already had nothing to look forward to except a short lifetime of dancing around the Old Emperor's moods.

[Query web,] he sent, for a repeat of the previous bank. When he had it, he sent [Magnify] with a pointer to the "lock" section. He was rewarded with another circuit diagram, simpler, with labels already attached. "Hood," "web," and "room": three circuits, all controlling a different level of locking. "Hood" and "web" were definitely what he wanted. "Room"? The room that the web was in? The room that Braniya and Julur were also in? That was distinctly tempting.

He sent [Query] and the circuits identified themselves in turn. He checked several times, to be sure he had memorized them; Julur was unlikely to be forgiving of any mistake he made. Then he carefully lightened his web control, mixing it with body control until he could hear the noises in the room around him, the rustle of armor-cloth, two people breathing and with nothing to say to each other. He dared not open his eyes, but the hood slid over from right to left; if he raised his right arm he would touch it. From then it would take a second to close the hood, a fraction of a second to operate all three locks. Then—he hoped—he would be safe from Julur and Braniya and they would be trapped until he decided to free them. Unless there was an override that could be operated from outside the web . . .

Hell, Julur could do nothing worse than he had already threatened. He raised his arm, closed the hood, triggered the locks. He had enough body control to hear Julur exclaim, Braniya run across the floor to find out what he had done. Through the darkly transparent hood, he could see her struggling to open it. When she dropped out of sight, he assumed she was trying to open the circuit access she had seen him open before.

Julur was asking sharp questions; there must be a sound pickup somewhere in the room that was relayed inside the web, Rafe decided. There would be even more questions asked when they realized that they were locked in. How long would it take to cut through the door, as sturdily built as the walls in this underground warren? Several hours at least. He had wondered about the thickness of that door when he first saw it; now he understood.

He let his body control fade. The web status bank now showed "Lock" was on, and there was a pulsing alarm signal.

To tell him that somebody was trying to tamper with the web, he decided. Now to find out what the other status banks would tell him.

"Complex" gave him a map. Working on the assumption that it was a map of the deep levels, he sent [Locate] and was shown a section of the map with one room highlighted, a figure *two* inside the room and a figure *ten* outside. Julur and Braniya and a squad of guards. [Query] gave him another circuit diagram. He ran through the identification sequence, finding "Lighting," "Temperature" and—most interesting—"Atmosphere." The presence or absence of atmosphere, he concluded, remembering the vacuum seal.

So. He had Julur locked in a room from which he could withdraw the air. Incidentally killing himself, since there was no independent air supply to the web, but it should be possible to convince Julur that he would commit suicide rather than remain a prisoner; the Emperor had been concerned enough that he would deliberately damage himself in the web. None of it would help him if he could not find a way off the planet.

"Surface" gave him a picture, several pictures that he could flick between. Most of them were blank; the others might be views of the surface of Old Imperial. The blank pictures worried him. Damaged sensors, or damage to the web itself?

He went back to the first status bank, puzzling over the lines he could not interpret. What he needed was a way to communicate, not only with Julur to put his demands—when he had decided what they were—but off-world as well. With Central. Whoever was in control—Rallya, or he did not know the woman—must have learned by now that he had not been Carher's prisoner. If he told the Guild where he was, made it possible for them to get in to collect him and out again safely. . .

The first line he tried gave him a diagram of his own web. Fascinated, he spared a few seconds to study it, defeated by the text but guessing that the highlighted section was a diagnosis of web-cramp. Or else the residual damage from the overload. The web must be probing his nervous system without him being aware of such an analysis. His mind balked at the level of sophistication that needed. This web was old, but it was not antiquated.

Another choice gave him a view of the room around him, of Braniya and Julur talking animatedly. There was extra data that might be sound, but he had never dealt with a sound input, could not begin to understand it. He watched them talk for a while; for once, Braniya seemed to be contradicting Julur. Regretfully, he filed the sound input among the things he would never have time to explore. If he needed to hear them, he could regain some body control.

His third blind choice brought him the comms circuits. Within the room, within the palace, system space, deep space. Rapid exploration of the deep space circuits taught him that they at least were familiar enough for him to use untutored. First, he had to target the message on Central. He knew the station's location to several decimal places; every Guild member did. He specified it. Immediately the web questioned it, offering an alternative that was different in the last decimal place on one axis. His mistake? No. He knew his coordinates were right. He overrode the alternation and the web gave in.

Next, before he brought anybody else into danger, he should be sure that he could control Julur and Braniya. He went through the sequence that identified atmosphere control. Demonstration first, demands afterwards? He was entitled to revenge for what Julur had done to him. This might be his only chance. For a long moment, he wondered if there was a way to take permanent revenge. To make Julur undergo an identity-wipe or a personality disintegration. Except that his personality was already less than intact. And the repercussions of any act of aggression against an Emperor were unthinkable, unless it never became known beyond the walls of this room. He would have to be content with teaching Julur what it was to be terrified and to have no means of escape.

He returned to the view of the room. Julur and Braniya were using the intercomm, arguing alternately with each other and with the comm. Rafe signaled for the atmosphere to be reduced. His captives were slow to notice the effects, but it was pleasant to see Julur's face when he finally realized what was happening. He watched until they had both passed out and he was beginning to feel the effects himself before he restored the air.

By the time they regained consciousness, he had withdrawn from the web enough to hear and to talk.

"I can do that whenever I want," he greeted Julur as the Emperor stood up unsteadily. He was obviously audible outside the hood; Julur jerked as if he had been struck. "I don't have to stop before you're dead."

The color fled from Julur's face, leaving him an unpleasant white. "You would not kill me," he said.

"Because you're immortal?" Rafe scoffed. "It doesn't mean you can't die. It means you haven't done it yet."

"You would die too."

"I have to do it sometime." Braniya was dragging herself to her feet. "Welcome back to the world of the living, Braniya. Temporarily, perhaps."

"You do not have to die," Julur said intensely.

"Given the choice between staying your prisoner and dying, I'll choose dying," Rafe said cheerfully. "You'll be pleased to know there's a third choice. You can allow the Guild safe conduct down here to fetch me. And out again, of course."

"No," Julur objected. "You cannot..."

"Breathe vacuum." Rafe dropped the air pressure in the room abruptly, restored it when he had made his point. "I shall be calling a Guild ship to fetch me. They'll come out of jump inside your defensive sphere and they won't be fired on. They'll send an armed team down here to collect me and they won't be stopped. They'll leave here with me and with you as a guarantee of safety."

"No," Julur insisted. "I will not leave this world."

"You want to die instead?"

"No." Julur's wits seemed to have deserted him, as if he could not cope with his loss of power. How long had it been since he had last been helpless? And how long would it be before he recovered?

Keep him off balance, Rafe warned himself; don't give him time to start thinking again.

"Order it done—and I can see everything that goes on in this palace," he exaggerated, "or die now. That's the choice you've got."

"We could have the crew of *Havedir* come down to fetch him," Braniya suggested calmly. Too calmly for Rafe to trust her...

"I want somebody I know," he insisted. "And if you're planning anything except obedience, don't. Any attempt to open that door before the Guild arrive, any attempt to get into this web, any attempt to override what I'm doing and I'll kill all of us. Now, do I send a message to Central, or do I stop the air?''

Julur flinched. "Send the message," he said hoarsely. "You're mad. You would kill both of us without understanding what you did."

*   *   *

Attention Commander Rallya. Urgent. Request transport for self and Emperor from Old Imperial. Advise extreme caution. Rafe.

Rallya reread the message flimsy before she handed it to Joshim. "That came in fifteen minutes ago," she said flatly. "The comms center have got a reck of it, if you think you could recognize his comms-style . . ."

Joshim shook his head grimly. "No." He handed the message on to Vidar. "If you want me to tell you whether it's genuine or not, I can't." He twisted the ring around his finger anxiously. "Even if there was some kind of proof in there . . ."

He did not finish, did not need to. Rallya knew as well as he did that nothing in the message could prove that the request was genuine, that Rafe had not been forced to make it. Julur had had him for long enough to strip every secret from him, every freedom of choice . . . And which was more probable, Rallya asked herself: that Rafe had somehow gained the upper hand over Julur, or that Julur was using him as bait in a trap?

"*Bhattya* is spaceworthy," Vidar remarked.

"I know that already," Rallya snapped. She also knew she had no choice. Joshim would never agree to ignore the request when there was any possibility that it was genuine. And neither would she, she admitted. It would be impossible to live with herself if she let Rafe down needlessly. Or if she sacrificed *Bhattya* needlessly. Even if it was not a trap, it was still dangerous. *Advise extreme caution*, Rafe had said, implying that he did not have everything under control, that something could still go wrong. Something can always go wrong, she reminded herself savagely. Gods and Emperors, she had put her ship at risk enough times before not to funk the decision now. Just because she could not go with them . . .

"What are you waiting for?" she demanded. "You'd better get moving."

"You aren't coming?" Vidar queried, surprised.

"No," Rallya said shortly. "Somebody has to stay here and

teach the Council their cursed business. Again.'' She saw disbelief on both their faces. ''You're big boys now, or you should be,'' she pointed out irritably. ''I'm not a faffing good-luck charm. You can manage without me for once.''

And the gods-be-cursed Council could not, she added bitterly to herself. Sometimes it seemed as if she was the only person in the faffing Guild who did not panic at the thought of rebuilding it from the inside out. And if that had been clear to Ayvar days ago—although she would see him in hell before she admitted to his face that he was right—it must be clear by now to Julur. Which meant—blood and hell!—that it was her duty to skulk safely at Central, out of Julur's reach. At least until the Guild could survive without her.

''You'd better get moving,'' she repeated. ''I'll have the comms center tell Rafe you're on the way. And be damned careful. I don't want *Bhattya*'s reputation ruined the first time I let her out of my sight.''

*   *   *

[Attention Rafe. Advise *Bhattya* will jump within one hour. Please confirm that arrival in planetary orbit has been cleared with the appropriate authorities.]

The response, half an hour after he had sent his message, woke Rafe from a dangerous half-doze. It was hard to fight the ache seeping through him, the result of nerves stretched with fear, of working too hard after too long out of the web. Gods, he thought gratefully as he monitored the repeat of the message, they *are* coming, in spite of all the reasons why they might have decided not to . . . And only an hour before they arrived in orbit—the length of time it took to calculate the jump from Central. Two hours, maybe three, and he would be on his way out of here.

''There'll be a ship jumping into orbit within the hour,'' he announced, startling Julur. ''You'd better give the orders to make sure that it arrives safely. And remember, I'll be monitoring them.''

Bluff, but it was the best weapon he had. He prayed that nobody on Julur's staff had any misplaced initiative . . .

''I'm waiting,'' he said sharply when neither of his prisoners spoke. ''All planetary defenses and the sector defensive sphere deactivated. Now.''

"Do it," Julur told Braniya abruptly.

Rafe listened to her give the orders. "Good enough," he conceded. "You'd better hope that everyone obeys you. Your lives depend on it."

"They'll obey," Braniya said confidently. She walked across the room to the locked web and studied him closely through the semi-transparent hood. "I assume we are expecting *Bhattya*. Shall I also give orders for a convenient shuttle-landing to be prepared, and guides to bring your friends down to us?"

"And for the crowd outside the door to move away," Rafe agreed. "All fifteen of them."

"Of course." She did not react to his accurate knowledge. "Immediately?"

"Immediately," Rafe agreed.

He faded out his body control before she spoke again. There was a message to send to Central, and . . .

The cramp hit him without warning, flooding signal circuits and control circuits, rendering him blind and deaf and dumb and helpless. As if acid was running along his nerves and spilling out into the web. He disengaged from the web before he could prevent himself, struggled desperately to re-engage before Braniya found a way to take advantage of the spasm. He must have passed out; when he could think and feel and see again, both Julur and Braniya were pulling furiously at the hood of the web, hoping that the lock had failed. It was a miracle that it had not, he thought shakily.

"Nothing so easy," he lied to them, blinking the tears out of his eyes and hoping he sounded better than he felt. "None of it depends on my even being alive." He grinned, although he did not feel like grinning. "You'd better hope I don't die in here. You'd starve to death before anybody worked out how to free you. Or can't immortals starve to death?" he added maliciously. "You can die from lack of air—we've already established that. What other ways are there of killing you? Are you really immortal, or are you just better than the rest of us at fighting off disease and old age?"

He was talking to hide the important things he was doing: cautiously re-entering the web, exploring his web-control, checking that the spasm had not done any damage that needed to be repaired, had not weakened his hold on Julur and Braniya. All of the locks had held; he offered a silent prayer of gratitude to the web's long-dead constructor. The diagram of his own web had several alarm signals pulsing, but told him nothing he did not already know. He realized suddenly that there might be a safety cut-out on the locks; if he lost consciousness for a prolonged period of time—or withdrew from the web to conserve his strength—the locks might open to give access to him. It was an unpleasant thought . . .

"You had some more instructions to carry out," he reminded Braniya, determined that they would not see how weak the spasm had left him. He could send a message to Central—he did it—and he could monitor his immediate surroundings, but to try anything more was to invite another attack. He had to save his strength until *Bhattya* arrived, until he had to assure the safe arrival of those coming through the palace to fetch him. Two hours, maybe three . . .

* * *

[Outward jump calculated and set in,] Vidar sent. [Return jump calculated and set in.]

[Acknowledged,] Joshim sent back, suppressing a wave of undisciplined relief that the interminable calculations were complete. [All teams report readiness. Jump in five minutes.]

This was worse than when the fleet jumped to Central, he reflected as he received the reports from around the web. The defensive sphere that Julur had thrown around Old Imperial was reputed to be impenetrable; two hundred years since the last attempt was made, and that had been as fatally unsuccessful as all its predecessors. True, they had Rafe's assurance that Julur had given the right orders. If it was Rafe on the far end of that comms channel. And if he was not acting under duress. And if Julur's orders were obeyed.

Joshim could not think of any way in which Rafe could have freed himself, put himself in a position to call for help, to propose removing the Old Emperor from his palace. He had said as much when he had asked for volunteers to crew *Bhattya* on this trip, and the idiots had still volunteered en masse, not one of the web-room agreeing to stay behind. He let his renewed gratitude at their decision seep into the web, wanting them to know how he felt, reckoning that it would do more good than harm.

[Four minutes,] Vidar sent. [Quit worrying and concentrate.] That was on a private channel. [Rallya will have our hides on her office wall if we foul up. And so will her successor.]

[Acknowledged.] Obediently, Joshim focused tightly on the jump and what they expected to find when they emerged. [Query status Rafe's comms channel,] he sent to Lilimya.

[Silent.]

[Acknowledged.] It had been silent since the message about the defensive sphere. But that did not mean that anything had gone wrong, Joshim told himself firmly. Only that Rafe had nothing new to tell them.

[Three minutes.]

If they were fired on, they had the return jump already set in; they could be safely back at Central within a few seconds. Rafe would not expect—would not want anybody's life put at risk when there was visibly no chance of success. If they were allowed into orbit unopposed . . . They would have to play it as they found it. An armed landing party, Rafe had specified, and again, extreme caution.

[Two minutes.]

Rallya had chosen a good time to send *Bhattya* off without her, he thought resentfully. The damned Council could surely manage without her for a few hours. Unless she thought this was too dangerous, that she was now too precious to risk . . . No, if she believed that, she would have locked them up rather than let them try it. Or kept Rafe's message secret; she was perfectly capable of that. What she was not capable of was giving in against her better judgment. She had sent *Bhattya* to fetch Rafe. Therefore it was possible.

[One minute.]

Rallya's successor, Vidar had called Rafe. It he wanted the berth . . . Even if he chose to continue webbing, he might not want to do it in *Bhattya*'s web-room. Not with Joshim, when there was still the tangle around Ayvar to unravel. Anyway, Rallya might not agree to step aside, might still find a way out of the Guild leadership. Although she was no longer struggling as hard as she might . . . Gods and Emperors, just two messages from Rafe—supposedly from Rafe, he reminded himself sternly—and he was reviving all the possibilities that he had promised himself to forget until he knew that Rafe was safe. And Rafe would never be safe if he did not concentrate on the web.

[Activating jump.]

*   *   *

"Your friends have arrived in orbit," Braniya said smoothly. "But you don't need me to tell you that, do you?"

"You don't expect me to answer that, do you?" Rafe countered, squirting a hasty query along his comms channel and receiving a prompt affirmative. "They're waiting for your clearance to land a shuttle."

"I'll have it transmitted," Braniya promised.

She walked to the intercomm. Rafe did not watch her, did not listen to her speak. He would only hear what she wanted him to hear, not the hidden messages in her choice of words.

[Trust nobody,] he sent to *Bhattya*, not caring that Rallya would laugh at the warning. It was such a long way through the palace to fetch him and there were so many traps that Braniya could set . . .

Odd that Braniya was the one who worried him most, that Julur seemed to have conceded defeat. If Ayvar had been in the same situation, he would have been the one at the intercomm, the one scheming to regain control. Or would he? Would the threat of death reduce him to the same mute acquiescence? Was that the price of being immortal, the sacrifice of everything that made you human to a desperate obsession with living forever?

Rafe shuddered uncontrollably. How must it feel, to live so long that there was nothing new left to experience? To share that empty existence with just one other man, until love and hatred were meaningless words for what you felt about them. To be caught between the temptation to take the crazy risks that Rafe had seen Ayvar take and the desire to shut yourself away from danger in a paranoiac cocoon. And—surely—always to know the fear that you were not truly immortal. The possibility that there was some disease to which you were not immune, some degree of damage that was too great to survive, some day on which you would start growing old. The fear that, in the end, you *would* die like everybody else.

[Shuttle on its way down.]

The message from *Bhattya* dragged Rafe out of his reverie. It was fatally easy to lose concentration; to feel the growing sickness in the pit of his stomach; to give in to the gathering light-headedness as his blood-sugar dropped and fatigue claimed him. To lose track of what was going on.

Shuttle on its way down. That meant it would be thirty minutes before they landed. Another hour making their way through the labyrinth of the palace. Could he last that long? He

could not ask them to hurry, could not warn them how shaky
his control of the situation was. Not when Braniya's people
must be monitoring his comms. He had to maintain his bluff.
Not only for his own sake now, but for *Bhattya*'s sake too.

*   *   *

"In here," the guard said sullenly, unlocking the riser. "You'll
be met at the bottom."

"I'll bet we will," Vidar said, exchanging a wary glance
with Joshim before stepping into the riser.

Joshim and Ajir followed him, Peri and Caruya bringing up
the rear, all of them careful not to turn their back on the guard.
The further they traveled from the surface, the harder it was to
believe that they were not walking into a trap. For the hundredth time, Joshim reviewed the orders he and Vidar had
given to Jualla, looking for any eventuality they had missed. If
Bhattya was fired upon, if they lost contact with the landing
party, if Rafe alerted them to any danger, she was to retreat to
Central. He prayed that she had the sense to do as she had been
told.

"How much further?" Peri asked quietly as the riser carried
them down.

"The gods know," Joshim said frankly. "Rafe told Jualla
that he was on one of the deepest levels."

He did not add what they all knew, that there had been no
word from Rafe since that message. No word, no indication of
why he could not come to meet them, no explanation for why
he was still relaying his comms through *Bhattya* instead of
using a direct voice-link. Injured, Joshim's treacherous imagination suggested. Or a prisoner, doing only what he was told.

"Bottom approaching," Vidar warned, readying his bolt-
beamer to cover the corridor that waited them. Joshim copied
him, gaining a false sense of security from his weapon. If it
came to shooting, they could not win but they could refuse to
be taken alive. That would be his choice, guessing how Julur
would react to the face he shared with Ayvar, knowing how he
could be used to torment Rafe, how Rafe could be used to
torment him . . .

The tunnel they emerged into was vastly different from the
corridors above. Joshim shivered, making a comparison with
the dungeons that he had known as Salu'i'kamai. The walls

pressed eagerly in upon him and their distance from safety seemed to double abruptly.

There was a single guard waiting for them, faceless in the same dark visor as their previous guide, carrying the same holstered weapon.

"That way," he greeted them curtly, pointing to their left.

"How much further?" Vidar asked.

"Round the corner, to the door at the end of the tunnel." He paused, listening to something inside his helmet. "Wait here. Orders are to clear the tunnel before we send you in."

"Why?"

"Orders," the guard repeated.

There was the sound of feet approaching from the direction they were to take. Joshim tensed, knew that the others with him were equally alert. Nowhere to hide, nowhere to run. As naked as the stone walls. From the corner of his eye, he saw Caruya's finger tightening on the trigger of her beamer, her aim steady in the center of the tunnel where it turned the corner. Joshim picked his own aiming point, ears straining for footsteps from the other direction, for the sound of more guards coming down the riser...

He breathed again as a group of maybe fifteen people came around the corner, both guards and civilians, their faces grim—the ones that were visible—but their weapons not in their hands. They seemed to be arguing among themselves, but fell silent as they came within earshot of the small group by the riser. All except one, who said loudly. "He won't get away with this. None of you will."

"The Guild looks after its own," Joshim retorted angrily.

"By threatening the Emperor's life?" the civilian demanded.

"If you care about it that much, you'd better get out of here," Vidar intervened. He reinforced the message by gesturing with his beamer.

Joshim watched without speaking as the riser carried them out of sight. Threatening the Emperor's life? If Rafe had a weapon aimed at the Old Emperor, that would explain a great deal. And Rafe—with his knowledge of Ayvar—was possibly the only person who could threaten to kill an Emperor and make himself believed. Gods be thanked, they might yet walk out of this safely...

"Left, around the corner to the door at the end," he repeated impatiently. "Let's go."

*   *   *

[Message for landing party,] Rafe sent, using the little strength he had been saving for this moment. [Maximum thirty seconds from reaching the door to enter. Expect two enemies inside plus self in web.]

The danger would come as Joshim and the others came through that door, when it would no longer be possible for him to control his hostages by threatening to suffocate them, when there would be a chance for Julur and Braniya to escape. He had done what he could to reduce the risk. He had forced them to remove their armor-cloth and force-shields, made Braniya drop her weapon, insisted they had the corridor outside emptied. It would have been safest to knock them out by withdrawing the air before unlocking the door but he could no longer do so, not with any certainty of remaining conscious himself.

[Landing party acknowledges,] *Bhattya* relayed. [Approaching door now.]

Rafe started to call up the schematic of the corridor outside, gasped as another onslaught of cramp racked him. Desperately, blindly, he released all the locks: door, web, and hood; he could not distinguish between them in the surge of pain before he passed out.

*   *   *

As Joshim pushed through the door, he saw Braniya fumbling inside an ornate metal case, Julur scrabbling on the floor for a beamer. He kept moving fast, to allow the others in. Behind him, the heard Vidar curse and fire. Julur dropped the beamer, clutching a hand burnt by the suddenly heated metal. One part of Joshim noted Vidar's marksmanship with approval, even as he took his own aim at Braniya.

"Leave him!" he snapped.

"Freeze or I pull this," Braniya countered. In her hand, she showed him the unmistakable braided linkage of a web-contact. "The shape he's in, yanking this could cripple him," she added, telling Joshim what he already knew. "If it didn't kill him."

"How do we know he's still alive?" Joshim demanded, thinking frantically. If he shot her, her falling weight would still

drag the contact away from Rafe's neck. He must be unconscious. Had he disengaged from the web? If not, could he
survive that degree of disruption so soon after the overload and
whatever Julur had done to him?

"You'll have to take my word for it," Braniya was saying.
"Although I can't guarantee that he'll survive long whatever I
do. Every attack of cramp he has is worse than the one before.
Would you care to speculate how long you have to resolve this
stand-off before his death does it for you?"

Julur was rising to his feet. Joshim spared him only a glance,
confident that Vidar and the others had him covered. Web-
cramp. Of course, after so long out of the web . . . How long
would Rafe remain unconscious? It depended on how many
previous episodes he had suffered, on how long it had been
since the first one. If he had not disengaged, if he had another
attack while he was unconscious . . . Joshim made himself remain calm, made himself remember that there were others
besides Rafe whose lives depended on his decisions now.

"If he dies, you die," he said brutally. "Julur we need to get
us safely out of here. You we don't." It was not an empty
promise, he assured the gods silently.

"Hardly a satisfactory resolution for anybody." Braniya
wound the linkage more tightly around her hand. "You and he
both seem remarkably careless with his life."

Julur was moving to her side. "Remarkable indeed, when he
expresses such a deep—if confused—affection for you under
gadrine." Devoid of recognizable emotion, his voice had none
of Ayvar's redeeming humanity. "I think, however, I must trust
his judgment about you, and believe that you would allow him
to be killed to save your companions' lives. For some curious
reason, he finds that admirable in you. I find it wholly
alarming." He glanced into the web. "You may wish to know
that he is conscious again."

"And in control of the air." The voice was thready, but
recognizably Rafe's. "Don't worry, Braniya. If I shut it off,
disconnecting my contacts won't restore it. You could go down
in history as the woman who killed an Emperor."

"You're bluffing," Braniya snapped.

"Call it," Rafe suggested. "But oughtn't you ask Julur's
permission first? He's got more to lose than the rest of us."

"Release the linkage," Julur ordered, chopping his hand

viciously down onto Braniya's wrist, pinning it to the edge of the web-casing. "I have decided. There will be no deaths. There is more at issue here than any of you understand."

"More than your sweating pink skin?" Rafe mocked. "Somebody get me out of here. Before I throw up."

He allowed Joshim to remove his web-contacts and help him off the couch, but pulled determinedly free of his support when he was standing upright.

"Somebody should shove the point of their beamer in Julur's ribs," he said. "To make sure he behaves himself on the way out. And to make sure that nobody tries to stop us."

"I have sworn there will be no trouble," Julur objected.

"We know how much that's worth," Joshim said grimly, following Rafe's advice. "Vidar, take care of Braniya. Peri, help Rafe if he needs it." Even if he did not want Joshim's help, he would be grateful for another shoulder to lean on. And Julur as hostage was a better guarantee of safety than any number of ready beamers.

*   *   *

"Message from *Bhattya*, ma'am." In his excitement, Fadir forgot to knock. "They're on their way back. With Rafe and the Old Emperor."

"I should hope so," Rallya growled. "Joshim and Vidar learned to look after themselves years ago. Which is probably more than you'll ever manage." She looked up at the apprentice, wondering why he had stayed to plague her instead of stowing away for the second time. "Tell me, Fadir, are your pants too tight, or is there some better reason for you to be dancing from one foot to the other?"

"Sorry, ma'am."

"Don't apologize. If you don't take the Oath, you could almost make a living as a clown."

"Not take the Oath, ma'am? But . . . ."

"It was a joke, Fadir. Now, get out of here. And tell my fool of a secretary to arrange accommodation for another damned Emperor."

From Central Station News

...The Emperors Julur and Ayvar are both currently visiting Central to discuss the renegotiation of their Oaths. This historic occasion is the first time the Emperors have met each other since the Empires were divided...

356/5043:
CENTRAL ZONE

"You've got the gods' own luck," Rallya accused Rafe. "Or has Joshim finally learned some prayers that work?"

"I knew you'd be pleased to see me." Rafe slumped into the nearest seat, wearing a hands-off look that was keeping Joshim at more than arm's length. "Especially if I brought you an Emperor to argue with."

"Two," Rallya said smugly. "The other one is here as well." And neither of them would be leaving before she had their new Oaths. Oaths so tight it would slit their own throats if they broke them.

"Ayvar's here?" Rafe's voice was flat with weariness and something beneath that. "Does he know I'm safe?"

"If Fadir didn't forget the message I gave him."

"Then he'll be here soon." Rafe glanced at Joshim and away again guiltily.

"You need some sleep," Joshim said. "Everything else can wait."

"About a year of sleep," Rafe conceded. "Is it Guild Commander Rallya now?"

"Gods and Emperors, no," Rallya said vehemently.

"She's the only one that doesn't admit it," Joshim contradicted her. "There's still a Council, but she decides everything important."

"Only until they can be trusted to get it right," Rallya insisted.

"A few years then." Rafe closed his eyes, hiding behind grey lashes. "Gods help us all."

"Huh. Why don't you stop making my office look untidy and let Joshim take you to bed?"

Rafe shook his head. "Nobody is taking me to bed. I can get there by myself, if I'm pointed in the right direction."

"It looks like it," Rallya said scornfully. It looked like Rafe was holding himself together by willpower alone. If he managed to leave that chair, it would only be because somebody picked him up and carried him. A pity Joshim showed no sign of doing it.

"He'll be in here, sir." Fadir's voice, as proud as if he had rescued Rafe personally.

"Thank you."

Ayvar came straight to Rafe's side, knelt beside him and kissed him on the mouth, long and lovingly. Rallya looked away, angry—hurt—for Joshim. Joshim did not move.

"Gods, Lin, I've missed you," Ayvar said eventually, gripping both Rafe's hands. "To think you were dead, and then to know that Julur had you . . ."

"I . . . didn't miss you," Rafe said shakily. "The identity-wipe . . ."

"I forgive you," Ayvar said lightly.

"You haven't much choice."

"I forgive you most things."

"Eventually."

"You should be in bed."

"So I've been told."

"The only question is whose," Rallya broke in, unable to bear Joshim's stillness any longer. Somebody had to make him fight.

"I've told you. Nobody's." Rafe pulled his hands away from Ayvar, stood up, managing not to take the help Ayvar offered.

"There's a spare bed in my suite, Lin."

"Please, 'Var...Rafe is easier..." He stopped by the door with his back to all of them. "I can't throw ten years away. Not any of it." Rallya could not see his fists but she could hear that they were clenched.

"I'm not asking you to. I'm not asking you for anything, Lin. Rafe."

"You are. You will." Rafe turned round with an effort. "I know what you'll ask me for. You'll ask me to stop webbing. You always do. Every time I'm in combat. Every time I get a new assignment to an active zone. And now you'll use what Julur's done to try to persuade me to stay with you. Won't you?"

"It wouldn't work. I know that." Ayvar made a gesture of resignation. "I'll admit, I don't want you in a patrolship. I don't think I could bear to mourn you again."

"You'll have to do it eventually," Rafe said harshly.

"You could stay in the Guild—still web—without being Commander of a patrolship. Commander Rallya doesn't want to stay on the Council. You could take her place..."

"Stop planning my future for me!" Rafe yelled. "I don't want to be on the Council any more than Rallya does."

"And I wouldn't stand aside for you," Rallya added drily. "Having seen the havoc you can wreak as a First, I dread to think what you'd achieve as Guild Commander." She looked across at Joshim, wondering how much longer he could be so blind. "There is another option, Rafe. Since I'm the only person I can trust to run this damned desk properly, *Bhattya* is short of a Commander. Temporarily. And since she's been mine since she came out of the construction dock, I've the right to choose my replacement."

Ayvar glared at her. Rafe looked past them both at Joshim. "Would you..."

Say yes, you fool, Rallya urged Joshim.

"Yes," Joshim said simply.

"You'd have to ask Vidar..."

"I have." Joshim moved, passing Ayvar to go to Rafe's side. "Even a Commander has to take Webmaster's orders," he said, smiling a little. "Especially a Webmaster who knows what Hafessya saw you doing. Bed. Before you fall over." He slipped an arm around Rafe to support him; Rafe did not fight it.

"Lin."

Rafe paused in the doorway, still holding onto Joshim.

"You'll come to me when you can?" Ayvar asked.

"Yes." Very quietly.

Thank the gods that was settled, Rallya thought as Joshim closed the door. The outcome had been obvious to anybody with a pair of brain cells, but like most spectator sports, love was chiefly enjoyable for the incompetence of its participants.

"Looks like you and Julur both lost him," she said to Ayvar with satisfaction.

"Temporarily." He sat in the seat that Rafe had left.

"He won't change his mind."

"I can afford to wait." Ayvar smiled broadly. "You're a loser too, in your own terms."

Rallya scowled around the office. "Tell me that when I've written you an Oath so tight even Julur can't break it." She lifted her feet onto the desk. There were some compensations—the painkillers for her hip for one, and the chance to see Råfe make fools of two Emperors. She frowned, thinking just what fools he *had* made of them. They were both so damned irrational over him, and so determined to keep him alive . . .

"Oh gods," she breathed in disbelief. "You *can* afford to wait, can't you?"

Ayvar smiled again. "A few tens of years," he confirmed.

"Does he know?"

"No, and it would be a kindness not to tell him. He'll have to live with it for long enough when he does realize. I want him to have what mortal life he can."

"Oh gods," Rallya repeated. "Two of you are enough trouble. Three of you, including him . . ." *Having seen the havoc he can wreak as a First, I dread to think what he'd achieve* . . . Her own words came back to her with force. Rafe as an immortal, as an Emperor . . . She shivered, for him and for all the people he would touch. "Over my dead body he gets control of the Guild."

It was the wrong thing to say about an immortal.